Praise for Ka

Sit. Stay.

"A cute and fun romance set in a small town. Great main characters that are easily relatable."—*Kat Adams, Bookseller (QBD Books, Australia)*

"This is a sweet romance about two lovely people growing together and falling in love as they help the people and animals around them."—*Rainbow Reflections*

"This is an easy romance to read. It's not overly fraught with angst, but there are some light drama to keep the plot moving forward. The obligatory separation of the leads near the end of the book didn't feel eye roll worthy, because, though dramatic, it was set up almost from the beginning of the book. I loved the characters, pacing and plot of this book. Very recommended."—*Colleen Corgel, Librarian, Queens Public Library*

Love on Lavender Lane

"Gentle romance, excellent chemistry and low angst…The two MCs are well defined and well written. Their interactions and dialogue are great fun. The whole atmosphere of the lavender farm is excellently evoked."—*reviewer@large*

"[*Love on Lavender Lane*] was very nearly my perfect romance novel. Lovely human beings for main characters who had fantastic chemistry, great humor that kept me smiling—and even laughing—throughout, and just enough angst to make my feel it in the heart. And a cute doggie, too!"—*C-Spot Reviews*

Seascape

"When I think of Karis Walsh novels, the two aspects that distinguish them from those of many authors are the interactions of the characters with their environment, both the scenery and the plants and animals that live in it. This book has all of that in abundance…"—*The Good, the Bad and the Unread*

Set the Stage

"I really adored this book. From the characters to the setting and the slow burn romance, I was in it for the long haul with this one. Karis Walsh to me is an expert in creating interesting characters that often have to face some type of adversity. While this book was no different, it felt like the author changed up her game a bit. There's something new, something fresh about this book from Walsh."—*Romantic Reader Blog*

"Both leads were well developed and you could see them grow as characters throughout the novel. They also had great chemistry. This slow burn romance made a great summer read."—*Melina Bickard, Librarian, Waterloo Library (UK)*

Tales From the Sea Glass Inn

"A wonderful romance about starting all over again in middle age. Karis Walsh creates an affirming love story in which relatable women face uncertainty and new beginnings, with all of their promise and shortcomings, and come out whole on the other side."—*Omnivore Bibliosaur*

"*Tales from Sea Glass Inn* is a lovely collection of stories about the women who visit the Inn and the relationships that they form with each other."—*Inked Rainbow Reads*

Love on Tap

"Karis Walsh writes excellent romances. They draw you in, engage your mind and capture your heart…What really good romance writers do is make you dream of being that loved, that chosen. Love on Tap is exactly that novel – interesting characters, slightly different circumstances to anything you have read before, slightly different challenges. And although you KNOW the happy ending is coming, you still have that little bit of 'oooh—make it happen.' Loved it. Wish it was me. What more is there to say?"—*Lesbian Reading Room*

"This is the second book I have read by this author and it certainly won't be my last. Ms Walsh is one of the few authors who can write a truly great and interesting love story without the need of a secondary story line or plot."—*Inked Rainbow Reads*

You Make Me Tremble

"Another quality read from Karis Walsh. She is definitely a go-to for a heartwarming read."—*Romantic Reader Blog*

Amounting to Nothing

"As always with Karis Walsh's books the characters are well drawn and the inter-relationships well developed."—*Lesbian Reading Room*

Sweet Hearts: Romantic Novellas

"I was super excited when I saw this book was coming out, and it did not disappoint."—*Danielle Kimerer, Librarian, Reading Public Library (MA)*

"Karis Walsh sensitively portrays the frustration of learning to live with a new disability through Ainslee, and the pain of living as a survivor of suicide loss through Myra."—*Lesbian Review*

Mounting Evidence

"[A]nother awesome Karis Walsh novel, and I have eternal hope that at some point there will be another book in this series. I liked the characters, the plot, the mystery and the romance so much."— Danielle Kimerer, Librarian, Reading Public Library (MA)

Mounting Danger

"A mystery, a woman in a uniform and horses...YES!!!!...This book is brilliant in my opinion. Very well written with great flow and a fantastic plot. I enjoyed the horses in this dramatic saga. There is so much information on training and riding, and polo. Very interesting things to know."—*Prism Book Alliance*

Blindsided

"Their slow-burn romance is a nuanced exploration of trust, desire, and negotiating boundaries, without a hint of schmaltz or pity. The sex scenes are sizzling hot, but it's the slow burn that really allows Walsh to shine…the deft dialogue and well-written characters make this a winner."—*Publishers Weekly*

"This is definitely a good read, and it's a good introduction to Karis Walsh and her books. The romance is good, the sex is hot, the dogs are endearing, and you finish the book feeling good. Why wouldn't you want all that?"—*Lesbian Review*

Wingspan

"I really enjoy Karis Walsh's work. She writes wonderful novels that have interesting characters who aren't perfect, but they are likable. This book pulls you into the story right from the beginning. The setting is the beautiful Olympic Peninsula and you can't help but want to go there as you read *Wingspan*."—*Romantic Reader Blog*

The Sea Glass Inn

"Karis Walsh's third book, excellently written and paced as always, takes us on a gentle but determined journey through two women's awakening…Loved it, another great read that will stay on my re-visit shelf."—*Lesbian Reading Room*

Worth the Risk

"The setting of this novel is exquisite, based on Karis Walsh's own background in horsemanship and knowledge of showjumping. It provides a wonderful plot to the story, a great backdrop to the characters and an interesting insight for those of us who don't know that world…Another great book by Karis Walsh. Well written, well paced, amusing and warming. Definitely a hit for me."—*Lesbian Reading Room*

Improvisation

"Walsh tells this story in achingly beautiful words, phrases and paragraphs, building a tension that is bittersweet. As the two main characters sway through life to the music of their souls, the reader may think she hears the strains of Tina's violin. As the two women interact, there is always an undercurrent of sensuality buzzing around the edges of the pages, even while they exchange sometimes snappy, sometimes comic dialogue. *Improvisation* is a true romantic tale, Walsh's fourth book, and she's evolving into a master romantic storyteller."—*Lambda Literary*

Harmony

"This was Karis Walsh's first novel and what a great addition to the LesFic fold. It is very well written and flows effortlessly as it weaves together the story of Brooke and Andi's worlds and their intriguing journey together. Ms Walsh has given space to more than just the heroines and we come to know the quartet and their partners, all of whom are likeable and interesting."—*Lesbian Reading Room*

By the Author

Harmony

Worth the Risk

Sea Glass Inn

Improvisation

Wingspan

Blindsided

Love on Tap

Tales from Sea Glass Inn

You Make Me Tremble

Set the Stage

Seascape

Love on Lavender Lane

Sit. Stay. Love

Liberty Bay

Love and Lattes

Mounted Police Romantic Intrigues:

Mounting Danger

Mounting Evidence

Amounting to Nothing

University Police Romantic Intrigues:

With a Minor in Murder

A Degree to Die For

Visit us at www.boldstrokesbooks.com

A DEGREE TO DIE FOR

by

Karis Walsh

2023

ISBN 13: 978-1-63679-365-8

THIS TRADE PAPERBACK ORIGINAL IS PUBLISHED BY
BOLD STROKES BOOKS, INC.
P.O. BOX 249
VALLEY FALLS, NY 12185

FIRST EDITION: JUNE 2023

CREDITS
EDITOR: RUTH STERNGLANTZ
PRODUCTION DESIGN: STACIA SEAMAN
COVER DESIGN BY TAMMY SEIDICK

A Degree
to Die For

CHAPTER ONE

A ntigone Weston paused—her breath held and her slender gold letter opener hovering in midslice—when she heard footsteps outside her office door. The sound of the heavy steps slowed momentarily, then continued, receding down the hallway. Tig exhaled with a sigh of relief and finished opening the padded mailer. She felt foolish for hiding in her office, but not enough that she was about to get up and open her door, inviting everyone to come inside and share their opinions about her leadership of the University of Washington's Classics Department. At this point, even conversations with the few who saw merit in the upcoming shift from a pure classics curriculum to the more inclusive Mediterranean Studies exhausted her. She'd had so many criticisms, compliments, and rambling debates thrown her way as she led her department through the transitional phase of this drastic change that she felt as tightly wound as a resonating piece of glass. One wrong move and she would shatter. So she was hiding behind closed doors, alone.

Well, *alone* if she didn't count the ghost of Laura Hughes. Laura had been one of Tig's favorite students and had recently—and far too briefly—been promoted to the status of colleague when she accepted Tig's offer just a month ago to be an adjunct professor at her old alma mater. She had been on campus for barely a day before an unstable and jealous student murdered her, erroneously believing that Laura and Professor Libby Hart might become romantically involved. The killer had then come far too close to murdering Libby and her new girlfriend, campus police officer Clare Sawyer. Losing

Laura had sent Tig reeling through grief. Losing her best friend Libby, as well, would have destroyed her.

And now Laura was back. Her memory, at least, if not her actual ghost. Tig had retrieved her mail a few days ago and found the letter-sized package among the usual stack of bills and professional journals. It was postmarked from Philadelphia, sent by Laura's fiancé. Tig hadn't known what to expect inside, and she had been carrying the unopened mailer in her briefcase for the past few days.

Tig sighed. She was usually the type of person who met issues head-on, often more defiantly than the situation warranted. She'd be the bull in the china shop, not the cow quietly tiptoeing through the daisies. Yet here she was, afraid to open her office door *and* her mail. Ridiculous.

She pulled the contents out of the mailer with a bit more force than necessary, and a handwritten sheet of blue paper fluttered to the floor. She ignored it for the moment, focused instead on the neatly printed and stapled essay in her hands. She remembered the title and topic, and a glance at the date confirmed that this would have been one of the first—if not *the* first—papers Laura had written for Tig as a freshman, for her Ancient Greek Novels course. She gingerly turned through the pages, skimming the handwritten notes she had crammed in the margins—correcting here, praising there. The paper felt fragile in her hands, its sides bent and torn, as if it had spent the past decade in a pile of books or other things that were slightly smaller, leaving only its edges exposed to the outside world.

She came to the last page. A-. Her final note said that Laura seemed to have an instinctive sensitivity to the subject and would likely be successful as a classics major if she was interested enough to pursue the degree. Tig sighed again, closing the paper and setting it on her desk. She fought the temptation to leap to the conclusion that Laura's death was now undeniably her fault. If she hadn't encouraged her to study this subject, she might be alive right now, happily teaching chemistry or economics or French literature…She shook her head. She had recognized her own passion for classics in Laura. She would have followed the same academic and career path even if Tig had written that she seemed to have no discernible talent and should probably consider any other major before this one.

Tig set the paper on her desk and bent down to retrieve the accompanying note. The delicately slanted handwriting of Laura's fiancé told her that Laura had kept this paper, even though she saved relatively few other sentimental items. He wrote that Laura had reread Tig's note whenever she was struggling in graduate school, and that Tig's message had seemed to give her courage to face her challenges and remain focused on the direction she needed to go. He hoped Tig might find the same comfort in the memento.

Tig carefully stowed the letter and essay in a file folder before resting her elbows on her desk and cradling her forehead in her palms. Maybe reading the paper would help in the coming days, reminding her of why she—like Laura—had chosen this career path in the first place, but she'd much rather have Laura herself to talk to. They had briefly discussed this upcoming curricular change when Laura had returned to campus last month, and she had seemed to have a like-minded approach to the new Mediterranean Studies plan. Neither Tig nor Laura liked change, especially when it came to their beloved subject and its reputation as a venerated university degree, but both of them recognized the need for the department to take steps toward mending some of its more racist qualities.

Tig tilted her head without raising it and looked around her office. This had been her space for almost fifteen years, but everything inside told an even older story. Her life was contained in the capsule of a room, with photos and mementos from family vacations, books her parents had used during their own careers as classical scholars, replicas of ancient Greek and Roman artifacts, and gifts from decades of Christmases and birthdays.

She hadn't even moved the furniture an inch in any direction since her first week as a professor at UW. Who was she to lead this department forward when she was the poster child for the status quo?

An outsider observing Tig's office and life would probably have bet a fortune on her being one of the more vocal opponents of this transition. Her life was modeled after those of her parents, whose careers were modeled after the generations of professors who had come before them. But despite the outward expression of her passion, she believed wholeheartedly in the need for an infusion of new viewpoints and in the importance of giving voice to the other cultures that had been so overshadowed by those of the Greeks and Romans that they were barely visible.

A loud rap on the door jolted Tig into an upright position and out of her maudlin musings. She momentarily considered ducking under her desk, but she had a pile of books and her laptop bag under there, and she probably wouldn't fit all the way. She doubted the other faculty members would have much faith in a director who was caught trying unsuccessfully to wedge herself into a hiding spot.

"Tig, I know you're in there. Open this door!"

Tig exhaled softly in relief. Ariella Romero's voice was sharper than usual, but she was a friend, and therefore on Tig's side by default.

"It's unlocked, Ari," she called in response.

Ari came in and shut the door behind her, giving her a look that Tig would have filed under the word *disdain* if she had been compiling a visual dictionary of expressions. Ari might be the smallest member of Tig's group of friends, but after only moments in her company, her stature seemed to grow beyond her physical size, and she was ferociously capable of expressing intense emotions and judgments with a mere glance. She sat down in the chair on the other side of Tig's desk and crossed her legs. She was wearing a simple long-sleeved black top and a pair of black jeans, but with intricately woven, sand-colored fingerless gloves on her hands. Tig shook her head. If she had worn those gloves, she would have looked like she had hurt herself and accidentally wrapped doilies on her hands instead of bandages. On Ari, the same accessories made her look as if her hands were about to bring forth something wondrously creative, like an intricate piano concerto or a timeless novel that would rival Heathcliff and his moors.

"What gave me away?" Tig asked.

"I could see that your light was on," Ari said. "If you're going to hide in here, you ought to use a jacket or something to cover the crack under the door."

"I was going to turn off the light and read by flashlight, but yours is a better idea," Tig said. "This is an old blazer, so I don't mind if it gets dirty on the floor."

Ari raised her eyebrows slightly. "I was joking, but I think you're serious."

"Just a little," Tig admitted, spinning her letter opener under her fingers until she realized it was making a divot in the wood surface of her desk. She had bought the massive cherrywood desk when she moved into her first apartment after college, and it was covered with years of chips and dents. Still, she didn't need to make it worse. She set the opener to one side and laced her fingers together. "I'm avoiding the angry hordes."

"I can give you a motivational speech, but it needs to be a short one since we're meeting Libby and Jazz in about twenty minutes. Libby wants to try the new hamburger place near the police station."

"On a Monday?" Tig asked, partly because she was surprised that Libby was deviating from her usual dining schedule, and partly to avoid what was more likely to be a motivational diatribe rather than speech. Libby used to make Tig seem wildly spontaneous in comparison, but she had relaxed her hold on her daily and weekly rituals quite a bit since falling in love with Clare. Tig quite liked Clare and thought she was perfect for Libby, but she was planning to avoid following the same path Libby had taken. She had enough changes to deal with in her professional life, and she didn't need to add upheavals in her personal life to the mix. Not that her personal life had included anyone new and exciting since…well, Tig couldn't exactly remember when, but she'd ballpark it somewhere between Ancient Greek times and about five years ago.

"I think she just wants to be near where Clare works," Ari said. "This might be the best time to convert her to being a gothic literature fan, while they're still in the lovey-dovey stage and emotions are running high. I'd normally wait until the breakup to really get someone hooked, but I have a feeling this one's going to last."

"I agree about it lasting," Tig said, "but I'll bet the real reason she wants to stick close to the police station is because she's hoping someone will accidentally leave a detective's badge or uniform lying around, and she can take it and pretend she's officially on the job."

Ari nodded thoughtfully. "You're probably right. Really, she helped catch one serial killer and suddenly she thinks she's Sherlock Holmes. If she starts making noise about giving up architectural history and joining the force, we'll have to have another intervention and try to get her back into her old rut. Still, though..." Ari hesitated, then leaned forward slightly. "She really was amazing, wasn't she? The way she noticed the symbols and details of the crime scenes was very impressive."

"Because they were designed for her," Tig said. The infatuated student-turned-killer had used Libby's lectures to send messages to her beloved teacher, speaking in a language they shared. Tig smiled, sharing in Ari's pride for Libby. "She *was* brilliant, though. If every future murderer makes explicit use of the architectural elements at their crime scenes, she could have a stellar career as a detective."

Ari grinned in response, then shook her head and the smile disappeared. "Back to your cowardly hiding. You distracted me, so now you get the super-abbreviated version of the lecture. I'm sure the three of us can expand on it for at least another hour during dinner, but here's the gist." Ari flicked one gloved hand as if chasing off an errant fly. "Just tell the complainers that they need to grow up and move with the times. You're doing what it takes to make this department relevant and to get more students interested in it, and they should appreciate you instead of complaining."

Tig sighed. Ari made it sound so easy to just shrug off the antagonistic attitudes of her colleagues, but Tig wasn't handling it with as much grace or confidence as Ari seemed to expect from her. She wanted to bring her faculty members together as a team—to convince them that this was the best way to keep the department alive—partly because she felt that her role as head of the department was to be on everyone's side, seeing problems and solutions from all angles. And, she admitted only to herself, partly because she was sympathetic to those who didn't want anything to change.

"It's more complicated than that," she said. "Classics has always been a respected major. It's foundational, for both our culture and our educational systems. I know those old ways need to be updated, and that we need to acknowledge and honor the civilizations and contributions of other ancient peoples instead of erasing them, but it's not easy for some to let go of the cachet that our type of department used to have."

"Hey, I get that. Don't you think I'd rather have Gothic Studies be its own major instead of just a tiny specialty within the English Department? Of course, the Classics Department has obviously survived on its own for ages, but according to you, just because it has in the past doesn't mean it should from now on. Didn't you say that you're not trying to dilute the department, but to make it stronger?"

Tig frowned. Ari was playing dirty, throwing her own words back at her. "Maybe I said those words, but you make them sound more convincing. I hereby appoint you spokesperson for the new Med Studies program."

"No way. It sounds like a thankless job." Ari grinned at her. "Besides, deep down you know you're the best person to do it. You'll be more effective if you're not shouting those words through your closed office door. You just need to have more confidence in yourself. And if you don't believe me when I tell you how great you are, maybe I should read some of your fan mail."

Ari grabbed the unopened envelope on the top of Tig's stack of mail and cleared her throat dramatically as she tore it open. "In the words of the illustrious classics faculty at Bryn Mawr, who are desperate to have you join them as a visiting professor—"

"Fine. Please stop," Tig said with a laugh. She was routinely courted by other universities—especially as a relatively well-known female professor in a heavily male-dominated subject—but she had no interest in leaving Seattle, no matter what difficulties she was currently facing. And she most definitely didn't want to hear Ari read one of those letters out loud. "I give up. I'm amazing. The best thing that ever happened to classics. A paragon of Greek virtue."

Ari grinned with a smug expression as she stuffed the letter back into the envelope. "Was that so hard? Now, come on, or we'll be late."

Tig gave the route of cowardice one more try. "I don't suppose the three of you would want to pick up those burgers and bring them back here, would you? We could have a picnic on my office floor. It'd be fun, eating by flashlight."

Ari's next look apparently meant *Get the hell out of your chair*. Tig sighed and stood up, following Ari out the door. Her hopes that all the other professors would be similarly ensconced in their offices were dashed when they practically ran into Chase Davies as they stepped into the hallway.

"Professor Weston," he said, with a nod of acknowledgment at both her and Ari.

"Professor Davies," she replied in kind.

"Wow. Objectively speaking, he's a very handsome man," Ari whispered after they had walked a few steps past him. "Snappy dresser."

Tig glanced over her shoulder. "Hey, we're practically wearing the same outfit."

Ari looked at her. Tan pants, a tweed blazer. Tig's shirt was pumpkin-colored and his was mauve, but still...

"You're right, sorry. Platonically speaking, you're—"

Tig held up her hand. "Save it, Ari. Everyone knows he's the hottie of the Classics Department. Probably three-quarters of our students chose this as their major because they're in love with him." She might be slightly exaggerating, but not by much. That was why she always had him teach at least one intro class every quarter. She wasn't above using him as bait.

"We seem to have similar wardrobes, and occasionally we look like we coordinated our outfits on purpose. Somehow, though, he always manages to look as if he's about to leap onto a desk and start spouting inspirational poetry, while I look like I might stumble over my own two feet and scatter all the loose papers I'm carrying across the floor."

Ari laughed and bumped Tig with her shoulder. "So, how many times has that actually happened?"

"I have no idea about the inspirational poetry, but the paper scattering has happened once." Ari gave her a look of disbelief. "Okay, twice. But I was grading papers in both cases. It's not easy to walk and correct grammar at the same time."

Their laughter faded slightly when they passed Professor Kamrick Morris and Tig exchanged the same terse greeting with him. He was wearing oddly similar clothes—Tig resolved to go buy some new, non-neutral outfits as soon as possible—but she decided she came out better in a comparison with him than with Chase. Kam's arms were full of books and files that looked ready to drop at any moment, and he had his usual scruffy, harried air about him.

Tig sighed in relief as they pushed through the glass-paned doors of Denny Hall and walked down the wide staircase, with its fall coating of damp, yellowed leaves. Only two encounters, and neither had resulted in a stressful conversation, probably thanks to Ari's presence.

"I'm not used to seeing you act so formal and distant with your colleagues," Ari said as they headed off campus. "Are they both opposed to the new department?"

"First one, yes. Second one supports it."

"Huh," Ari said, batting at an oak leaf that twirled out of a tree and into her hair. "I really can't see why you're hiding in your office when the worst that happens is maybe a briefer nod or a slightly cooler tone."

Tig shook her head. She couldn't explain it, but she felt more at work under the surface than was indicated by those two short hellos. "We've gotten pretty good at keeping our conversations to a minimum if there are students or people from outside the department around, but it feels like a fragile sort of control to me. I can't shake the feeling that everything is going to explode one of these days."

Taking out both her and her career when it happened.

CHAPTER TWO

Y our ass is mine, Sawyer."
 Clare Sawyer sighed as she turned around and faced her latest hopeful jailer. For the third time since she had stepped foot in the University of Washington's campus police station, she handed him the doctor's note she had been holding at the ready like a shield.

"You don't have to sound so gleeful, Landry. We're supposed to be friends."

"We are," Derek Landry said. He had been the first officer she met when she initially came to the department as a lateral, and one of the first people here that she had considered an ally. "Usually we are. But there's a beach in Hawaii calling my name, and I want those extra vacation days and the cash Kent's offering for your capture."

Clare shook her head. Her sergeant must have upped the ante after she caught Clare on campus a week ago. She had only been walking casually around the dorms at night, and it was just sheer coincidence that she had been in the right place to break up a fight on the lawn in front of Willow Hall. She hadn't even been in uniform. And the stomach wound she had sustained when her girlfriend Libby's student-turned-murderous-stalker shot her had been close to completely healed. Still, Kent had overreacted with a vengeance, and the resulting lecture—delivered loudly in front of the dorm—had caused quite a scene. Even the two squabbling students had forgotten why they had been fighting and had banded together to cheer Kent on. And, although there had originally been only extra vacation days to the officer who captured Clare sneaking back to campus, Kent had apparently added drinking money to the incentive package.

"Read the note," Clare said. "I'm fully cleared for duty, so Hawaii's going to have to exist without you for a while longer."

"Hmm. Hold these while I check this out," Derek said, handing her his pair of handcuffs as he scanned the paper. "In fact, go ahead and put them on. I'll uncuff you if this is legit."

Clare put the cuffs in her pocket in case he decided the note looked like a forgery and wanted to chain her up in a holding cell while he investigated farther. He scanned the paper and held it out to Clare with a rueful grin.

"Looks like you're officially back, dammit," he said. "No hard feelings, right? Can I have those handcuffs back?"

Clare snatched the paper out of his hand, then pulled out the cuffs and let them dangle from one finger. "I should keep these. Tell Kent you left them out somewhere and Libby got hold of them. Maybe she'll give *me* those extra vacation days."

"You wouldn't dare." Derek actually looked worried as he grabbed for the cuffs, and Clare wondered if Kent had offered a similar bribe to anyone who caught Libby impersonating an officer and launching some sort of investigation. Clare couldn't hide her smile at that thought. Good luck to anyone who tried to cash in on that bribe. Libby was a force to be reckoned with, and Clare was secretly relieved that the rest of the department might be helping to keep an eye on her. Clare had already discovered a study guide for taking a detective's test hidden among Libby's architecture books. She hadn't mentioned to Libby that she would need to have experience as an officer first because then she'd be applying for the police academy, or bypassing that route altogether and setting up shop as a private investigator.

She'd be a great one, too, with her intelligence and logic, but more than anything, Clare wanted to keep Libby safe, and being a professor was much less dangerous than Clare's line of work.

Well, usually, at least. Not lately.

Derek snapped his cuffs onto his duty belt. "See you in turnout," he said. "Glad to have you back."

"Yeah, right," Clare scoffed, but she smiled as she turned toward Kent's office. She was glad to be back, too.

Or she would be, as soon as she made it past Kent.

Clare walked down the hall, with its warm wood paneling that was covered with photos of past department chiefs, award plaques with lists of honorees, and bulletin boards full of notices about upcoming meetings and items for sale by the campus officers. The homey, comfortable feel was a contrast to the more steel and glass look of the public-access foyer, and completely at odds with Kent's office. Clare saw her through the open door, sitting at a desk that was piled with paperwork and an incongruous yellow mug with a hand-painted smiley face on it. Everything else in here was work related, from the framed service awards and certificates on the walls to the shelves with their tidy rows of procedural manuals. Clare didn't need to look closely at them to know that they were in strict numerical order.

Adriana Kent was just as tidy and ordered as her small office, aside from the messy stacks of paper and file folders on the desk in front of her. Her dark brown hair was neat and short, with a few gray strands that Clare figured were the result of annoyance at her subordinates rather than age. Her uniform was starched and creased until it looked as if it could walk around the department and issue orders without Kent inside it, if necessary. She was filling out a form with aggressively blocky printing, and Clare hesitated before knocking on the door, reluctant to disturb her when—

"Make it easy for me, Sawyer," Kent said without looking up. "Just keep hovering in my doorway until I finish this paragraph, and then I'll arrest you. I don't need the vacation days, but it'll give me great personal satisfaction to throw you in the holding cell with last night's drunks."

"I have a note," Clare said, sounding in her mind ridiculously like a student offering proof that she had permission to leave class and use the bathroom.

Kent looked up, her hazel eyes surprisingly warm and large, when one might expect to see chips of ice blue instead.

"Do you expect me to read it from here?" she asked. "Come *in*, Sawyer."

Clare stepped inside the office and handed her sergeant the note, pulling her arm back as quickly as she could without making it obvious. Kent would likely be less DIY with the handcuffs than Derek had been, and Clare had a feeling she'd be attached by her wrist to the arm of Kent's chair before she even saw her sergeant move. She took a step back and leaned casually against the doorjamb. Yes, she was perfectly at ease. Not scared of Kent at all.

Kent looked briefly at the note and then placed it on top of a pile of papers near her left elbow. She rubbed the bridge of her nose before glancing back in Clare's direction.

"What, are you on break right now? We're not paying you to lounge around, so get back to work." Kent returned her attention to the work in front of her, but not quickly enough to hide her smile from Clare. "Really," she muttered, "I'd have thought a month off would be enough R and R for you, but apparently it wasn't."

Clare grinned, feeling a weight rise off her heart as she left the office and headed back toward the building's entrance. The first time she had left Kent's office—barely over two months ago—she had been much less enthusiastic about this job. She had been worried over her rash departure from Seattle PD, and uncertain about her future as an officer. She paused in the hallway. Now, such a short time later, she felt as if she had just come home.

She started walking again, only to stop again a few seconds later when she spotted Libby standing in the foyer. Her heart might have felt light moments ago, but now it felt full, heavy with love. Libby had been the catalyst that turned Clare's life and career around when a murder case had brought the beautiful professor into Clare's world. Libby had been determined to stay there—at first, because of how intrigued she was by the investigation, but hopefully now because of Clare herself.

Mostly, at least. Clare wasn't a fool.

She hurried across the lobby, torn between the desire to pull Libby into her arms and kiss her—which she shouldn't do because she was at work and in uniform—and the urge to push Libby out the door before she asked for a job application.

She settled on standing close to Libby without technically touching her. Being able to feel the heat of her breath didn't count as touching, did it?

"I'm happy to see you, of course, but what are you doing here?"

Libby let her gaze travel down Clare's front, lingering in just the right places to remind Clare that she intimately knew what was under her uniform.

"I'm here to see you, of course. I've been missing you all morning."

Clare didn't say anything but merely raised her eyebrows slightly.

Libby laughed, the sound always striking Clare like musical notes. "Don't worry, I'm not hanging out waiting for someone to leave a criminal file unattended. Jazz is meeting me here. We're having lunch with Tig and Ari just around the corner."

"Just around the...wait..." Clare leaned closer. Libby was going off schedule. Clare wasn't sure why yet, but it was probably leading toward trouble. For her, most likely. "On a Monday? What are you up to, Lib?"

"Nothing, sweetie. I'm just..." Libby leaned to one side and peered around Clare. "Oh, hello, Sergeant Kent. It's nice to see you, as always."

"Professor Hart," Kent said, walking up behind Clare. "Suspicious to see you, as always."

Libby smiled, unfazed even though Clare had a nauseating feeling that she had figured out Libby's plan far too late to stop it. "I was just meeting a friend here...Oh, here she is now. She's always very punctual."

The three of them turned toward the glass doors in time to see Jazz walk through. She was as stunning and imposing as ever, even in her casual black sweater and trousers. She looked around the reception area as if she was claiming the territory for the Vikings.

Clare tugged on Libby's sleeve. "What are you doing, Libby?"

she implored, her voice pitched low. "Trying to get me fired on my first day back?"

"Shh," Libby said, patting her hand where it rested on Libby's cardigan. "I know what I'm doing." She raised her voice when her friend got closer. "Jazz, this is Clare's boss, Sergeant Kent. Sarge, this is Jasmine Harald, the director of—"

"Suzzallo Library," Kent finished for her, shaking her head at the nickname, but letting it slide. "Nice to meet you, Ms. Harald. Quite an impressive building you have there. I got to know something about its history during our investigation. I'm sorry a murder landed on your doorstep."

"So am I," Jazz said. She grimaced, probably at the memory of the few hours her library was cordoned off by crime scene tape and off-limits to her. "But I appreciate how quickly you took care of that mess. You seem to run an efficient department here."

"Thank you. We try." Kent glanced at Clare. "Some harder than others, apparently."

"Nice to meet you, Sergeant," Jazz said. "I'm going to leave now, so I don't have to watch the two lovebirds say good-bye."

"Likewise," Kent said, "to both statements."

The two women went their separate ways, with Kent heading toward the turnout room and Jazz going out the front door, where she stood under the awning and out of the steady autumn rain.

"*Efficient*," Clare repeated once she and Libby were alone. "Wow, that was really hot."

Libby punched her playfully on the arm, but her sigh was heartfelt. "I expected more fireworks with those two. I really thought I was making the match of the century."

"I expected something more along the lines of an explosion, leaving nothing but a crater where the station had been. The disaster of the century. Instead, that was almost..."

"Boring," Libby finished for her.

"Exactly," Clare said, smiling at her. "At least *we're* not boring."

"You're right," Libby said, leaning toward her without touching.

"We're so adorably in love we make people leave the room to get away from us."

"Damn right," Clare agreed. "There's nothing but passion when the two of us are together." She looked out front, where Tig and Ari had joined Jazz, then at the desk, where the officer on duty was looking awkwardly absorbed in the file he was reading. "Well, maybe not right at this moment."

"No," Libby agreed, then gave Clare one of her smiles that made her feel as if the world around her was about to explode. "But tonight, yes?"

"Most definitely yes," Clare said. She watched until Libby had walked out the door and joined her friends, turning back to wave at Clare before they moved out of sight. Then she hurried down the hall to join Kent's meeting before she was so late that she got suspended for another month.

Kent continued sharing campus news with her swing shift officers, barely acknowledging Clare's entrance to the meeting room except by the merest of headshakes, as if chiding her for being late. She noticed with amusement that most of the others in the room saw Clare walk in, and then immediately looked to her, as if wondering whether Sawyer was allowed back yet, or if they could battle each other to grab her and claim the vacation prize. Their disappointment when it became obvious that Kent was allowing her back to work was quickly replaced by smiles of welcome, and Kent pretended to be searching for some notes to give everyone time to greet Clare.

She continued after a few moments, acting as if the day was a normal one when to her and Clare it was anything but. She had seen Clare's potential in this department from the start but had had serious doubts about whether she'd ever fit in with the other officers or with the slower pace of university work compared to the bustle of Seattle. The murders had given Clare a chance to prove herself far sooner than Kent would have liked, but she had risen to the occasion far better than anyone could have expected.

Kent had seen the expression on Clare's face earlier when she had told her to get back to work. She was happy to be here, and not just because she saw the small department as a stepping-stone in her career. She was relieved to be back.

Not half as relieved as Kent herself, she thought as she stood to one side as the shift's supervising officer handed out assignments for the afternoon and evening. She had never had one of her officers get hurt as badly as Clare. The gunshot wound could have been fatal or career ending if it had strayed millimeters in another direction. Kent felt sick when she thought about it. She had been terrified the first time Clare had been attacked by the murderer and dazed by a concussion, but the second attack, the bullet through her stomach—incurred while she was attempting to rescue Libby—had been something else entirely.

Kent might not be old enough to be the mother of everyone in her department—although at times she felt old enough to be their great-granny—but her sense of responsibility toward these people and her desire to keep them safe were as strong as a parental bond. She had hated feeling so helpless while Clare was off duty, and her incentive plan for the other officers was as much meant to keep Clare off work long enough to heal as it was a way for her to keep tabs on Clare's movements. She had a feeling the other officers had guessed this, because they came to her every time they saw Clare, even when she was in civilian clothes and not attempting to stop brawls or enforce campus policies. Kent had gotten used to the informal reports she got every time a shift ended. *Hey, Sergeant, I saw Sawyer near Denny Hall with Professor Hart. They were eating sandwiches on a bench, and she wasn't in uniform.*

Ridiculous, but Kent had never discouraged these reports. Clare was out and about and doing well. She'd appreciated every mundane detail about Sawyer's movements because they meant she was still alive.

Kent watched the officers file out of the room, among them Sawyer and Landry, who were mock punching each other and most likely trading good-natured insults. She gathered her notes, turned off the lights in the meeting room, and went back to her office. She always felt a little twinge of loneliness when shifts started and she was left behind as an administrator and not a patrol officer, and today the pangs were slightly more intense.

The truth was, she liked Clare. And Libby. She'd met two of Libby's friends, also—Jazz today, and Ariella during the murder investigation—and they seemed nice, as well. Kent was able to admit to herself that she would like to allow these acquaintances to possibly grow into friendships, but her job meant she always had a strict hierarchy to obey. Clare was her subordinate—for the moment, but likely not for long, given her intuitive knack for the job. And since Claire was her link to Libby and Libby's friends, they were effectively out of bounds as well.

She sat down at her desk with a sigh. The constant assessing of relationships and how close she was allowed to get to people was tiring, but worth it because she believed the work she did was important enough to make sacrifices for it. She worked too much to give herself time to meet many people outside the department, and the ones inside were almost always on rungs above or below her on the ladder.

So, while today she might be regretting the distance she had to keep between herself and Clare, the reassurance that Clare was healthy enough to be back was more than enough to compensate for any sense of isolation Kent might feel.

She pulled the next file off the stack beside her and got back to work.

Chapter Three

A fter about an hour of paperwork, Kent couldn't take the inactivity any longer. She had been drawn to police work because of the near constant movement it entailed. Walking, chasing, fighting, helping...While some officers were content to spend as much of their days as possible sitting in a patrol car or coffee shop, waiting for the call that would force them to abandon their comfortable perch and act, Kent had always had a restless quality about her. Whenever possible, she'd choose to go on foot over driving and to mingle with the citizens she had promised to protect over hiding away and hoping her radio would remain silent. She had been good at being a patrol officer—often more proactive than most of her colleagues— and being always in motion had mentally settled her.

Fortunately for her career—but unfortunately for her temperament—she was even better at leading other people. She was organized and efficient, and she intuitively knew just how far and in what way to push her officers in her quest to have the best damned department in the state. She had been promoted far too quickly for her own comfort, and now she had a job for which sitting behind a desk all day was a requirement, not an escape.

She pushed her chair back and stood up. She had powered through her work in half the time it should have required, so she deserved a break. And she was hungry. Well, not very hungry, since she had finished her lunch just before the shift meeting, but she could manage to eat a cookie or something small like that. Or get some coffee. Of course, she could get coffee at over a dozen places in the U District, more than half of which were within a two-block radius of the station, but she really should stick to campus in case any of her officers needed her. They were shorthanded on all shifts at the moment, since a nasty flu was working its way through the department, and one of her most senior officers—Cappy Flannery— was away on family business.

She really had no choice but to leave her desk, bring her radio along, and head to campus.

She smiled as she locked her office door behind her, comforted by the logic of her internal reasoning. She would get back to that never-ending pile of reports, duty rosters, and memos a little later. For now, though, she would spend some time on patrol—er, *going for coffee*. She'd walk among her civilians wearing a uniform that would mark her as merely a campus police officer to most of them, since very few recognized her or the insignia of her rank. She'd get that coffee, and if by chance someone stole a laptop or shoplifted a pair of purple-and-gold socks from the HUB or needed directions to the Burke Museum…well, she'd be shirking her responsibilities if she didn't step in and help, wouldn't she?

She told the duty officer where she was going, attempting to look like her usual stern self and not like a child who'd just heard the bell for recess, and left the station. She hadn't even decided which coffee shop to choose when the call she had been hoping for came over the radio.

A fistfight at Denny Hall, near the western edge of UW's sprawling campus, and mere yards away from Kent.

Yes.

She keyed her radio and put herself en route to Denny. Fights were more common in the evenings and on weekends, especially near the Greek houses or dorms, where students and alcohol tended to congregate, but daytime scuffles weren't unheard of. Most likely a couple of kids squabbling over a mutual love interest, or maybe a plagiarized paper. Nothing exciting. Still, Kent was relieved to hear that she was the closest officer to the scene. She jaywalked across

15th Street, and then broke into a jog, skimming in and out of the crowds and splashing through puddles as she left the concrete paths and made a beeline to the building.

She reached the back entrance of Denny Hall. Its bland stone block and brick exterior made it look like a completely different building from the front, where it was decorated with ornate towers and turrets and archways. Kent would bet that Libby could give her a five-hour lecture on the architectural elements of this old building—likely needing very little prompting to do so—but for now, all Kent cared about was the plain gray metal door that stood between her and the latest cause of disruption on her campus. Once inside, she raced up a steep flight of stairs, relieved that she kept up on her workouts at the gym even though her current job didn't demand the same level of fitness she used to need. She wouldn't have made a very imposing figure if she'd shown up sweaty and disheveled.

The heavy use of glass and metal in the renovated interior made it easy for Kent to locate the fight using her ears alone, and the slap of her boots on the marble floors added to the echoing shouts coming from her right.

From the sound of things, the fight was still in progress. From the size of the crowd in front of her as she turned onto the main hallway, the entire population of the building had gathered around the brawl, like a pack of Romans at the gladiatorial games. Kent pushed her way through the cluster of students and faculty members. The people at the very edge of the crowd grudgingly moved out of her way, but once they seemed to notice her uniform, a tunnel of space opened up in front of her. She knew she was likely disappointing many of them by arriving so quickly to shut this down, especially those who were happy to have an unexpected afternoon entertainment or those students who were relieved to have an excuse to be late for class.

She paused for a moment as she made it past the last layer of humanity and the makeshift boxing ring they had created as they pressed close—but not *too* close—to the action opened up before her.

Kent visually scanned the scene, nearly two decades of experience enabling her to collect numerous details in a matter of seconds. The majority of the onlookers seemed to be students, most wearing jeans and hoodies or sweaters. The professors were likewise easy to distinguish, with their more formal and very uniform blazers and slacks. Two adults stood together across from Kent, notable in their lack of earth-toned clothing. The woman was wearing a silky peasant-style tunic with visible flecks of gold thread and matching deep purple trousers that were gathered at her ankles, and a blood-red head wrap. The man had on a well-cut black suit and tie with a deep navy shirt. They had similar light brown skin tones, but where hers was warmed by an amused-looking expression that crinkled the corners of her eyes and mouth, his was hardened by stony gray eyes and a sneer of contempt. She didn't know if that was his usual attitude or if it was simply a reaction to the scene playing out in front of him.

And then there were the two combatants. Well, three if she counted the woman standing between the two men, but she seemed to be trying to keep them apart rather than joining in the battle. Where Kent had been expecting to find students misbehaving, she found instead two grown-ass men flinging insults and erratic punches at each other.

"Worthless dandy!"

"Mediocre scholar!"

The scene would have been as ludicrous as a Three Stooges film if these two weren't brawling on Kent's campus, disturbing the peace she devoted her life to maintaining.

"Plagiarist!" the sandy-haired man shouted, eliciting gasps from the gathered crowd, as he swung wildly at his adversary. He missed—which anyone could have predicted given his untrained delivery—but connected with the woman who seemed to be in the process of trying to protect him by dragging the other man away.

Kent reflexively stepped behind her and caught the woman in her arms, holding her for a brief moment until she seemed steady enough on her feet, and then moved her as gently as possible out of the way of the other two. Once her arms were free of the woman, Kent grabbed a fistful of tweed in each hand, holding the two men at arm's length.

The fight had already left them, however, as they stared at the victim of their scuffle.

"Tig...Tig, I'm so sorry," the taller of the two stuttered.

"You hit her," the other said in a whiny, accusatory voice. Whatever the initial cause of the argument had been, he now seemed to be gearing up to renew the hostilities, this time defending the woman called Tig. "You son of a—"

Kent's sharp whistle was punctuated by a hard shake of her hands, and the men finally turned their attention to her. They seemed surprised to see an officer standing there, holding each by the shirtfront.

Before she could say anything else—or do anything rash like bang their heads together, and she really wanted to do that—she heard footsteps racing up behind her. Sawyer and Landry each took hold of a combatant, twisting an arm behind their backs to keep them from running, even though they now looked more likely to faint than to flee. The shorter man with a paunch was panting heavily and he sank into a sitting position, nearly pulling Landry with him.

Kent glanced around to make sure the scene was secure. Most of the crowd had dissipated at the arrival of the campus police, but a few lingered, probably prepared to give witness statements if needed. A couple of professors were gathering papers that had scattered across the floor. The two people Kent had marked as out of place were nowhere to be seen. She wasn't happy about that, but the campus community was small. She'd be able to find out who they were if she decided it was necessary.

She turned to check on the woman who had been sucker punched and barely contained her groan of annoyance when she saw Libby Hart standing next to her, dabbing at her bloody face with the end of her scarf.

"Really, Sawyer," she hissed in a low voice to keep from being overheard. She was too angry to save the lecture for a more private time, however. "You brought your girlfriend on a call? Do I need to get HR involved to prove to the two of you that she isn't actually an officer?"

"She was here when I got here, Sergeant," Clare said quietly. She hesitated then continued, "They're...she and Tig are friends."

Shit. Of course Libby would manage to be involved somehow. Kent shook her head and returned to a normal tone of voice as she quickly filled Sawyer and Landry in on what had happened before they arrived.

"Get their statements," she said, gesturing at the now-defeated looking men. "And then talk to the witnesses. I'll take care of this mess."

She wasn't sure what mess she meant. The bloody victim, the wannabe detective, or the entire fucked-up event. All three, she decided.

"Hart, I'll take it from here. You can go." She fished a clean handkerchief out of her pocket and handed it to Tig, who pressed it against her nose. The bleeding seemed under control, and Tig didn't look likely to pass out at the sight of her own blood, so Kent felt a small sense of relief. Still, she wrapped her hand around Tig's upper arm just in case.

"But she's hurt," Libby said, obviously distressed at her friend's situation. "I should—"

"You should get back to work. And by work, I mean professor types of things. Read a book. Give a lecture. Write a paper. Somewhere else."

Libby glanced at Clare, and the two of them seemed to conduct an entire conversation in just a few seconds of looking at each other. Clare's desire to keep her job apparently won Libby over, because she nodded and turned back to her friend.

"Call me if you need anything," she said. "I'll be in my office. And I'll come check on you later, so let me know if you're here or if you have to go to the emergency—"

"Hart!" Kent said.

"Libby, please," Clare said at the same time.

"*Yeesh*, I'm going," Libby said, turning after a final wave at Tig and a pained-looking smile at Clare.

Kent ran her free hand through her hair, keeping the other firmly on Tig's arm. "How do you feel?"

"Okay, I guess," Tig answered. "I suppose I would have bled out by now if it was going to happen."

"Yes, well, I had to deal with some staffing issues. Meaning someone thinks she's on my staff when she actually isn't."

Tig laughed and then winced. "Don't underestimate her. If she decides she really wants a career change, she'll probably be your boss in a year or two."

Kent shook her head, more in acquiescence than denial. "Let me check your nose," she said, stepping in front of Tig. She moved the handkerchief aside and carefully ran her fingers over the bridge of Tig's nose and her cheekbones.

Kent had to force herself to concentrate on checking for swelling instead of noticing how soft Tig's skin was, and how her breath smelled sweet, like chocolate, when Kent leaned closer to look for broken blood vessels in the whites of Tig's lapis-blue eyes. She felt the whole of Tig's body as if the energy of her was pressing physically against Kent, though they remained inches apart.

She was checking for an injury, dammit, not getting ready for a slow dance. She had done this exact same thing for Keaton the other day, after she tripped over a chair and face-planted into the conference room window. That had been a purely neutral experience—well, maybe a little funny—but nothing sensual or alarming. Kent had sent Keaton off to get checked by a doctor, wiped the blood smear off the window, and filled out an incident report. All without noticing the color of Keaton's eyes or the way her breath smelled.

She stepped away and handed the stained handkerchief back to Tig, feeling the lack of her warmth almost immediately.

"Well?" Tig asked.

"Well, what?" Kent snapped defensively, as if Tig was able to read her wandering thoughts.

"Is it broken? It really hurts."

"It doesn't seem broken, but we'll get you checked just in case. You might have some bruising, but it shouldn't be bad, plus the bleeding's already stopped. It was a weak punch."

Tig frowned, then winced again and returned to a more neutral expression. "It sure didn't feel weak."

Kent had to laugh at Tig's reaction. Weak punch or not, she had still been hit hard enough to give her a headache for the next day or two. Instead of looking like a wounded, delicate flower, she looked affronted by the experience, and like she wanted to do some punching of her own. "I take it you haven't been hit in the face before?"

"Of course not. I take it you have?"

Kent shrugged. "Well, yeah. I grew up with three brothers, and I'm a police officer."

"I grew up with one sister, and I'm a classics scholar. We're not exactly a rough crowd."

Kent raised her eyebrows at that, not even bothering to gesture toward the two men who had been separated and were talking to her officers.

Tig grimaced. "Usually. They're not going to get in trouble, are they?"

"They might. Depends on who started the fight, and who might want to press charges. Do you have an office in the building?"

Tig nodded. "One floor down."

"Let's go there and talk. Just for a few minutes, and then I'll let Hart take you to the emergency room for a checkup."

"Oh, okay," Tig said, pulling a cell out of her blazer's pocket. "I can call her and let her know."

"Don't bother. I can see her standing outside on the front steps." Kent shook her head. She really hadn't expected Libby to actually leave the vicinity. She pushed aside the unexpected wish that she'd be the one who needed to take Tig to the ER. The sooner she got Tig's story and handed her off to her friend, the better.

She looked across the hall and made eye contact with Clare, gesturing toward Tig with her head, and Clare nodded her understanding. They'd collect their stories and then meet back at the station and try to piece together something close to the truth from three different interpretations of it. Although Kent wanted to throw the lot of them into a holding cell for a day or so since they had disrupted her formerly peaceful campus, she knew they'd all be released. Tig, because she was an innocent bystander, and the two pugilists because they weren't likely to be flight risks. By next week, the entire incident would probably just be an embarrassing memory for those involved, and nothing more than a reprimand from the Dean of Faculty would come out of this.

And then the Classics Department would settle down to its usual unruffled state, and Kent could go back to her paperwork.

And if Libby ever brought this friend to the station on their way to lunch? Well, Kent would have to kick them both out. She looked at Tig, who had an intriguing expression of simmering fury on her face, and recalled in vivid detail how it felt to stand so close to her.

Yes, she'd definitely kick them out of the station. She didn't need this kind of trouble in her well-ordered life.

CHAPTER FOUR

Tig led the way down the stairs and to her office. She felt as if she was forcing her legs to work like normal through willpower alone, and the moment she let her concentration slip, she would crumple to the floor like Kam had done. She was glad she had to focus on the simple act of walking, step-by-step, because it kept her mind from far more upsetting thoughts. Such as, what was going to happen to her colleagues because of this? And how was she going to explain the fight to local businessman Max Adel—one of her department's primary local donors—and Samiya Ayari—the recently hired Professor of Comparative Mediterranean Art and Architecture—who had both managed to arrive at Denny just in time for the day's headliner boxing match?

And, most pressing, how was she going to keep from clubbing both Kam and Chase over the head with her replica of a caryatid statue as punishment for losing control the way they had?

While she was at it, she might also take a swing at the police officer who followed her into her office. She was sure that the officer would be able to deflect her blow, but it would feel damned good to try.

She had no idea why she felt so angry toward her, when the officer had managed to stop the fight, and her fingers had been gentle and careful on Tig's tender face. And she had radiated confidence in the situation, making Tig want to rest her head on those beautiful, competent shoulders and let her take care of—

Okay, that was why. This department shift was unpleasant,

and Tig wasn't happy with the rifts it was causing, but they were *her* rifts. The people involved were *her* responsibility as their new director, and *her* friends after so many years working together. As long as she had to handle the differing opinions and high tension around the transition, she wanted to do so on her own, and from within the department. Now, there might be arrests, or whatever happened when someone pressed charges after a fight. And not only were the students witness to today's embarrassment, but outsiders—including the campus police—had seen the outward expression of the faculty's inner turmoil as well.

She couldn't give in to any temptation to let a stranger take control of her emotional state or her department.

Tig entered her office and collapsed into her chair. She'd meant to sit down gracefully but failed. Her body had been on high alert from the moment she put herself between Kam and Chase, and now the adrenaline seemed intent on evacuating her system as quickly as it had arrived. And come to think of it, she usually got queasy at the sight of blood. She tried to avoid looking at her hands or the front of her shirt and, instead, glared at the officer who was standing by the closed office door.

"Are you going to sit down, or is remaining on your feet some sort of power play?" Tig asked. She knew she sounded testy, but she gave herself a pass this once. Even though *some* people might think getting punched in the face was a normal part of life, Tig wasn't one of them. She was overwhelmed by the number of emotions that seemed to have been rattled loose by Chase's fist—fear, pain, anger, and an unexpected sort of weepiness. She didn't welcome any of those feelings at the moment. "If it *is* a power play, you win. I give up because I don't know if I can stand up again just yet."

The officer remained as cool as she had been from the start, not remarking on Tig's tone. "If this was a power play, I'd have my gun out of its holster," she said evenly, walking over to the chair across from Tig and sitting down. She managed it with all the grace Tig had tried—and failed—to show, even though her duty belt didn't give her much leeway between the armrests. That didn't help Tig's mood at all.

"I'm Sergeant Adriana Kent," she said, pulling a small spiral notebook out of the breast pocket of her uniform and flipping it open. "Your name and your relation to the two men, please."

Tig pulled her gaze away from the sergeant's chest and met her eyes. Tig thought she noticed a flicker of amusement in them, as if she had noticed where Tig's attention had momentarily strayed, but she wasn't sure. She wasn't easy to read.

"The three of us are colleagues. Friends." That was a slight liberty to take with their actual relationships, but Tig wanted to show her support for her people. Solidarity of the masses, or whatever. She was still furious with them, but that wasn't Kent's business. "I'm the chair of the Classics Department. Well, director now. Of Mediterranean Studies." What else had she wanted to know? Oh, right, her name. "Professor Antigone Weston. Tig."

"Professor Weston," Sergeant Kent repeated as she made a note in her book, as if dismissing the more intimate nickname. "I don't know you. I know almost all the professors and staff on campus, and quite a few of the students, as well, but I don't know you or your colleagues. Do you know why?"

Tig opened her mouth to answer, but Sergeant Kent took care of the response herself.

"I don't know you because this department usually stays out of trouble. Now, I expect to be called to break up fights at Greek houses on weekends when the liquor is flowing, but the people who *study* Greek? They're usually well-behaved. Care to explain what happened to change that?"

"There are extenuating circumstances," Tig said. "Look, Sergeant. Or Adriana. Do people call you Adi?" Judging by her expression, Adi was *not* the right choice. "Ana, then? Or Dri?"

"No," she said, with a surprised expression, as if Tig had started spouting gibberish instead of offering potential nicknames. "No to all of those. People call me Sergeant Kent. Or just Kent if they think I'm out of earshot. How about you stick with the first one." She looked a bit disarmed by Tig's query, as if they had strayed from the interrogation script she usually used. Tig decided she liked seeing her off-kilter. She did a cute pinching thing with her eyebrows when she was.

"Kent it is, then. Sergeant Kent takes too long to say." Tig shrugged, adding Kent's eyebrows to her list of things she shouldn't look at. Brows, blood, breasts…she had quite a list going, and she hadn't even made it past the *B*s yet. She tried to hide her chuckle at her own goofy joke. She was definitely more shaken than she had thought.

"Yes, and this conversation has really been a time-saver." Kent made another note in her book. "We should probably have you checked for a concussion, too, while you're in the ER. Now, what were you saying about extenuating circumstances?"

"Ah yes," Tig said, trying to collect her wandering thoughts. "Growing pains, that's all it is. We're transitioning from a major focused strictly on the ancient civilizations of Greece and Rome to a broader Mediterranean Studies department. Some people are happy about the change because it has the potential to attract more students and because we'll be shedding more light on ancient cultures that are sometimes overlooked. Others are angry about this change because they want to keep the major more traditionally focused."

"*Oh*," Kent said, drawing out the syllable and nodding. "A curriculum change. That explains everything. No wonder those two grown men were trying to beat each other to bloody pulps."

"Exactly," Tig said, relieved that Kent understood. The stress of this transition had pushed them all too close—or actually past, in some cases—their breaking points. "It's a big deal. Tensions are high, and they got a little carried away with—"

Kent held up a hand, palm out, and stopped her. "Professor Weston, I was being sarcastic. World hunger is a big deal. A disruptive fight in the public hallway at my university is a big deal. A change in the course offerings for a major is *not*."

Tig fought to unclench her jaw at Kent's words. "You don't understand. A lot is on the line here." She paused. Well, the things that were under contention might not sway Kent toward her side. Losing the clout of studying what had long been considered a distinguished field might be interpreted by an outsider as academic snobbery. And Kent wouldn't likely understand Tig's own fears and her single-minded sense of purpose, how she had spent her life focused on this passion of hers and now was expected to lead a program that would contain fields she knew relatively little about. She tried to remain vague yet still convey the enormity of what was at stake. "Change is difficult, but if our department doesn't become more inclusive and attract more students as majors, we might disappear altogether."

Kent shrugged. "Would that be a great loss to the university? If there isn't enough interest in a field, why waste the resources on supporting it? And if a faculty can't settle their differences without leaving a bloody hallway in their wake, then maybe they don't deserve a place on this campus."

Okay, that was it. Tig was definitely throwing something at her. The caryatid statuette was across the room on her file cabinet, but she had a nice solid plaster bust of Homer's head sitting next to her right hand...

"Are you looking for something to throw at me?" Kent asked mildly. "That might not be the best way to prove that your department isn't too violent to exist."

"Of course I'm not going to throw anything at you," Tig said, as haughtily as someone who had been considering that very thing could manage. "I settle differences with words and logic, not with violence. And so do most of the people here. We've had debates and meetings to discuss all sides of this issue, and this one semiviolent outburst was an anomaly and certainly won't happen again."

She hoped.

She had been worried about just this type of eruption earlier today, and she felt wholly unprepared to deal with it. She could get her people through this change as long as the worst that happened was an occasional swear word during a Socratic dialogue about the pros and cons of the new course of study. She was way over her head if violence became the norm. Truth was, she was as bothered by the fight as Kent seemed to be, and she desperately wanted to hide that fact from the sergeant.

"Besides," she continued, "*bloody hallway* is an exaggeration.

I was the only one who was bleeding, and that was pretty much contained to my shirt." She gestured at the front of her, making the mistake of looking down at her bloodstained hand and top. She swallowed tightly and forced her attention away from the sight.

"Yes, but next week it might be two professors who are better at throwing punches. Do you really want another innocent bystander to get hit then? Or worse?"

Tig didn't answer because Kent already knew what she'd say. Of course she didn't want that to happen.

Kent nodded, as if content to have proved her point. "So, our two boxers. Are they members of opposing factions? Separate alliances? Warring city-states?"

Tig tried to give her a look of contempt, but in reality, the third option captured the feeling she had while trying to unite her faculty. One side had been subsumed by the other—well, technically, one side had won the war and the other had no choice but to accede. Athens and Sparta were pretending to coexist. "Chase Davies has been opposed to the new department, and Kamrick Morris has been for it."

In truth, Davies had been one of the most fanatical of the opponents, surprising her with his vehemence at times, when he had always seemed pretty easy-going and cheerful. Morris had been neutral for the most part, until he realized which side was winning, then he offered his lukewarm support as if he'd been one of the proponents the entire time.

Kent watched her silently, as if guessing that Tig was glossing over the details. "And the one who hit you?" she asked after a pause.

"Well, he didn't really mean to…I got in the way, and it was an accident."

"Davies," Kent said, making another note.

"He seemed sorry," Tig offered. It was a weak defense, but he was one of her professors and her loyalty had to be toward him and not anyone outside their department. Of course, that didn't mean she was going to be all sweet and forgiving the next time she and Chase had a chance to speak in private, without the cops listening in.

"One more question. There were two people in the audience

who didn't seem to fit the mold of either classics professors or students. One wearing all black, the other in bright clothes. Do you know who they are?"

Damn it. Kent had managed to spot the two people Tig had been most upset to see at Denny Hall's impromptu spectacle. Did she have to answer? Couldn't she plead the Fifth, or whatever it was they said on legal dramas?

"I have all day," Kent said. "You, however, have a short window of time before your nose sets and you have to live with that bump. And constant snoring."

Without making a conscious decision to do so, Tig reached up to feel her nose, which seemed as straight as it always had been. She figured Kent was lying, and that she didn't really have a fracture, and that there was no real statute of limitations on fixing it if she did, but she chose to answer anyway. For one, she really wanted to get her hands on some painkillers. Also, almost anyone else in Denny would be able to identify the two people for Kent.

She reluctantly gave their names. "Max Adel is CEO and owner of SEATRINT, an international trading company that offers a full scholarship to outstanding students who are classics majors, and we have usually one or two recipients every year. Samiya Ayari is one of the people who have been involved in implementing the new department. She was an external member of the steering committee and a visiting professor here a couple of years ago, and she'll be joining our faculty starting next quarter. She was a professor at UC Berkley, but she's been in Tunisia on sabbatical until she starts teaching here. She comes to UW every month or so, and she's here for a week this time to help finalize the curriculum and manage the logistics of office space, classrooms, and so on."

Kent took rapid notes. "And you're not happy that the two of them witnessed today's fight," she commented without looking up. She didn't seem to be asking a question that needed answering, so Tig stayed silent. She desperately needed the support of both Max and Sami, and she wanted their respect. Max's financial contributions to the department were significant, and Sami was going to be Tig's Vice Director and colleague. Plus, even though Tig hadn't spent much time with her socially when she had taught at the U, she felt a kinship with Sami that she knew would easily turn into friendship. She felt a growing pressure behind her eyes, and she carefully rubbed the bridge of her nose, trying to ease her growing headache. Kent suddenly tucked her notebook away and stood up. "We need to get you to the ER now. I might contact you in the future if I have any more questions, but honestly, I hope I don't see you again, except to nod hello if we pass on campus sometime. I want to go back to ignoring Denny Hall because the people working inside it keep their noses clean and their hands off each other. Can you try to make that happen?"

Tig nodded. She wanted nothing more than to get her department off Kent's radar. And once everything here was under control, maybe they would pass on campus sometime. Maybe they'd say hello, or stop and chat. Go get coffee together. In the future when everything in Tig's world didn't seem so fragile. For now, staying as far away from each other as possible seemed like the best course of action.

"I'll do my best, Sergeant."

"Good." Kent walked over to the door and opened it, sticking her head outside. "I see you down there, Professor Hart. Get in here."

She stepped back again, and Libby walked into the office. "I work in this building, you know," she said to Kent with a scowl.

"I know you do. And if you can make time in your busy schedule of skulking in hallways, I'd like you to take Professor Weston to the hospital to get her nose checked and to make sure she doesn't have a concussion."

"A concussion?" Libby repeated, looking at Tig with a worried expression. "Was she punched that hard?"

"I didn't think so, but she's acting a little...erratic."

"Hey," said Tig, annoyed with both of them for talking about her like she wasn't in the room. And not very politely, either. "I'm perfectly..." Un-erratic? No, that sounded silly and would add evidence to Kent's unfair diagnosis.

"Stable," Libby offered before turning her attention back to Kent. "That's just Tig. I'm sure she's all right."

"Still, doesn't hurt to check. I'll call ahead and let them know to expect you." Kent looked at Tig and tapped her radio with a fingernail. "I don't want to hear the phrase *Denny Hall* on this thing again, okay?"

She left the office without another word, and Tig didn't throw the bust of Homer at the back of her head. A successful truce.

"Come on, then," Libby said with a sort of forced cheerful tone. Tig knew her friend must have been worried about her, and she figured the lurking in the hall was as much to be there if Tig needed her as it was to be on hand during the course of even a minor investigation. "Do you need to hold my arm for support, or can you walk?"

"Of course I can walk. Davies hit my nose, not my legs," Tig said, hoping she wouldn't embarrass herself after that statement by toppling over as soon as she tried to stand. She felt much steadier on her feet, though. The few minutes of rest and the anger she had felt toward Kent over her casual dismissal of Tig's department seemed to have joined forces to banish Tig's momentary weakness.

She buttoned her blazer, trying to hide as much of the blood as she could, and frowned at Libby. "And what the hell did you mean when you said *That's just Tig*. What's just Tig?"

Libby shrugged. "You're sort of scattered. We find it endearing, but Kent must have misinterpreted it as the result of a blow to the head."

Tig picked up her scuffed leather messenger bag. "Well, I wish you hadn't told her that."

"It's cute. And why do you care what she thinks, anyway?" Libby paused, and her expression visibly brightened. "Unless you… say, did you notice any fireworks while the two of you were talking?"

Tig scoffed. What a ridiculous question. She might have felt a sparkler or two while sitting here in such close quarters with Kent, but who could blame her? Kent's uniform fit *really* well. She wasn't about to admit anything of the sort to Libby, though.

"By fireworks, do you mean beautiful multicolored lights cascading through the night sky or a rocket that goes off while you're still holding it and takes off a few of your fingers, and then your friends have to try to find them and put them in a baggie of ice in the hope that the doctors will be able to sew them back on at the hospital?"

"Um, the first one."

"Sorry, then, but no. She has no idea what it's like, trying to hold this department together while it's falling to pieces around me. She thinks we should just shut it down. Shut it down! Can you imagine a university without a Classics Department? What would I do?"

Tig's last question was delivered with a bit of a wail, which would have made Kent underline the word *erratic* in her little notebook if she'd been here to hear it. Tig's words were telling, as she moved in one stream of thought from bemoaning the decline of classics as a symbol of scholarship and tradition in a university setting to her too real fear that her career, her passion, was becoming obsolete.

Libby just regarded her steadily. "Well, since most of the classes I teach are connected to this department, I can understand your concern. But Kent's responsibility is to keep her campus and the people who live and work here safe. According to Clare, she'd do just about anything to make that happen. Closing a department to avoid letting the Mediterranean Studies conflict endanger others would be a no-brainer for her." She put her hand on Tig's shoulder. "I have faith in you. You'll get your people back in line. By the time the department switches over to the Mediterranean format, they'll be ready to welcome the new faculty and students with open arms."

❖

A few hours later, Tig walked along the rain-soaked path leading to the back of Denny Hall. She had parted ways with Libby just a block ago. Libby—calmed by the doctor's assurance that Tig had neither a concussion nor a broken nose—had headed toward the apartment she and Clare shared just a short distance off campus. Tig, with nothing medical to worry about except a purpling bruise and a screeching headache, was running back to her office for a reference book she had forgotten before she went home to painkillers, a bath, and then bed.

Although she didn't share Libby's optimism about the open arms, she was determined to get back in control of her people. They could handle this in a civilized way. After all, they were all about symposia and debates in the forum, not gory gladiatorial games. She'd convince them that the time to argue was over, and the time to plan and get excited about the new program was upon them. She had logic on her side, as well as necessity.

She had just passed Parrington when she saw the elegant figure of Professor Ayari walking toward her. Great. She didn't feel up to doing damage control at the moment, but she seemed to have no choice. She veered to the left to intercept her newest colleague.

"Sami," she said once they had reached each other and come to a halt. "I have to apologize for today's fight. I'm sure it was just a spirited discussion that got out of hand. We've all been stretched as we work to develop the new program, and everyone is exhausted, but excited. Emotions are running high…"

Luckily, Sami stopped Tig before she rambled on. None of the reasons she was giving explained why Davies and Morris had been fighting, and neither of the men had actually been contributing to the work. Chase, because he'd be likely to sabotage it, and Kamrick because he didn't really seem to care one way or the other. As long as he could still study and teach the works of his favorite historians, he was content.

"You remember, I worked with both of these men when I taught here," she said, in the slightly formal tones of someone for whom English wasn't a first language. "I am not surprised by their behavior today. Disappointed, perhaps? But not surprised." She put her fingers, cool to the touch, under Tig's chin and turned her head gently to one side and the other. "You are not seriously hurt?"

"No, just bruised," said Tig as Sami released her. She didn't mention the headache.

"I am glad. Although, I also feel much consternation over

the events of today. Max Adel, also, has been worried. We were discussing how the death of Laura Hughes and now this public display are damaging to the department. He might need to remove his endorsement and pull his scholarship if his reputation is in danger."

Tig frowned. She hadn't realized the two were friends, although they had had plenty of opportunities to meet over the past years, while Sami taught classes here and, more recently, as she traveled between her old university and this new one. "And you?" she asked.

Sami was under contract—her job with the university was a done deal, as was the entire Mediterranean Studies program—but Tig didn't know if there was some sort of *afraid of getting punched* clause that might let her out of it.

"I am committed to this university, and to the program you and I have created." She gave a small laugh. "When we began work on this program a few years ago, I had initially hoped to be named director, to be in charge. But now…what is the saying? Better you than I?"

"Close," Tig said, not trusting herself to say more. She hadn't realized Sami had originally wanted—and maybe expected to get— her job. Tig had assumed that she had been chosen over the more renowned Ayari because the university wanted to placate alumni and members of the Classics Department by keeping one of their own in charge. Eventually, Sami would probably have her chance at the position, and Tig would step down. It was tempting to make that happen this very night, but while she often complained about having to lead this charge toward a more progressive curriculum, she believed what Ari had said—she was the best person for the job because she cared so much about classics, and about her people. But maybe this fiasco wouldn't have happened if Sami was the faculty's leader.

Sami rested her hand briefly on Tig's shoulder. "I have faith in you, Antigone. Tomorrow, we will start fresh. We will work together to repair the rifts and make our program a proud one."

Tig just nodded, then stood and watched Sami take the path

that would lead her back to the U District and her boutique hotel. She finally started walking again, both concerned and encouraged by Sami's words. She focused on the positives.

Yes, they'd start pulling together and maintain the integrity of their department. Morris and Davies—and likely everyone who witnessed the debacle—must understand now how this had gotten too far out of hand. They'd turn back into the reasonable adults she knew they could be, and Sergeant Kent would have no need to come back to Denny Hall.

Tig reached the back entrance to Denny and paused next to the metal door, fishing her key ring out of her messenger bag. A light overhead cast a circular aura, and she leaned into the brightness to help her pick out the right key. As she moved out of the light, she saw a flash of something pale and out of place in a clump of rain-darkened leaves under an evergreen shrub.

Something that looked like a hand. But it couldn't be a hand. Not possibly. Not on the ground like that, looking so lifeless and still.

She took a couple of hesitant steps closer, then pulled aside some branches. Yes, it was a hand, attached to an equally still and lifeless body. Even facedown, she was able to recognize Chase Davies. Even with a bullet hole in the back of his head, and with his usually tidy hair mussed and matted with blood.

Well, shit.

Chapter Five

Kent pulled the last report in front of her and tried to focus on its contents. Her unplanned jaunt as a patrol officer had put her behind in the actual work she was supposed to be doing, and she had already stayed in the station an hour after her shift was meant to end. No one who walked by her open door seemed surprised to see her still there, since she tended to take her scheduled hours as a guideline rather than a rule and often worked beyond them. She was finding it more and more difficult these days to concentrate on administrative tasks, not because she had too much to do or because the work was too hard, but because she was so damned bored with it. Getting back out into her community and dealing with humanity in all its imperfect glory had been exciting, and she vowed to take advantage of Cappy's absence and fill in the gaps on patrol. Really, her people needed her to be out there with them. She wasn't doing this for selfish reasons at all.

Well, maybe a little. It had been a while since she had felt the rush of dodging fists and grappling with public brawlers, and she realized that she had been missing this kind of excitement in her life. She had been concerned over the last few months about her growing ennui when she came to the station and had been considering taking a vacation or even a leave of absence to reinvigorate herself. Turned out all she needed was a couple of inept professors to start throwing punches around.

And maybe meeting Tig had been a teeny bit invigorating as well.

Kent wasn't sure why. Tig was attractive, sure. She had a face made for smiling, with her slightly upturned lips, and the hint of lines at the edges of her mouth and eyes were signs that she often did. Those lips looked soft and made for kissing, too, but Kent only noticed that in a detached, highly professional manner. She was trained to notice every small detail about a person, and that's the only reason she had made that observation.

She cleared her throat and squinted at the paper on her desk, trying to return her concentration to her job. No matter how kissable and intelligent and muleheaded Tig seemed—all very attractive qualities in Kent's opinion—she and Tig weren't likely to have any sort of relationship beyond their discussion in Tig's office and the brief moment when Kent touched her face to check for broken bones.

Okay, maybe that wasn't the best line of thought for someone who was trying to get her attention *off* Tig, not more deeply on her. Focus on the things keeping them apart, not the ones that involved touching. They had vastly different priorities, for one thing. Kent wanted her campus to be in order. The safety of her community was more important than any other consideration. Apparently, Tig and her faculty were more concerned with what classes were being offered in their department, and an occasional fistfight over course options was perfectly acceptable and understandable.

Ludicrous.

Still, she recognized passion when she saw it, and Tig obviously felt that toward her department, just as Kent did toward the community she was sworn to protect. Intensity and integrity were qualities Kent appreciated in herself, and she could tell that Tig had them, too. Unfortunately, those shared values put them at odds right now, when Tig was willing to tolerate her faculty acting like hoodlums because they were ostensibly defending their beloved Classics Department, while Kent hadn't been bluffing when she said they should just shut down if their professors couldn't handle a course change without turning the university hallway into a boxing ring.

Kent looked back at the report she was meant to be reading. She hadn't gotten more than two sentences in when her radio chirped to life and the dispatcher put out a call with the code for a dead body. Behind Denny Hall.

No fucking way.

Kent ran her hands through her short hair, contemplating pulling out big chunks of it. That'd be an appropriate Ancient Greek type of response, wouldn't it? For one short moment, she wondered if this was a joke. She had just told Tig she didn't want to hear that particular hall's name over her radio again, and now here it was, with a dead body attached for good measure. She could easily imagine Tig coming up with this idea as a prank, but she knew her own people wouldn't go along with it. They were too scared of her, so this had to be real.

Too bad, though, since it would have been funny. A chuckle escaped from her—probably caused as much by her sudden launch to high alert as by the imagined joke—and she quickly smothered it with her hand. She heard Sawyer respond to the call from the station's changing room, where she had probably been getting ready to head home after her shift, and Kent went to find her.

Sawyer stepped into the hallway just as Kent arrived at the changing room door. She was pulling on her navy raincoat, and when she saw Kent she hesitated for a moment, then continued to tug the jacket over her duty belt.

"Are you coming to the scene, Sergeant?" she asked. "If we hurry, we might be able to beat the forensics team."

"My thoughts exactly," Kent said, buttoning her own coat as they hurried through the glass doors and out into the night. The rain had dissipated into a light drizzle, which settled on Kent's hair and the wool of her lapels and trouser legs, the places where the raincoat didn't cover her uniform.

They settled into an easy jog, cutting across the street and up a short flight of stairs leading to campus, retracing Kent's route from earlier in the day. Denny was close enough to the station that it was quicker to cover the distance on foot rather than taking a patrol car and parking in the lot behind Denny. It was fortunate to have the building so close, since it had suddenly become the hotbed of campus crime.

"Who else is assigned to this with me?" Sawyer asked as they slowed to a walk and scanned the area while approaching the scene.

Kent was impressed. A little over a month ago, when Clare had arrived for her first day of work, she had been much more hesitant and unsure. Not unsure of her abilities or ambition, but of her decision to join the campus police force. Now, she simply assumed she would be the one to take point on this case, especially since Cappy wasn't here to challenge her for the lead position.

"You're looking at her, partner," Kent said, opening her notebook to a blank page. She pulled her hand holding the notebook into her sleeve to protect the paper from mist. When Clare halted and stared at her, Kent paused, too. "I'm the only other officer with significant experience as a detective," she continued. "Same as I said the last time we found a dead body on campus—I want us to handle this case, not Seattle PD. The two of us together have the best chance of doing that."

Sawyer nodded, then resumed walking, but Kent reached out and touched her arm, bringing her to a halt again.

"Listen, Sawyer, this isn't a test. You're not being observed and judged. You've proven yourself as an officer and as a detective, and now you're just going to do your job and solve another case. We need to work together to get this done, so for this brief moment in time—and only when we're directly working on this case— we're partners and not sergeant and officer-who-is-still-in-her-probationary-period, got it?"

"Yeah, thanks for the reminder," Clare said. She looked at Kent for a moment, clearly processing Kent's words, then gave her a nod. Kent knew she had fully accepted the terms and would treat their partnership like any other she would have with another officer. Maybe not with the same amount of teasing and camaraderie she shared with Cappy, but with enough trust and ease to make their partnership function smoothly.

"Rock paper scissors for who gets to be in charge?" Clare asked as she resumed walking toward Denny, glancing sidelong at Kent. She snorted. "In your dreams, Sawyer. Sergeant smashes all three."

"Well, so much for equality," Clare said with a laugh.

Kent smiled. Okay, maybe there would be a little teasing. She wasn't happy with the circumstances, but at the same time she was excited at the chance to do fieldwork again. Experiencing some companionship along the way was an unexpected bonus. She normally held herself slightly aloof from her officers, but she had to honor the same promise she had extracted from Clare—to be true partners for the duration of the investigation. She was looking forward to both the job and the partnership.

Officer Pickett had already cordoned off the area behind Denny with yellow crime scene tape and a tarp, and she was standing to one side, keeping onlookers away. Kent assumed her partner Larson was just around the building's corner, detouring pedestrians away from the walkway. Kent heard two more officers declare themselves at the scene over the radio, and they immediately set themselves in positions to widen the perimeter of protected space.

Careful not to disturb any evidence, Kent went as close to the body as she was willing to go before forensics had a chance to examine the scene. Clare swept the beam of her flashlight over the body and the surrounding area. Kent immediately recognized the sandy hair and clothes of the victim without needing to see his face.

"Professor Chase Davies," Clare said, confirming her guess. "I interviewed him after the fight today. Whatever got him fired up enough to start throwing punches had drained out of him by the time I got him back to the station. He was ashamed of acting like that in front of the students and faculty, and he seemed honestly remorseful about hurting Tig. Um, Professor Weston."

"Well, apparently someone wasn't ready for the fight to be over. So, any insightful clues from the placement of the body? The building's architecture?"

During the last murder spree, Clare had been the first to notice that the victim had been posed like one of the figures decorating Suzzallo Library's entrance. In this case, the body suited the scene yet again, but in a much less helpful manner. There was just a man lying facedown, with what looked from Kent's position like a bullet hole in the back of his head. No posing, no symbolic clues. As plain and unadorned as the back of Denny Hall.

"Nothing so far," Sawyer said, "but maybe there will be something to see when we get closer. We could always ask Libby to—"

"Don't you dare call your girlfriend, Sawyer," Kent said, hoping to nip that in the bud. "Or did you already? The last thing we need is…" She faltered to a stop when she noticed that Clare was laughing. She was rustier than she thought. It had been too long since she had let herself relax and enjoy someone else's company—probably since she had been promoted to sergeant in a department where she had few peers of equal rank. She really needed to make some friends outside of the campus police community. Unfortunately, she knew how to meet cops and criminals but wasn't as good at meeting other kinds of people.

She wouldn't mind spending some more time in the company of a certain professor, but said professor was now a possible suspect in a murder, having recently been punched by the victim, making a relationship with her highly inappropriate.

Kent sighed and returned her attention to the scene. Her instincts told her Tig was innocent, but they might be slightly biased in this instance.

"Well"—she continued their conversation about Libby—"even if you haven't called her, she's probably around somewhere. Hiding in a shrub or up in a tree."

Clare smiled, obviously in love. "I'm sure you're right. I caught her with a catalog that sells night vision goggles, so she could be anywhere, watching us."

"You sound strangely proud of that, Sawyer."

Clare just grinned, then her expression sobered. "Forensics," she said simply, gesturing with her head toward the parking lot.

They moved even farther away from the scene and out of the

way while the forensics officers and techs scurried about. She hated this part, watching other people look for clues that should be hers to find and handle the victim's body that was hers to avenge. Judging by the glower on Clare's face, she felt the same way.

Finally, one of the officers approached them. He didn't introduce himself—they rarely did—but instead launched into discourse without preamble.

"Time of death, eight thirty-six or so. Close range gunshot wound, probably with a silencer. We'll know more after the autopsy. We didn't find anything that looks like evidence, and there are hundreds of footprints around this area, but none that stand out as being connected to the scene. It appears he was shot, maybe as he was opening the door, then dragged a short way into the bushes. Someone from the coroner's office will be here soon to remove the body, but the scene is yours until then."

He handed Kent some pages of notes, then marched away, heading toward the parking lot. The other forensics techs followed, soon leaving Kent and Sawyer standing alone in the misty, silent night. Pickett and Larson were shadowy shapes, standing outside the ring of lights that were aimed at the scene.

Kent mentally overlaid a grid pattern on the scene and methodically worked her way from the outside in toward the body. Clare did the same, but in the opposite direction, so they passed occasionally and double-checked every inch of the space. When they got to the body, Clare used her phone to take a few pictures, even though the forensics team had brought a photographer. The pictures he had taken were surely high quality and numerous, and probably already uploaded for them to access when they got back to the station, but Kent liked that they would have a few of their own. Sometimes a shift in angle made a shift in perception, and clues were brought to the forefront where before they had blended in with their surroundings. She trusted Sawyer and knew she had the best chance of instinctively getting the exact right shot that they needed.

If there were clues to be found, of course. It didn't look extremely likely.

"It's like a scene from a beginner's textbook on solving

crimes," Clare said. "Not staged, like the other murders, but bland. Nondescript, like we're looking at a generic murder."

Kent nodded. "Quick and efficient. The murderer was probably in and out of the scene in seconds."

She pulled on a pair of nitrile gloves and carefully lifted the victim's head an inch off the ground. It was Davies, of course. The fight hadn't left a mark on his handsome face—in fact, Tig had been the only one to be bloodied in the brawl—and Kent couldn't see any signs of struggle or defensive maneuvers. He probably hadn't even realized the killer was behind him as he went to open the door.

"Looks like a .22," she said as she gently set his head down again. A small, quiet gun with little kick was ideal for this kind of murder, and they were practically made for silencers. Small, yes, but just as lethal as a bullet packed with more firepower if you knew how to use it. And this murderer had known what they were doing. Kent didn't like that. She liked criminals who were stupid and inexperienced because they made mistakes.

Sawyer picked up one of his hands, his skin pale against her black glove. His knuckles showed some slight bruising—probably where he had hit Tig—and his short nails were grimy and rough, as if he had been doing work with his hand. She checked the other, and it was the same.

"We're probably not going to find anything else here," Sawyer said after a few more moments, and Kent nodded her agreement. The scene was too clean, too careful. Still, the two of them spent another half hour after the body had been removed, taking photos and jotting down notes about their observations.

By the time they got back to the station, Kent's hair was drenched even though the mist hadn't gotten any heavier while they were out. She pulled off her dripping raincoat and hung it by the door in the station's foyer, not wanting to get water all over the station's floor. Clare did the same thing.

"Arrange to get our other fighter in here for another chat," Kent said, mussing up her hair to help it start to dry. "I think it's time I had another talk with Professor Weston."

Clare hesitated, as if wanting to suggest that they switch duties, probably so she could protect her friend, then nodded and walked away. Kent tried to ignore the small part of herself that would be glad to see Tig again. This was business, not pleasure, and if she found out the murder had anything to do with the Classics Department and its dramatic changes, she would be head of the campaign to shut the whole damned thing down.

Kent started down the hallway and came to the open door of the conference room where she had been told Tig had been waiting for the past few hours. After calling 911, Tig had been informed that she needed to come to the station and wait. Kent felt a twinge of regret about that—at a larger police department, she would likely have been interviewed and sent home while Kent and Clare had been busy at the crime scene. As it was, she had been a suspect from the moment she stumbled across her colleague's body, and her officers had been right to keep her at the station.

They apparently hadn't been overly convinced about her guilt, though. She was in the room usually reserved for talking to families of victims or holding meetings with high-ranking members of the department, sitting in a leather armchair with a blanket around her shoulders and a cup of tea on the table next to her. She had her shoes off and her legs tucked under her, with an open book lying in her lap. She wasn't reading but instead was staring into the distance, toying with an ice pack that was most likely meant to be on her face. Her skin was paler than it had been when Kent met her earlier, making the bruising under her eyes stand out in sharp contrast. She appeared fragile, but Kent wouldn't be foolish enough to tell her that—Tig would probably repurpose the book on her lap for throwing if she did, and it looked heavy. Still, the dark circles under her eyes and the air of sadness about her were probably why she was being treated by the officers at the station like an honored guest and not someone who might have recently put a bullet in the back of another professor's head.

Tig didn't look up, seemingly unaware of Kent's presence. She was likely in a state of shock after today's chain of events, and Kent would need to shake her out of it. Soon. Right now, Kent walked past the room and into her own office, taking a moment to collect herself before she started the interview. She found herself wanting to tuck the blanket a little more snugly around Tig's shoulders, to make sure her tea was warm enough, and to hold the ice pack to her cheekbones. Kent was devoted to her university and its people, but that usually didn't include wanting to make sure they were comfy cozy enough. She needed to snap back to her usual gruff self before she went into that room and acted like a complete fool.

She tapped her fingers against the table as she opened the preliminary reports from forensics. As she had suspected, there were numerous photos of the body and the scene, as well as the coroner's initial findings. Cause of death, bullet wound to the head. Duh. Time of death, eight thirty-eight. Ha. The smug officer at the scene had been off by a whole two minutes. She made a quick call to the ER, then closed her laptop and headed back to Tig.

CHAPTER SIX

That ice pack will do a much better job if you hold it to your face instead of twirling it around in your hands."

Tig jumped, caught by surprise at the sound of Kent's voice. The sergeant walked into the room and sat in the chair across from Tig, crossing her long legs and making the dark wool fabric stretch tautly across her thighs. She rested a legal pad on her lap and clicked a ballpoint pen open. Her hair was damp and standing up in places as if she had just come in from outside and shaken off the raindrops. Or maybe as if she had just gotten out of bed, all sweaty and rumpled and sexy.

Rain. It was definitely rain. Tig held the ice pack back to her face, wishing it was still frozen so it would do more to cool her down. Still, it wasn't nearly as hot as her cheeks felt at the moment, so that was something. She had been through too much today, and her thoughts were jumpy and rampant, not nearly as controlled as usual.

"Maybe those bruises will stick around until Halloween," Kent said, tapping her lower lip with her pen and looking thoughtful. "You could go trick-or-treating as a zombie without needing to buy a costume."

Tig bristled. Somehow Kent managed to make her swing from being attracted to her to wanting to kick her really hard. She spoke without stopping to consider what she was about to say. "Oh yeah? Well, you wouldn't need a costume to go as a..." Kent raised her eyebrows, and Tig paused, rethinking her comment. Murder investigation. Cop with the authority to put her in jail. Maybe. Tig wasn't certain, but she wasn't about to push her luck. "As a police officer," she finished weakly.

Kent surprised her by laughing. "I'll pretend I don't know what you were really about to say because you look like hell. You've been through a lot today, and I'm sure you're exhausted and not thinking clearly, so let's get this over with and get you home and into bed." Kent frowned and changed the cross of her legs. "You know what I mean. Someone will get you home. Probably Professor Hart, who might, at this moment, be watching from the other end of our monitoring system. But she'd better not be!" The last sentence was spoken in a raised voice and aimed at the small security camera in the corner of the room. Kent looked at Tig again and shrugged. "I do that every once in a while, just in case."

Tig had to smile at that, and Kent nodded in a satisfied manner, as if she had meant to put Tig at ease before talking about more serious matters. Like Tig's now-deceased colleague. Tig steeled herself to get through the following minutes, glad that one of the officers had gone to the pharmacy a couple hours ago and picked up her prescription for her. She couldn't face the questioning without something to calm her headache. A month ago, she had spoken to a different officer after Laura's death in this same station, and even though she wasn't nearly as close to Chase as she had been with Laura, the situation brought those memories scrabbling to the surface.

"So, Professor Weston," Kent said, all traces of laughter gone. "Even after I explicitly told you I didn't want to hear Denny Hall on my radio, you went and called in a murder. At Denny Hall."

"Maybe I should have told the 9-1-1 operator I was at the building across from Savery instead," Tig suggested. "Would that have been better?"

"It might have caused less of a spike in my blood pressure, but not by much. Interesting how I've spent my entire career as a campus police officer without so much as crossing paths with you or Chase Davies, and in one day I get two calls to your building, you get punched in a fistfight, the man who hit you ends up dead, and you discover the body. Fascinating set of occurrences."

"I didn't kill him," Tig said. The phrase *I am going to kill that man* might have crossed her mind a time or two since this afternoon, but she had meant it more in a figurative way, not in a *Where can I buy a gun?* kind of way. And she hadn't said it out loud.

"Did I say you did?" Kent asked.

"Well, no, but it sounds sort of suspicious when you put everything together like that. Do you believe me?"

Kent made a half-shrug, half-nod sort of gesture. "I believe the ER nurse who said you were discharged two minutes before the time of death and couldn't possibly have made it across campus in time to kill him. Does that count?"

Tig thought about it. "Not as flattering, but it'll do. Anything that keeps me out of jail, I suppose."

"Yes, that is usually the goal. Now, tell me about what happened tonight."

"I was at the back door of Denny, looking for my keys—" Tig started, but Kent held up a hand and stopped her.

"Farther back. Start when you left the hospital."

Tig closed her eyes and retraced her steps in her head, recounting them to Kent. She was surprised by the amount of detail she remembered when she wasn't starting her narrative at the traumatic point where she found Chase's body. She felt calmer while telling it, too, which might be some sort of police trick Kent was using—allowing her to back away from the emotion-ridden moment and then slowly approach it again. She considered leaving out her conversation with Sami, but she knew there were some security cameras around the campus, and she didn't want to be caught in a lie.

"And then the 9-1-1 operator told me to wait at the scene," she finished. "They said not to touch anything, and to try to keep anyone else from approaching. A few people walked by on the way to the parking lot, but it was fairly quiet, and no one came close. Then two officers got there, and one of them drove me here."

Kent nodded, her eyes on her legal pad as she scribbled notes as quickly as Tig was speaking. When Tig fell silent, Kent scanned the page and then looked up at her.

"In your conversation with Professor Ayari, did you feel threatened at all?"

Tig frowned, caught off guard by the question. She had assumed they'd talk more about the body, but Kent seemed interested in everything on the periphery.

"Threatened? Do you mean by the gun she was waving around?" Tig slapped her hand over her mouth. "Sorry, that was sarcasm. No, not threatened, and she obviously didn't have a gun. She didn't seem likely to punch or shoot me."

"Be careful with the sarcasm, please. Just answer my questions directly," Kent advised. She shook her head. "Although I'm beginning to see why you and Libby are such good friends."

Tig grimaced. "We share a rather inappropriate sense of humor."

"Control it if you can, while you're in here. And I didn't mean physically threatened. It sounded to me as if she wants your job."

Tig thought back to the interchange with Sami and tried to remember how she had phrased Sami's comments while telling Kent about it. "Maybe she does, but that wouldn't have anything to do with Chase, would it? At the time, I guess I was more concerned by what she said about Max, and how he might end his scholarship. We have some very generous donors in the Seattle community—alums and families of some of our graduates. If he pulled out, we could lose a lot of them, as well. We're able to offer our students some great resources because of those donations. Research materials, subsidized travel and other events, some of the art and sculpture exhibits in our gallery. If someone wanted to make me feel threatened, he'd be the one able to do it. If Sami really wants to be director, she can have the job. It involves more black eyes and dead bodies than I anticipated."

Kent squinted slightly as she scrutinized Tig's face. "You're lying about that. Your eyes got very shifty. You might not find the responsibility as simple as you thought it would be, but you've taken it on, and now you don't want to let go."

"And how would you know that?" Tig asked, trying not to be shifty looking, which was harder than she expected.

"Because it's exactly how I feel. Sometimes I'd rather just be a patrol officer, but I've accepted the role of sergeant, and now I'm the one who's responsible for my people. If I said the word, I could be back where I used to be. Someone else would gladly take my place, and they'd be the one to deal with the worries and the paperwork while I only had my own job to consider. But I won't say that word, and I don't believe you would, either. And please, stop staring like that. You've gone too far to the opposite side of shifty."

Tig smiled and let her expression relax back to what she hoped was some semblance of normal. The comments about her staring were spoken in a cranky-sounding tone, and Tig sensed that the delivery was a defensive reaction on Kent's part. She had a feeling Kent didn't often share information about herself like that, and she understood that it meant something to have been the recipient. She also wanted to respect Kent's touchiness about disclosing personal information, so she didn't remark on it and kept the focus of her comments on herself and Sami. "You're right. I could have backed down anytime during this process, and if Sami really wanted the leadership role during this transition, I'd have been leaving the program in very capable hands. So no guilt involved. But I didn't. Or at least I haven't yet. I think the university wanted someone from the Classics Department to remain in charge to make it seem like we were expanding, and not being annexed. They might reconsider my appointment given what's happened today, though."

"They might reconsider the entire department," Kent said casually, flipping through her pages of notes again.

"What do you mean?" Tig asked sharply. Kent had said before that she'd be happy to shut the department down if its faculty members didn't stop fighting, but even as annoyed as Tig had been by those words, she hadn't believed Kent had any power to make her threats come true. The university, however, did.

Kent looked up from her notepad. "You've had two dead bodies in as many months. Your professors are fighting in the halls. The powers that be might overlook some in-house squabbling over departmental policy and the expanding major, but how long do you think they'll let these serious crimes happen before the entire Classics Department becomes too great a liability?"

"I don't know. How long?" Tig asked, really needing Kent's answer. She had seen the curriculum expansion as not only the right thing to do but the pragmatic one, as a way to avoid obsolescence, but she hadn't truly considered that the university might regard them as a liability and shut them down. She had assumed that if they didn't make changes, they would slowly fade away with a sense of grandeur over the course of a decade or two, giving her time to reconsider her entire life's purpose. Now, she was being told she might have to do so immediately. Kent's comments rang true, and they shifted her perspective in a very uncomfortable way.

"I don't know," Kent repeated, looking a little surprised at Tig's question. Or maybe at the vehement tone in which it had been delivered. "We don't really have precedent here. With Davies and Hughes, you've beat the record for number of faculty murders in a single department over the course of one term. Which isn't even over yet, by the way."

"I can't let them close us completely. Can you imagine the university without a Classics Department, even if it's part of a broader field of study and not its own entity?" Tig hesitated. "Well, I know *you* can imagine that, but I can't."

"I understand that this is very personal for you, but my focus is on solving this case. Finding the killer before anyone else gets hurt."

Anyone else…Tig had a dozen professors on her faculty. Sami. And a handful of emeriti. Add another ten if she was including affiliated faculty members, like architectural historian Libby. No, Tig wasn't going to count them. They couldn't possibly be in danger. Not Libby. So, around fifteen, with another eight that would be added in the first year of expansion. Her people. She couldn't lose anyone else. She wondered if Sami had made it safely back to her hotel in the dark. Tig wouldn't handle it well if another person she'd had a personal stake in bringing to campus was killed. She fought to steady her breath but felt as if she was gulping air.

A DEGREE TO DIE FOR

"Can I help?" she asked, ready to do whatever it took. "What can I do?"

Kent uncrossed her legs and leaned toward Tig, resting her elbows on her knees. "Nothing that puts you in danger. Just be aware of what's going on around you, and don't hesitate to trust your instincts if something doesn't feel right. Anything—a person, a place, a meeting. And keep me informed if you notice anything unusual or suspicious as you're going about your day. Or if any of the discussions around the new program get more heated or threatening than they should."

Tig nodded. She had been determined to keep Kent and the other officers out of her department's business, but now she was rethinking that decision. What good did it do to protect their privacy if they were closed down? None at all.

Kent continued. "Since this murder might be connected to your department, you can use your expertise in classics to help us if you notice any connections we might miss since we're unfamiliar with your subject."

"Well, there is that lost play of Euripides that has a character being shot to death with a gun, so there might be something there," Tig said, looking thoughtfully toward the ceiling as if she was trying to recall the exact phrasing of dialogue. "Only a few fragments are extant, though, so I can't do much without the full text."

Kent watched her for a moment before speaking. "Didn't we already cover sarcasm?"

"Yes, but I don't have any serious answers for you. I'm not Libby, with some intuitive sense of what a murderer is trying to say," Tig said, her frustration evident in her voice. "I feel helpless and unhelpful. Besides, those murders were meant for Libby to see and understand. No one knew I'd be going back for a forgotten book, so anyone could have found his body. And by the time I got back to campus the next morning, someone else surely would have."

Kent sighed and rubbed her temple. "I know. Look, you asked me what you could do to help, and answering my questions is a big part of that. Some of them you might not be able to answer, or they might not end up being relevant to the case, but eventually some question will spark the right response, or a new idea, or something to help us catch this killer. I just need you to remain calm and try not to detour into deflective humor whenever you get upset."

Tig wanted to protest that she was calm, and not upset in the least, but neither was true, and Kent was well aware of that. Instead, she nodded her agreement, not trusting herself to speak without inserting a flippant remark.

"Okay, then," Kent said, referring back to her notes. "Just a couple more things to cover, and then we'll let you go. In our previous conversation you said you and Professors Davies and Morris were friends. How true is that? Did you spend time together outside of work? Do you know their families or go out to lunch together every Wednesday?"

Tig fidgeted with her ice pack, which was now room temperature. She still felt haunted by the vision of Chase lying on the ground, and she regretted his death, but she seemed sort of numb inside. She could talk dispassionately about their relationship now, but when she returned to Denny and saw his empty office...well, then she would probably feel more sadness at his loss. "I meant friends more in the *we work in the same building* kind of way."

"Colleagues," Kent said, clarifying.

"Friendly colleagues," Tig amended. Most of the time. Sort of.

Kent looked unconvinced. "Tell me more about Kamrick Morris. Were he and Davies reasonably friendly with each other, too? Was the fight an aberration or a physical manifestation of an antagonistic relationship?"

"They were...different," Tig answered, rethinking her earlier conviction to be completely honest with Kent. She had a feeling they were coming to the dirty laundry part of the conversation, and she wanted to avoid it. "They traveled in different social circles, and they just seemed so unlike each other. I don't think they were ever especially civil. Even before the Med Studies stuff, they'd snipe at each other during meetings and in the hallways. Nothing like today, but still..."

Kent nodded and wrote more notes. Her hand holding the pen

grew still, but she kept her gaze on the page and not on Tig, letting her know she wasn't going to like the next question. "During the fight there was a lot of schoolyard name-calling. Most of it seemed harmless and rather silly, but when Davies called Morris a plagiarist, it caused a reaction from a lot of people in the crowd."

Tig groaned inwardly, while externally trying to keep a balance between shifty eyes and staring. She wasn't sure how the result looked, but it felt very unnatural. She gave it up and just spoke normally and quickly, before Kent could accuse her of deflecting by making goofy faces.

"Kam published a paper on Xenophon in a prestigious professional journal, oh, about five or so years ago. He was accused of plagiarizing another professor whose article appeared in a lesser-known journal more than a decade earlier. The evidence was ambiguous and the similarities subtle and the lawsuit was ultimately dropped, but those sorts of accusations don't just disappear. They can taint a reputation forever. He's naturally very touchy about the subject, and Chase hit a sore spot when he used that insult." Tig paused and took a breath. "I'm uncomfortable talking about this. He was cleared, and the university let him stay, so it's not right to use this against him."

"Being cleared because there wasn't quite enough evidence to tip the scales is vastly different from having the claim dropped because everyone realized it was completely unfounded," Kent said, matter-of-factly. "What's your opinion?"

Tig sighed and looked up at the ceiling again, hoping for inspiration. She considered both lying and breaking into a full-blown comedy routine to avoid answering the question honestly but eventually rejected both options.

"I read both papers. Kam's was definitely derivative, and borderline…well, I believe he had read the other journal, and it influenced his work, but whether he intentionally copied it or not is unclear. He could have read it years before and forgotten about it as a source. Or he could have found it and hoped no one else would remember it and make a connection between the two."

"Risky, if he went on that assumption," Kent said, then gave a small laugh. "Obviously, since someone did exactly that. You believe he plagiarized."

The last was made as a statement and not a question. Tig gave a brief nod, as if not wanting to fully commit to her answer, but it was the truth. She had read other papers by Kam, and he was smart, but dry in his delivery. This paper was more passionate and vivacious, and it matched the tone—even if not the exact wording—of the original.

"I think it would be clever to choose an older, less frequently read publication if you want to steal someone's work, but the topic was fairly narrow. Just some simple keyword searches in academic databases would have resulted in only a few entries, with the older article as one of them. Even if Kam hadn't intentionally borrowed from the journal without citing it, he should have discovered that it existed while researching his own article."

Tig finished speaking and leaned back in her chair. She felt almost more drained by this confession than she had by anything else she had experienced that day. These were serious accusations to make against any academic, let alone someone she had worked with for about twelve years, and she had never spoken her honest opinions about the case out loud.

Kent steepled her hands and frowned at Tig. "This hurts you, doesn't it? The lack of integrity, the dishonesty. But still you let him teach, and you were tempted to protect him from me."

"I have no authority to fire him," Tig said. "And I'm not sure I would if I could. He's a good teacher, and knowledgeable within his specialty. The claim went through the proper channels and was dismissed, so my personal beliefs about it don't have any bearing on whether he should stay or not. And I protect him because I want to protect my department from having this unearthed again at such a delicate time. Do I think what he did was slimy and in opposition to everything I think academic scholarship should be? Yes. Do I think he was hurt and embarrassed by Chase's insult? Again, yes. But I don't believe he would kill someone over a word he's heard applied to him far more often than this once."

Kent didn't respond, and Tig wasn't sure whether she thought accepting Kam as a colleague was a shameful, dishonorable thing for her to do, or whether she understood Tig's decisions on the subject. She had spent many hours contemplating this topic, and she had made her choice based on a lot of soul-searching. Did she need to have Kent's respect or approval? Not at all. Well, maybe a teeny tiny bit, but she was going to ignore that part of herself and dismiss it as being influenced by weariness and pain.

Kent stood up and reached out a hand to Tig. She accepted the help out of her chair but immediately stepped back once she was upright. She knew exactly how it felt to stand close to Kent, and she was worried she'd sway into her before she could stop herself. She was not in the right condition to make good choices.

She put the blanket on the chair and picked up her book and messenger bag before following Kent out of the conference room and back to the foyer. Clare and Libby were sitting on a bench by the front entrance, waiting for them. Rain ran down the window behind them in irregular ribbons.

She heard Kent sigh. "Are those two connected by some sort of invisible tether?"

Tig smiled at her exasperated tone. "I think the tether is pulling Libby to the station, not to Clare. She's just really happy when Clare happens to be here, too."

"Sawyer," Kent snapped.

"Yes, Sergeant?" Clare asked, seemingly unperturbed by Kent's irritable tone.

"You'll get her home safely? And take that one with you?" She gestured at Libby, who merely grinned back at her.

"Yes, Sarge," Libby said cheerfully.

Kent shook her head, then faced Tig. "Sleep. Take care of yourself. I'll contact you if we have any more questions."

She turned on her heel and left the foyer without another word. Libby and Clare, who was now wearing street clothes, came over to her.

"How did it go?" Clare asked, obvious concern on her face and in her voice.

Tig shrugged. "Exhausting," she admitted. "But okay, I guess. I wasn't very helpful."

Well, she might have made Kam seem even more like a potential suspect, but she wasn't sure.

"I'll drive you home in your car, and Clare will follow us," Libby said, in a tone Tig recognized all too well. It meant there would be no arguments. Not that she was about to make any. She'd probably fall asleep at the wheel while trying to find the ignition if left on her own.

Libby linked her arm in Tig's and led them toward the door. "So, your first dead body," she said. "And you got punched in the face, too. That part didn't happen to me."

Clare groaned as she followed them out into the rain. "Lib, can you please try not to sound jealous of that?"

Tig smiled as the banter continued on the way to Denny's parking lot and her car. She was glad to be back with her friends, and very relieved that they were kindly managing the entire conversation without requiring any effort on her part. Kent was an intriguing woman, but her questions had worn Tig out. She was sure there'd be more of them in the future, too. Tig tried to be upset about the prospect, but the thought of seeing Kent again was enticing enough to make her fail completely.

Yes, she definitely needed sleep.

Chapter Seven

K ent got to the station early the next morning and hurried through the most pressing items on her admin to-do list. She would need to spend most of the day with Clare, looking more deeply into Chase Davies's life, but she still had a sergeant's duties to perform.

Even with her pressing timetable, she managed to spend more time than she should have thinking about Tig. Tig was thoughtful and contemplative, carefully making decisions based both on values and real-life practicality. She had taken the responsibility of her new position to heart and was protective of her people. She also was funny, and Kent had needed to force herself not to laugh every time Tig went on one of her deflective tangents.

She'd also had to control her physical response to Tig, especially since they had been sitting so close to each other, in a room that seemed homier than an interrogation room should be. Next time Kent needed to ask her questions, they'd be sitting in hard plastic chairs with a sturdy metal table between them. That would take the romance out of the interview.

And Kent would need to remember not to mention taking Tig home and getting her in bed.

Her interviewing techniques were apparently rustier than she had realized. Her next scheduled chat was with Kamrick Morris later this afternoon, so Kent figured she'd have no trouble keeping her hormones under control in that situation, at least.

First on the agenda, though, was a trip to Denny Hall to look through Davies's office. She had put an officer on guard duty through each shift, making sure nothing of his was touched before she and Sawyer had a chance to search for evidence. And although she knew she'd be less distracted and better able to do her job without Tig there, she planned on stopping by her office and asking her to join them. She could handle being in close quarters with Tig because it was a necessity. Tig had been in Davies's office before and might notice if anything was out of place, and she'd recognize anything that seemed unusual for him to have in his space.

Tig could handle the classical side of things while she and Sawyer would look for other, more mundane reasons for someone to murder him. Drugs, weapons, illicit photos. She hoped they would have a clearer idea of the type of man he was once they were done since at the moment Kent only had a vague image of him as a decent enough professor who had been opposed to changes in his department and who didn't know how to fight. It was hardly enough to go on when solving a crime.

Kent pushed away the pile of reports she was reviewing. They could wait until she finished her detective work. She left her office and wove through the officers who were leaving their morning meeting and heading out on patrol until she reached the foyer where Sawyer was waiting for her, along with Officer Miles Larson, unofficial resident tech expert. The three of them geared up for the walk through the morning's heavy rain and headed out on the now familiar walk to Denny Hall. Kent kept her hood down, not wanting to obscure her vision or hearing, and by the time they crossed Fifteenth, her hair was soaked, and rivulets of water were finding their way through gaps in her uniform and trailing down her back and neck.

Chase's office was just two doors down from Tig's, and Kent unlocked the door for the other two before going to Tig's office.

Tig's door was open, and she was sitting at her desk, staring at her computer screen with a frown on her face. At least she seemed less pale this morning, and her bruises hadn't gotten any worse. From a distance, she just looked like she'd been really heavy-handed with her eyeliner, but from her vantage point, Kent could see a couple of popped capillaries in the whites of her eyes, and the way the bruises faded to purple on her lids. Chase's off-target punch had managed to do more damage than he ever could have intentionally done. Too bad he hadn't been aiming at Tig—then she wouldn't have a mark on her.

"Hey," Kent said, stepping into the office. "You look better this morning."

Tig laughed and snapped her laptop shut more quickly than the average innocent person would. "I look like a slightly-less-undead zombie, you mean."

Kent smiled. "I think you might have to buy a Halloween costume after all. Please tell me you're not googling *how to become a detective*. We're really not planning to recruit from the university faculty, despite what Libby might have told you."

Tig's expressions shifted in a way Kent was beginning to recognize, as she seemed to consider making up a story, then settled on telling the truth. She gestured with her head for Kent to shut the door, which she did before walking over to the chair she had used the previous time she was in here.

"I've been sending some emails. Researching other jobs," Tig admitted, lowering her voice even though no one would hear them unless they had the office bugged. "In Classical Studies, not police work. I guess I had been seeing two options for the department. Either a slow decline, or a drastic switch to the new expanded program. But what you said yesterday…Well, you're right, of course. It's a very real possibility that the university will just shut us down without enough notice for all of us to find new placements, so I decided to get a head start."

She said the words matter-of-factly, but Kent saw a redness in her eyes that had nothing to do with Chase's punch. She reached across the desk—wanting to touch Tig and offer some comfort, but feeling uncomfortable doing so—and tapped on her closed laptop instead.

"Anything promising?"

Tig shrugged. "A couple. I've been offered positions as a visiting professor at several universities. Boston and Bryn Mawr. Northwestern."

"You wouldn't want to stay here in Washington?" Kent asked, unsure why she felt hurt by Tig's choices. She'd naturally look for universities that were good fits for her, not ones that would keep her close to Kent. She wasn't sure exactly when she had started thinking they might have the potential to be friends after this case was closed. More than friends? Yes, that had definitely crossed her mind as well. But now it seemed that Tig didn't share those hopes.

"Yes, I would," Tig said. "My friends are here, and my family is close, since my parents and my sister are all in Oregon. I thought I'd be here until I retired, and then I'd settle down somewhere closer to the ocean, but still in the area."

"Then why…?" Kent started, then stopped when the rest of the sentence nearly came out as *Then why not stay close to me?* Only yesterday, closing the entire department was no big deal. As long as it kept her campus safe and quiet, she would have been just as neutral about razing Denny Hall to the ground. Now, the department was Tig. Close it, and she would leave. Kent didn't feel nearly as neutral about that.

"The field of classics is a small universe." Tig shrugged, fiddling with her laptop, a notepad, a blue-and-chrome pen. Anything within reach. "Lots of programs are closing or downsizing until they only offer minors in the subject instead of full majors. Others are merging with larger, more general departments like comparative literature or art history, so that fewer classics-specific professors are needed. Add to that the new PhDs who are graduating every year, and it means that competition for the few openings available at any given time is fierce. The positions I've been offered are temporary, but they're sort of an audition. A mutual one, since both the existing faculty and I are trying to see if we'd be a good fit. I have an advantage since I'm sort of…well…being headhunted, but it's a slim one. It takes a strong department to be able to court someone with my experience and reputation, but that also means that plenty of applicants will be courting them in turn. And if a dozen of us from here are let go at the same time, it'll change the situation as well. I'll have to take what I can get as far as high-quality departments go, and I'm limited in how choosy I can be over location."

Kent exhaled slowly. Tig didn't look any happier about this situation than Kent felt, but there was nothing they could do. She had a feeling Tig was downplaying how appealing she'd be to these other schools, but even assuming she was being modest, Kent understood how challenging it would be for her to find a new job that fit the criteria of being both suitable for her level of experience and in her preferred location. "Then we should get to work and solve this murder as quickly as we can," she said, with a false sense of cheer. "That might be enough to keep the department open."

Or it might not. There were already two dead bodies connected to the Department of Classics. Kent doubted it could withstand much more.

"Sawyer and Larson are already in Chase Davies's office. I thought you might be able to give us a hand while we search. Let us know if things look out of place, or if you see anything else that draws your attention."

Tig nodded and stood up. "I'd rather be helpful than just sitting in here moping. Let's go."

Tig locked her office door behind her, and Kent followed her to the other room. She watched as Tig paused on the threshold before walking inside. Tig didn't need to have been best buddies with Davies to mourn his death as a person and colleague, and from the look on her face, Kent sensed she was doing just that, but she appeared to put aside any discomfort she might feel at going through his belongings and stepped resolutely inside.

"Hi, Tig," Clare said, looking up from the pile of papers she was carefully sifting through. She handed Tig a pair of gloves. "How are you feeling?"

"Sad, worried, and a little headachy," Tig said. "All to be expected, though. What do you want me to do?"

"First, just look around without disturbing anything too much,"

Clare said. "Let us know any observations you have, no matter how insignificant they might seem to you. If you notice it, say something about it."

"Once we've gone over what we can see on the surface, we'll move deeper," Kent added. "Then you can sort through drawers and bookcases more thoroughly."

Clare nodded. "I've taken photos, but nothing has been moved."

Tig headed toward one of the bookcases first—Kent would have bet a month's salary that she'd start with the books. She didn't want to hover and make Tig feel self-conscious when she needed to focus on what she was seeing, so she went over to the desk and hovered behind Larson instead. He had Davies's laptop open and was meant to be hacking into his accounts but instead appeared to be doing some online shopping.

"Any progress, Larson?" she asked, her tone sarcastic. "Oh, yes, look. They're having a sale on hammers. Good job."

He continued typing, apparently unperturbed by her comment. "I got into his Home Depot account. If you can crack the passwords for sites with less security, it's usually easy to get enough info to hack the more protected ones. Unsurprisingly, most people aren't very savvy about passwords, and they'll often use the same core word or phrase over and over. They believe that changing one number or symbol makes it unbreakable, but it just narrows down the options and allows me to…"

He paused and tapped another key. "There you go. Bank and cell accounts. This thumb drive has encrypted documents, but they're accessible now."

"Let's see those first. Tig, can you come look at these?" Kent said. She paused, then continued. "Good job, Larson. I'll buy you one of those hammers as a bonus."

He just grinned and opened the drive's menu. Tig walked over and stood next to Kent, close enough for her to feel a welcome pressure from her nearness, even though they didn't touch. Kent wanted to inch away but couldn't find a reason to do so without being obvious about it. She didn't want to feel either comfort or excitement from having Tig close because there was a good chance that, within a few months, she wouldn't even be in the same state. Kent needed to remember that, and not let herself hope for anything beyond this moment with her.

Tig leaned forward slightly and pointed at one of the folders. "Can you open that one?" she asked Miles, her voice subdued.

"Xenophon," Kent said, reading the folder's name. "He was the topic of the plagiarized article, wasn't he?"

"Allegedly plagiarized," Tig said. Then she sighed. "But, yes."

Larson opened the file and slowly scrolled through the scanned document. It was a typed paper but had handwritten notes and sections crossed out with pen. The scrawl was barely legible to Kent, but Tig was apparently able to read enough to decipher its meaning.

"Shit," she said.

"Care to elaborate?" Kent prompted when she didn't seem prepared to add anything else.

"It's a draft. I'd need to reread the original article, the one Kam was accused of plagiarizing, but I'd be willing to bet these crossed out parts more closely match it than his final article did."

"Blackmail?" Clare asked, coming over to join them in a semicircle around Miles.

"If it's what I think it is, then possibly," Tig said. "Kam would probably give anything he could to keep this quiet, but I doubt Chase would have gotten much from him. Kam's a single dad with three teenagers. He makes a decent salary, but I'd be surprised if he has tons of cash to spare."

"Power play, maybe?" Kent suggested, surprising herself by considering the lesser explanation. "If he and Morris didn't get along, maybe he just liked having this to hold over his head."

"That actually makes more sense," Tig said with a nod. "Unless Kam has some rich relatives who are willing to help him out, blackmailing him wouldn't be a long-term lucrative venture. No wonder Chase kept his day job. Oh, can you open Oedipus Rex?" she asked as Miles closed the Xenophon file and returned to the menu.

"Why that one?" Clare asked, echoing the question Kent had been thinking.

"It might be something to do with me. Everyone started calling me that when I was first named chair of the department, Oedipus the king, you know? My sister and I were named after his daughters, Antigone and Ismene." She laughed. "We used to call our dad Brother, and Mom was Grandma. They weren't thrilled about that, but they should have thought the names through more carefully before they chose them."

Kent and the other two turned to stare at her.

"Killed his father and married his mother? Oedipus?" Tig explained.

"Got it," Kent said. "And I'm beginning to understand why you're so obsessed with nicknames."

Tig nodded. "I used to call my sister Meany. She hated me."

The last was said in the nostalgic tone of someone who was most definitely not hated by her sister or anyone else in her family. Even those brief comments told Kent that their childhoods had been far from similar. Her three brothers had protected her and acted as surrogates for her indifferent, older parents, even though they had their own lives and friends, but she sometimes had felt as if she existed on the periphery of her parents' lives. She'd never been abused or gone without either the basic necessities or extras like toys and books, but she hadn't experienced the teasing, playful, loving type of parents that Tig's words had conjured up in her mind.

"Did she really try to give you a nickname?" Sawyer asked Kent, with a mixture of disbelief and awe in her voice.

Kent nodded, leaving the memories of her nontraditional childhood behind and coming back to the present. "I think *Adi* was the first attempt," she admitted. Larson and Sawyer both looked at her with their brows furrowed, as if not understanding where the name came from. "Short for Adriana," she explained, which didn't seem to help their comprehension. "My first name."

"You have a first name?" Clare asked. "Really?"

"I thought her first name was just Sergeant," Miles added, shrugging at Clare.

"You're both fired," Kent said, fighting to hide her smile. "Now open that file so we can see the goods he had on Professor Weston."

"Oh, those are just some of my exam questions from last spring," Tig said, after skimming through the pages. "We were talking about our methods for designing tests, and I sent him that file. I wrote them myself, based on topics we had discussed in class, so there's nothing I'd even pay him a nickel for as hush money."

"Could he have used them for his classes?" Kent asked. "Passed them off has his own?"

"Well, I suppose so," Tig said skeptically. "But his students would have been confused by all the questions about Aeschylus's plays when they had spent the quarter studying Virgil's *Aeneid*."

"Can you ever just answer a question without adding sarcastic commentary?" Kent asked mildly.

"No, she can't," Clare answered for her, earning herself a playful elbow in the side from Tig.

Kent kept her attention on the computer screen, and off their antics. She didn't really mind Tig's inability to keep from inserting her own brand of humor into every conversation. In fact, she liked it, more than she should. If they just kept to plain, impersonal words, then she wouldn't find herself growing more and more intrigued by Tig. It was too late to undo the attraction she had already developed toward her, but she could do her best to keep from adding to it.

They went through the rest of the files without finding anything else incriminating. Kent could sense when Tig read through some of the documents with more intensity than others, as if something about them bothered her but she couldn't explain why. Once they finished, Miles went back to the station with orders to print the files for Tig to read more closely when she didn't have the others to distract her.

Once he had gone, the three of them wandered through the office, eventually opening drawers and pulling out stacks of notes. Tig was reading through one of the heavy texts from the bookshelf— Kent couldn't figure out if she was still investigating, or if she had gotten bored with it and was simply reading a book. She was leaning against the bookcase, with a plaster bust of some Greek or Roman perched near her elbow.

"Do all classics professors collect copies of statues and vases?" Kent asked, turning a large vessel she had just taken from a high shelf behind Davies's desk in her hands. It had been partially hidden by a stack of composition notebooks and a dying fern.

"Most of us, I suppose," Tig said, looking up from the book. "It makes you feel closer to the past, to have these replicas of artifacts near at hand. We're always seeking to deepen our connection to ancient history, and these physical objects can help."

"You have a statue of a woman in draped robes in your office," Kent said.

"Yes, she's a small-scale replica of a caryatid from the Acropolis. They were used in place of columns on the temple Erechtheion."

"Ah. And the one you were going to throw at me?"

Clare looked up at that comment, and Tig gave her a quick shrug. To her credit, she didn't even pause to consider denying it. "A bust of Homer. And that's a black-figure amphora you're holding. The design with horses and chariots might mean it was made as a prize that would be given to the winner of a race. It would have been filled with precious oils."

"I like how they aged it to seem more authentic," Clare said, coming over to stand beside Kent, and tracing a sealed crack in the vase with a gloved finger.

Tig joined them. "I don't remember seeing that amphora before, but I think he used to have a couple others in here. Can I hold it?"

Kent handed the heavy vase to Tig and watched as she examined it more closely. She and Clare exchanged a curious glance as Tig frowned and moved so she was directly under the ceiling light.

"Holy crap," she said. "This might be authentic."

Chapter Eight

Tig felt all her recent concerns fade into the background as she gingerly held the amphora in her hands. Chase's death, the possible loss of her job, her confusing feelings toward Kent. Those things weren't going to disappear anytime soon, but for this moment, she allowed herself to pretend they didn't exist. She held the vase closer, squinting to see the details in its design, grateful that she already had gloves on before she picked it up.

"Authentic?" Kent repeated. "How is that even possible? Wouldn't it be in a museum somewhere?"

"Art theft and blackmail," Clare said. "This is getting more interesting by the minute."

Tig shook her head. "Ancient pieces come up for auction now and then, so it's not unheard of to have one in a private collection. An amphora this size, in this condition, would bring well over one hundred thousand, probably double or triple that. More? I don't know. Don't get too excited, though," she said, speaking as much to herself as to the others. She had looked into the prospect of buying a tiny ancient object for herself—a drinking cup for wine or water, maybe—but she hadn't been able to justify the cost of even a small artifact that was in poor condition. This was the exact opposite. She couldn't imagine how Davies had managed to acquire it. "I'm not an expert at all, so this might be something he picked up for five dollars at a kiosk outside the Parthenon."

"But you don't believe that," Kent stated.

Tig met those beautiful hazel eyes that seemed to have gotten very good at looking right into her. And now, she knew, Kent's observant eyes were most likely seeing the excitement in her own—excitement Tig wasn't even bothering to hide.

"I don't believe that," she agreed. She could cite her reasons, starting with the way the foot, neck, and handles of the jar had been made separately and attached with slip, while most modern replicas were fired as single pieces. But she was convinced more by the feel of the object in her hands than by her rudimentary knowledge of Greek vases. Even through the layer of her gloves, she felt an ancient energy emanating from the terra-cotta vessel. Some part of her, deep inside, resonated in turn.

She was *not* telling Kent any of that.

Clare gave a low whistle. "Maybe Professor Morris was a better blackmail subject than we thought."

"Or there were others," Kent said. "If he was willing to blackmail one colleague, why stop there? Or why not add another crime, like embezzlement or theft?"

"Or he saved up and bought it," Tig said, still wanting to protect him, or at least to offer a less morally bankrupt explanation. "He's single with no kids. He has a house in Pinehurst, which couldn't have been cheap, but he might have been extremely frugal in the rest of his life in order to splurge on this."

Okay, he wasn't frugal with clothes. He always wore well-tailored good clothes. He and Tig might share the same basic aesthetic, but she doubted they shopped at the same stores since his outfits always had a high-end quality about them. Hers had a nice midrange quality she preferred. And his car was newer and fancier than most of the other ones in the faculty parking lot. Nothing extravagant, but not an old beater. Maybe he ate rice and beans every night.

Kent watched her silently, probably aware that she was refuting her own explanation in her mind.

"So, he saves a shit-ton of pennies and buys this," Kent said, after a moment. "Why hide it on a shelf and not tell his colleagues about it? You'd think it would be worth bragging about. Tell me, if you bought something like this, what would you do with it?"

"I have no idea," Tig said, hugging the amphora gently to her. "Why don't I take this home for a week or two, then I can let you know?"

"I'm going to need that back now," Kent said, reaching for it, but Tig turned evasively to one side.

"Fine, I was kidding. I'd probably keep it in my house for a few weeks." Or months. Maybe years. "I'd want it close. But eventually, I'd give it to a local museum or place it in our gallery in Denny's basement. It would be safer there, better protected than I could manage in my home, and I would want other people to be able to see it. I'd want my name on the plaque, though," she added, in the name of honesty.

"So, part of the joy of having it would be sharing it with others," Kent said.

"But plenty of art collectors just want pieces they can enjoy in private," Clare interjected. "They have no interest in sharing, and some of the thrill of ownership comes from knowing no one else can see what you get to stare at every day."

Tig nodded. That sounded more like Chase Davies than she wanted to admit. "Keeping it here, but hidden, would play into that as well," she said. "How exciting to know that other people are close to your treasure but don't realize it's there."

"That explanation makes sense to you, doesn't it?" Kent asked her. "It fits the man you knew."

"Yes, and stop reading my mind," Tig protested.

Clare laughed. "You're an open book, Tig. We can practically read your thoughts like you have the words scrolling across your forehead."

Now she knew why she had never won at a poker night in her life. "Chase liked to be in control," she said, disregarding the commentary about her and focusing on the matter at hand. "He liked taking charge at meetings, that sort of thing. Until yesterday, I'd never seen him act out on it physically, but it was always present in his interactions with us. He was the one who started calling me Oedipus Rex, and it had a definite passive-aggressive tone when he started it. Once everyone else joined in, though, it turned more playful."

Tig paused, gently cradling this secret, wonderful thing that Chase had been hiding under her very nose. "Although we're assuming he *could* display it but chose not to."

"Stolen?" Clare asked, at the same time as Kent's "Smuggled?"

"Either one," Tig admitted. "The trend with artifacts is increasingly that they rightfully belong to their country of origin. In the past, anyone with enough money and some knowledge of where to dig could go pillage archaeological sites and take whatever they found back home. But with increasing regulations on trade comes a corresponding increase in illegal movement of ancient artifacts across borders. I don't know if Chase was involved in anything like that, but it's another possible reason for keeping it hidden."

Kent nodded, then gestured toward the amphora again. "How ancient are we talking here?"

She snapped the question at her, but Tig didn't take it personally. Clare was correct that the case had gotten more interesting, but Kent was probably focused on the fact that it was now much more complicated.

"Maybe sixth century BCE? Somewhere around there. I know an art history professor who would be able to give us more information."

Kent rubbed her eyes and sighed. "If you're about to say the name Libby Hart..."

"Alexis Matthiou," Tig said quickly. She knew, though, how excited Libby would be by this office visit and everything they had found so far. Tig had a feeling Clare was thinking the exact same thing. She was equally sure neither of them were going to share that with Kent. "She's a visiting professor from Greece. Her specialty is sculpture, but she teaches a couple Museology courses, too, so she must have some credentials in that area."

Kent took the amphora from her again, and Tig congratulated

herself on not keeping hold and starting a tug-of-war, although that was more because she wanted to protect the vessel than because she had a superhuman amount of self-control. "Fine, then," Kent said. "I'll contact her and see if she can help us. Tomorrow, we'll go to Davies's house and see what other treasures we can unearth. Tig, I'd like you to go with us."

Tig nodded, not in agreement with Kent's request, but because she was already planning on accompanying them. If there was any chance of finding another artifact like this one, she wasn't about to be left behind.

"I'll be there. And while we're waiting for Professor Matthiou to check that out, I can keep it in my office." Tig reached for the amphora, but Kent held it out of reach. "Hey," Tig protested, "I'm just trying to do my part."

Kent shook her head. "I have enough on my plate without needing to chase you across the country when you run away with it."

"I would never…" Tig started, trying to inject as much of an air of affront as possible into her words. Clare and Kent were both staring her down, though, so she gave up the pretense. "I would never leave enough of a trail for you to find me."

"Ha. I'd have you in custody before you left the county. Now, I'm taking this over to the Art History Department. Sawyer, make sure this office is guarded, and get Professor Weston's class schedule for tomorrow so we can plan our trip to Davies's house for when she's not teaching. And both of you"—she stared at each in turn—"remain silent about this. We don't even know for certain what we have here."

Tig didn't hear much conviction in her last order. After only one day of knowing each other, Kent believed her, even though she didn't have the expertise or equipment to prove that her gut feeling was correct. Kent's trust in her gave her a feeling of almost physical warmth in her belly, but even though she knew that trust was not given lightly, she had to merely be grateful for it and then let it go without letting it take root. The amphora was an exciting find, but it didn't change the fact that Tig's future was uncertain.

Tig went back to her office and emptied some old files out of a box and piled them on the floor so Kent could use it to transport the vessel across campus in a less obvious way than tucking it under her arm. She carefully covered the vase with an old sweater she found draped over her coat rack, to protect it from the rain, and then Kent took the box and left her and Clare behind.

"Are you gazing wistfully after my sergeant, or after that vase thing?" Clare asked, breaking Tig out of her reverie as they left the office behind Kent.

"That *vase thing* is potentially an authentic prize amphora. And I'm not wistful. I'm just concerned because she might trip and fall, and I really should be there to catch the box if she does."

Clare grinned. "You were watching Kent walk away, weren't you? I'm telling Libby that you're in love with her."

Tig turned on her, indignant even though Clare was completely right. About the walking away part, not the rest of it. "First of all, I was not watching her. Second of all, who could blame me if I did when she manages to make wool uniform pants look so sexy from the back? Third, don't you dare tell Libby anything about this. You know what a matchmaker she is—she'll never leave me alone."

"Come on, you have to let me tell her," Clare said as they left Tig's office and headed toward the stairs. "She's going to smell it on us, that we found something interesting. I need a diversion, and you're it." She paused at the top of the steps. "Although I might promise not to say a word to her if you vow to never mention anything remotely related to my sergeant's ass around me again."

"Deal," Tig said with relief. It didn't mean she'd stop noticing it, but she could certainly manage not to say anything out loud to Clare.

"Good. Now you need to get that dreamy look out of your eyes, no matter the cause, and go teach your class. I'll see you at the restaurant tonight."

Tig nodded. "Pizza Tuesday. Wouldn't miss it."

She walked down the hall toward the room where her advanced Greek students were waiting to translate lyric poetry, sternly telling herself that she would *not* go off topic and embark on a lecture about black-figure vases when they were meant to be discussing Callimachus, no matter how tempted she was.

She was distracted enough by her internal monologue that she yelped and jumped about a foot to one side when Kam stepped out from a doorway and into her path, as if he had been waiting there for her. Which he might likely have been doing, since he knew her course schedule. He was holding his usual armload of loose papers, and Tig wondered if he just swept everything off his desk and carried it with him each time he left his office.

"He's dead," Kam whispered.

Tig didn't even bother to ask who Kam meant. Chase Davies, of course. Unless someone else had been killed in the past hour.

"Yes," she said.

"You found his...his body?"

Tig nodded, unsure what she was able to tell him and what was part of the investigation and needed to be kept from the public, especially when said public might be a potential suspect. She had called 911, though, and she knew anyone could access that information.

"The fight, Kam," she said, going on the offensive before he could ask her more questions that she wasn't sure she could answer. "What the hell were you thinking?"

He shifted, looking over his shoulder, and a piece of paper came loose and wafted to the floor. Tig picked it up and glanced at it. It looked like a random page from a student's essay. How did he manage to grade papers when they were all tumbled together? She tucked the page back into his armload.

"Not here," he hissed. The hallway was fairly quiet, but a few students were walking past on their way to and from class. "He was done with me. He was going to...Not here. I'll call you."

She nodded, filing this away as an unusual occurrence that Kent would want to know about. Not a very informative one, but still. Unusual, even for Kam.

"I have to talk to the police today, after my class," he said.

Tig wondered why Kent hadn't mentioned the interview to her, then stopped herself because she was quickly approaching Libby territory. After the fight and the reappearance of the plagiarism scandal, it was only logical that Kent would want to talk to Kam. She had no need to inform Tig about it.

"Yes. I had an interview, too," she said vaguely. She wasn't about to let him know how his name had come up. "Just be honest with them, and it'll be okay."

He looked at her as if she had told him to jump on the table during the interview and start doing some impromptu disco dancing.

"Honest," he repeated.

"Yes. Don't lie. They can tell." Tig frowned at him. He was acting flaky, even by Kam standards. "Did you kill him, Kam?" she asked outright.

"No, of course not!" He seemed genuinely surprised by the question, even though she thought he couldn't have acted guiltier during the entire conversation if he'd been trying.

But Tig believed him. God knew why, when he was nearly hopping from foot to foot in an agitated way. She had seen the files and had heard Davies call him a plagiarist while they fought in the hall, dredging up old, nearly career-ending pain. She also thought he had questionable professional ethics, at best. But when he looked at her and said he hadn't killed Chase…Well, she just believed him.

"Look, I need to get to class now," she said. "But call me. We'll talk, okay?"

He nodded and scurried away from her. She moved more slowly, dragging out her walk to her classroom while she replayed his words and mannerisms in her mind in case Kent wanted to hear about the encounter. She wished she had more than intuition to give as the reason why she thought he was—at least where this crime was concerned—innocent, but she didn't. Between this and the amphora, Kent was going to think she was a wannabe psychic.

She smiled. She and Libby should join forces and solve crimes. With her psychic abilities and Libby's natural flair for detective work, they'd be the most sought-after investigative duo in the state.

That is, if Kent didn't toss them both in jail first, under no other charge than coming up with the idea in the first place.

Chapter Nine

Clare sat in one of the conference rooms and flipped through the crime scene photos for the hundredth time. There was nothing, not even a niggling sense that a clue was present, and she hadn't yet seen it. Just nothing. A man facedown, shot from behind, and partially moved into the bushes. The latter act was most likely not an attempt to hide his body, since the shrub wasn't especially thick, and the area would be well-trafficked during the day, but more to give the killer time to leave the scene in case anyone walked by and found the body quickly enough to notice someone fleeing.

She spread a few of the photos out on the table. In her previous case, the numerous symbols and carefully chosen locations related to the crime scenes had helped her solve the case—with Libby's invaluable help, of course. Surprisingly, in this current investigation, the sheer lack of clues gave her hints about the killer's mind. This seemed personal, as if Davies had been sought out on purpose, then shot execution-style. There was anger behind this, or a desire to punish him. At the same time, the way the body was left had a dismissive feel to it since no attempts were made to cover, thoroughly hide, or otherwise handle the corpse. He still had his wallet with some cash in it, as well as his car and house keys, likely ruling out an opportunistic robbery.

Someone wanted to get rid of Chase Davies, but they couldn't be bothered to do more than shoot him, then leave the mess and the body for other people to clean up. The coldness of the act gave her the creeps because she had the sense of a sociopath being behind it, someone who was likely able to pass as an average, nonmurderous human being in daily situations, but who was hiding the icy soul of a killer.

All of which was just an instinctive way of seeing clues in the absence of any significant ones and wasn't yet helpful in terms of catching the killer. She sighed and stacked the photos into a pile. She might not have anything solid to go on, but she knew she had to warn Tig about the possible duplicitous nature of the murderer. Tig needed to understand that she couldn't trust anyone right now. She was kind and always willing to overlook faults and give people the benefit of the doubt. All very nice attributes to have, but they could put her in danger in this situation. Clare needed to protect Tig because she was Libby's closest friend, but also because she had come to care for and respect her in the short time they had known each other.

Kent came in the room and dropped heavily into the chair opposite her. Clare put a finger on the corner of one of the photos and slid it toward her.

"Cold," Kent said. "Barren. With the other murders, you could see the passion behind them, but this is detached, somehow."

Clare nodded and repeated the observations she had been making before her sergeant had entered the room. Kent nodded thoughtfully.

"Share that with Tig," she said, then ran a hand over her eyes with a sigh. "Professor Weston, I mean. She's brilliant but very trusting, and I think our killer will likely be someone capable of seeming worthy of trust. Be vague, but encourage her to be suspicious of everyone until this person is caught."

Clare smiled. Libby had picked the wrong friend to bring to the station yesterday. Clare hadn't seen any overt signs of fireworks between Kent and Tig, but she had noticed enough hints that some were simmering under the surface, kept under wraps by these two very controlled and outwardly calm women. And, in the course of one short day of acquaintance, they had seemed to develop a mutual respect for each other, which Clare personally thought was much more valuable in a relationship than fireworks that could burn out. Luckily, she had both in spades with Libby.

"Oh, stop," Kent demanded. "I can tell by the look on your face that you're thinking about Hart. We have an interview coming up, so for God's sake try to look like a cop and not someone who's about to race to an airport gate with a bouquet of flowers in the last act of a romantic movie."

Clare laughed. "Did my expression really convey that entire scene, or are you projecting your own romantic daydreams onto me? Partner?"

She added the last word to remind Kent that they were on equal footing during the investigation, although she wasn't sure it was necessary since she had noticed a definite softening in her sergeant since they had started working together. She smiled more easily—some of the time, at least. Clare wasn't sure how much was to do with Tig, because Kent had definitely been almost playful at times this afternoon in Davies's office, comparatively speaking, of course. She had a feeling Kent liked being a partner and not a superior for at least a small part of her day. Not the entire day, but a part of it.

"I assure you, I am not prone to daydreams, romantic or otherwise. I keep my mind focused on my work. You should try it sometime."

Clare grinned. "Sorry, but I've become rather fond of romance. I'm looking for a balance between the two, slightly leaning toward the Libby side." More than slightly, but Clare wanted to keep her job. It was best not to let her boss know which had become her true priority, but inside she knew that, from now on, Libby would always win, no matter what.

"What happened with the vase thing?" she asked.

"Professor Matthiou is going to run some tests at the Museology Department, but it looks like Ti…Professor Weston was correct. Matthiou rather rudely told me she was busy and didn't have time to play *Antiques Roadshow* with every person who had found something vaguely Greek looking in their attics. I pulled out the vase while she was in the middle of that rant, and suddenly she had all the time in the world. She practically grabbed it out of my hands and ran out of her office to examine it more thoroughly." Kent shook her head. "The next hallway fistfight we have to break up will probably be her and Tig arguing over who gets to take it home."

"Um, Professor Weston, you mean?" Clare asked innocently, laughing at Kent's expression as it shifted between what was clearly annoyance aimed at Clare and embarrassment for using the more familiar name for Tig. Clare had seen the first look many times since she had transferred to this department. The second was new to her and made her sergeant look suspiciously like a real human being.

The desk officer leaned into the room, her hand braced on the doorjamb. "He's here. Want me to bring him in?"

"Yes, we're ready," Kent said, looking relieved at the interruption.

Clare gathered the photos and put them back into their folder while Kent walked around the table and sat next to her, leaving the chair across from them vacant for Kamrick Morris.

Clare watched him walk into the room almost on tiptoe, as if afraid to put his full weight on the floor. Landry had interviewed him after the fight, while Clare talked to Davies, so she hadn't spoken to him before now, but Derek had told her he had been overly chatty, in a nervous sort of way, and determined to prove that he was innocent and Davies was at fault. Her interview with Davies had been almost the opposite, as he had been close to catatonic and only spoke to say how sorry he was, and how ashamed.

Today, Kam still exuded that nervous energy that Derek had described, and it seemed almost palpable as it filled the room. Most people were stressed when they had to face a police interview, but this was something different. It made her feel tense just to watch him move, and she took deep breaths to relax and detach herself from his contagious anxiousness. She heard Kent exhale in a long, soft sigh and wondered if she was feeling the same thing.

He sat down gingerly—again, as if he was trying to hold himself at a distance from everything in the room.

"Thank you for coming in, Professor Morris," Kent said evenly. "We just wanted to—"

"I didn't do it," he said. "You can't keep me here. I want a lawyer."

Kent's sigh was a little less soft this time. "We're not accusing you of anything, Professor, nor are you in custody. We know you were at your son's football practice last night at the time Professor Davies was shot, so you are not a suspect. We asked you here because you were a colleague of the victim, and any information you can share about him might help us solve this case."

"I don't know anything about him," Morris said. "We barely spoke to each other."

"You were trying to beat each other up in the halls yesterday. Apparently you spoke enough to get into a fight. Care to tell us what that was about?"

He crossed his arms over his chest. "No."

Well, that was helpful. "Who started the fight?" Clare asked. He had told Derek that Davies had thrown the first ill-timed punch.

"I told that officer yesterday. It was a misunderstanding, that's all."

Clare was beginning to understand why Landry had seemed so exasperated after his interview with Morris.

"Who misunderstood first?" she asked.

He looked somewhere beyond her left ear. "I don't remember."

"He called you a plagiarist," Kent said, tired of his noncooperation and going directly for the topic that would shake him up. "That seemed to upset you. Care to explain why?"

"I'm an academic," he said. He seemed to be trying for a condescending tone, but failed since he only sounded whiny. "It's a nasty name to call anyone in my profession, so of course it upset me."

"Hmm. I thought it might be because you were accused of it in the past. Did Davies ever remind you of that fact? Did he ever bring up the evidence against you in conversations?"

"I want a lawyer."

"Fine. We'll speak to you again when you have representation."

Kent went to the door and called for Keaton, who came and escorted Morris out of the room.

"That went well," Clare said as they gathered their files and notepads and left the room.

"Irritating man," Kent muttered. "I think I'll leave his next interview to you."

"Rock paper scissors for it?" Clare asked hopefully. Kent gave her a look that was more sergeant than partner. "Oh, yeah. I forgot."

"Go home, Sawyer. I'll see you in the morning."

Kent parted ways with her in the hall, and Clare watched her walk back to her office, where there was likely a stack of administrative work for her to finish before she could go home, too. Clare sighed and went to change out of her uniform.

❖

Less than ten minutes later, she was walking into the new pizza place in the U District, just a block from the station. Libby had surprised all of them by picking this place for dinner—she wasn't deviating from Pizza Tuesday, but switching from their usual Italian restaurant to this one was a big deal for her.

Clare spotted her at once, sitting in a booth near the door and laughing with Tig, Jazz, and Ari. She walked over and gave Libby a kiss, earning the two of them a chorus of groans and complaints from the others.

Clare sat down next to her. "I kissed her on the cheek. What's to complain about?"

"Nothing really. It's become a habit now," Jazz said, waving a breadstick at her.

"And we hope that some proactive grousing will keep the two of you from getting out of hand," Tig added.

"We're perfectly in hand, thank you," Libby said with a haughty sniff. "And yes, I meant that exactly the way it sounded."

Clare grinned and relaxed in her seat, with her arm resting across the back of Libby's chair. The day had been a long one, with time spent on the investigation combined with a few hours of patrol duty. The department was small and currently short-handed, so detective work had to fit in with her regular campus police duties.

She'd never complain about the busy days, however, because she was having the opportunity to do more interesting and varied work with this department than she had anticipated. Still, she welcomed the chance to get away from the station and hang out with friends.

"So, Tig," Libby said, leaning back until her shoulders touched Clare's arm, "guess who I saw in the Art Building today?"

Clare and Tig exchanged a quick glance, wondering if the answer was Sergeant Kent, carrying an ancient Greek artifact.

"Who?" asked Tig, her voice sounding wary.

"Professor Ayari. Or, Sami. That is what *you* call her, isn't it?"

"That's what most people call her," Tig said mildly, sipping from her glass of wine.

"Well, she's very beautiful, no matter what name you use. Have you thought about asking her out? You're sort of running out of options."

Tig choked on her wine and sputtered for a moment, apparently unable to decide which part of Libby's comment to address first. Clare shook her head. She had a feeling this was another miss on Libby's part.

"I'm going to be working closely with her over the next year… That's not what I meant by *closely*, you two, so stop laughing." She turned and addressed Jazz and Ari, then faced Libby again. "We need to be able to work together to make this new department a success. I wouldn't jeopardize that just to get a date. And what do you mean by running—"

She had to stop when their pizzas arrived at the table. Clare leaned to one side to make room and noticed Sergeant Kent walking into the restaurant wearing civilian clothes. Kent saw her at the same time and momentarily looked like she was considering walking out again, but then she straightened her shoulders and came over to their table.

"Good evening, Sawyer, Professors, Ms. Harald," she said.

"Hey, Sarge," Libby responded. Clare bumped her with her knee. "Why don't you join us?"

"Thank you, but I was just going to pick up some dinner and eat in my office. I have a lot of work to do. Enjoy your meal."

"Come on, you should stay. It's what partners do," Clare said as Kent was starting to walk away. She didn't like the thought of Kent eating alone with only a stack of paperwork for company, plus this would give her a chance to spend time with Tig.

Jeez, she was getting as bad as Libby.

"We're partners when we're working directly on the case," Kent said, lowering her voice. "That isn't going to happen at this table."

"No, but if you don't stay, I might accidentally start talking about the case," Clare whispered back. "It'd be better if you were here to keep that from happening."

Kent raised her eyebrows. "Blackmail, Sawyer? Really?"

Clare pushed the empty chair next to her toward Kent. "Don't think of it as blackmail. Think of it as an offer of free pizza."

Kent sat down. She looked uncomfortable at first, but everyone else continued chatting and filling plates with pizza slices, so she seemed to relax a fraction.

"We were just discussing Tig's love life, Sarge," Libby said. "She's run through all the eligible dates in the humanities departments, so I suggested she date Professor Ayari. New blood."

"Libby!" Tig said, dropping her piece of pizza on her plate. "I haven't dated my way through anything."

"Yes, you have," Libby said, pulling off a piece of pepperoni and eating it.

Tig paused for a moment. "Well, maybe," she admitted. "But we're talking two or three women since I've been teaching here. You make it sound like I've gone through dozens."

Jazz leaned toward Kent. "I keep telling her she needs to branch out into the sciences."

Tig shook her head and looked at Kent. "Maybe you should get back to that paperwork."

Kent grinned and took a piece of cheese pizza. "Are you kidding? This is turning out to be much more interesting than those stuffy old reports. So, what's wrong with the sciences?"

"Their buildings are too far away," Ari chimed in. "She thinks they're inconvenient."

"I never said anything like that," Tig protested. "Really, can we change the subject?"

There was a chorus of *No!* from everyone at the table, and even Tig joined in the ensuing laughter, shaking her head at Kent in an exasperated sort of way.

"Oh," Libby said softly as she watched them exchange that glance, drawing out the syllable. She looked at Clare. "I've had it all wrong, haven't I. Did you know about this?"

"Yep," said Clare, smug even though she had only recently guessed at the connection forming between the two. She smiled as the conversation continued and Kent was absorbed into their group.

CHAPTER TEN

Tig rather desperately tried to change the conversation's topic, but the others seemed determined to remain focused on her. The best she could hope for was a distraction. An earthquake, maybe? They had a lot of those in the Northwest. She'd prefer that to having her unsuccessful love life discussed in front of Kent, of all people. Kent, who seemed to be enjoying Tig's discomfort far too much.

She wasn't even sure how she'd like Kent to see her, nor did she want to delve too deeply into why it mattered to her at all what Kent thought. Still, the fact remained—not too closely examined, but present—that she *did* care how Kent saw her. With her friends trying to outdo each other with their exaggerated descriptions of her, she sounded in turn like a player and a social recluse. The truth was somewhere in the middle. She might have dated her way through her section of campus, but she hadn't been lying when she reminded everyone that the pool from which she had to choose was very small. And, yes, she hadn't had a relationship for well over a year now—she wasn't about to count months, and instead settled on that vague estimate—but she had been too busy with not only her teaching, but also with her departmental responsibilities to squeeze in time to spend on dating.

And she had her friends to fill her evenings and weekends, although she was currently rethinking the wisdom in that.

Kent laughed at something Jazz had said while Tig was distracted by her own thoughts. Judging by everyone's gleeful reactions to whatever comment she had made, Tig was relieved to have missed it. They never laughed that hard at the flattering remarks anyone made.

Kent nudged her with an elbow as the laughter faded. "It's funny to tease about, but the four of you really have narrowed down your available dating options when your friend group is made up of the majority of eligible women on this side of campus." She nodded toward Libby and Clare. "Or three eligible, and a newly ineligible one and her girlfriend. Haven't any of you ever dated each other?"

"No," Libby and Jazz said in unison, at the same time that Tig and Ari said, "Yes."

"The two of you dated?" Libby asked incredulously. "And you never told us?"

Tig shrugged. "It was a one-time thing, and it was before you and Jazz came to campus. Not much to tell."

"Ooh, bad date, hmm?" Clare asked, reaching for another slice of pizza. "We need the full story."

Tig laughed. "Not at all. Best date I ever had."

Ari grinned at her. "Me, too. I've never laughed so much with someone I'd just met."

"So, what are you saying?" Jazz asked. "Are you secretly married and raising a family of little Tigs and Aris?"

"No. We had absolutely zero chemistry," Tig said, smiling at the memory. She and Ari had realized this after only about ten minutes together. She had never regretted the fact that their relationship hadn't had the hope of evolving into something romantic, since she had gained a best friend in the process. "We brought it up right at the beginning of the date, which you'd think would have put a damper on the evening, but it turned into a running joke the entire night."

Ari laughed. "We'd say things like *I think I'm starting to feel hot for you. Oh, never mind, it was just the spicy jalapeños in my burrito.*" Tig joined in her laughter, but the others were watching them, still apparently in shock at the revelation. "Well, I guess you had to be there," said Ari with a shrug. "We thought it was hilarious."

"So, which one of you asked the other out?" Clare asked. "My money's on Tig."

"You win," said Ari. "I hadn't even been here a week when she made her move."

"I'll admit I was the one who asked," Tig said. "But you happened to be standing outside my office at the time. As far as I know, you've never taught a single class in Denny."

"I was new," Ari protested over the laughter of the others. "I was lost."

Tig turned to Kent and grinned at her. "She was holding a campus map at the time."

"Fine, it's true," Ari said. "I had heard there was a cute, single classics professor in Denny, and I wanted to check you out myself."

Tig sighed with relief as the group's teasing turned in the direction of Ari, and she took a bite of the pizza that had been sitting uneaten on her plate during the earlier part of the conversation. Their news wasn't exactly an earthquake, but it had done the job.

Kent leaned toward her. "So," she asked, speaking quietly so the others couldn't overhear. "You can tell if you have chemistry with someone right away?"

Tig looked into Kent's eyes and felt something stir inside her, making her want to lean forward in turn and fall into whatever this was, no matter the consequences. She loved her friends and thought they were beautiful, wonderful people, but none of them had ever made her feel this same way. She knew she should be sensible, aware of how precarious her future was, and just shrug off Kent's question with a joke or neutral answer.

"Immediately," she said, instead. She held Kent's gaze for a few moments longer, then dragged her focus away and back to the table in general. Even without eye contact, though, she still responded to Kent's presence, her mind and body alert to every breath, every sigh.

This was not good.

She spent the rest of dinner doing something she rarely had to do when they were all together—she had to force herself to smile and laugh in the right places, and to fight to keep her attention on the others and not drift into her own mental space. She had spent the time between her last class and this dinner updating her CV and actually reading and considering the letters she had received from other universities. It wasn't fair to Kent for Tig to encourage any sort of relationship when she was already preparing her exit strategy. And this whole situation was damned unfair for Tig herself, to finally find something that felt real when her career was developing fractures that might result in irreparable breaks. She could imagine the two of them together, curled up with each other in the evening and talking or kissing, or at a dinner like this one, with their chairs pulled closer together and Kent's hand resting on her thigh as they chatted and laughed with friends. But she could also clearly picture herself packing up her belongings and traveling to wherever her next job might be. Her career was everything to her. Her passion, her past, her future. What was between her and Kent was intriguing in the present, but nothing more.

Right. She made herself laugh at something Libby said, barely hearing it and joining in with the others after a few seconds' delay. Somehow, she made it through the rest of dinner without doing anything to draw attention to herself—although that in itself probably alerted her friends that something was wrong. She just couldn't shake the awareness that in all likelihood, she was going to have to say goodbye to whatever potential she and Kent shared.

And she'd be saying goodbye to her friends, as well.

❖

They proved themselves to be as perceptive as usual, although they only figured out half of Tig's reasons for being as distracted as she was. As soon as they stepped outside the restaurant, the four of them barely said good night before they scattered as if they had prearranged it, leaving Tig and Kent alone on the sidewalk. If her friends had known everything that was weighing on Tig's mind, they would have stayed instead, protecting her from starting a new relationship that would only end up with her in pain, nursing a broken heart in an unfamiliar city.

"Your friends aren't exactly subtle," Kent remarked.

Tig shook her head in exasperation. "They're not. But don't worry, I'll be swapping them out for new ones tomorrow."

It was a comfortable old joke that she and her friends often made when one of them was being driven nuts by the others, and she said it without thinking. She rubbed her eyes and sighed.

"They don't know yet, do they? What we talked about, if your department is shut down."

Tig shook her head. "We all share the belief that our specialty is vital to the university, and I don't think it would occur to any of us that classics or architectural history or gothic novels might be expendable and could vanish on the whim of the university. I guess it needs to be pointed out to us by an outsider for it to seem real."

"Yeah, sorry about that. Let's walk." She tugged on Tig's sleeve until she started moving, then dropped the contact. "Is your car in Denny's lot?"

Tig nodded. "I'll walk you to the station on the way."

Kent laughed. "How about I walk you to your car, then walk myself back to the station."

Tig playfully gave her a push. "I'm perfectly capable of taking care of myself and protecting you at the same time."

"Of course you are."

Tig stuck her hands in her pockets to keep from reaching out to touch Kent again. "Thank you. Now, if you could just say that again without rolling your eyes, it would be a bit more meaningful."

"I could try, but I doubt I'd pull it off. What I can say is that normally that might be true, but tonight why don't we let the armed person who doesn't look like she might start crying at any moment be the bodyguard?"

"I'm not crying," Tig protested.

"I said *might start*."

"Oh. Well, then, okay. You can be the muscle just this once."

They walked in silence for a while, weaving through the busy U District streets until they reached the relatively quiet campus. Tig had a hard time believing that about twenty-four hours ago she had walked along these same paths and had discovered Chase's body.

Some parts of her day had been very normal—teaching classes, being with friends. Others had been so strange, like her conversation with Kam and assisting as the police searched Chase's office. She felt disconnected from all of it, but she decided that was understandable given the situation. Somehow, having Kent at her side helped ground her when she felt like she was becoming unwound from the life she had built here.

"Oh, hey," she said, coming to a halt. "I forgot to ask about the amphora. It's real, isn't it? Can I have it if no one claims it?"

Kent laughed. "Do you mean like things that are left in the lost and found? No. If it turns out he acquired it legitimately, it belongs to Davies's estate, at least once the investigation into his murder is finished. Until then, it's potential evidence. Professor Matthiou still needs to examine it, but she had the same fanatical look in her eyes that you did when she saw it, so I believe she thinks it's authentic, too."

"Maybe I should go over there, just to check on it."

"By *check on it*, I hope you don't mean *break in and steal it*," Kent cautioned her. "I don't know if it factors into this investigation, but it seems like it might be connected."

"Speaking of things connected to the case, I've been meaning to tell you about some weird things Kam Morris said to me today when he accosted me outside my classroom."

Kent listened quietly to Tig's recitation, then moved them next to a lamppost and had Tig repeat the conversation while she took notes in its light.

"Honest," she repeated when they started moving again. "We had a completely worthless interview with him today, but I suppose he was honest about not wanting to give us any information."

"Is he a suspect?" Tig asked. His behavior, combined with the hints of possible blackmail, made him seem like a likely candidate. His personality made the idea of him as a murderer seem laughable.

"No," Kent said. "Good alibi."

They got to Tig's car, but Kent didn't seem inclined to rush away, so Tig kept her keys in her pocket and rested her hip against the front fender.

"You have good friends," Kent said, leaning against the car next to her. "You're lucky."

"I know," Tig answered quietly. She heard the edge of wistfulness in Kent's voice. "Is it hard to make friends in your job? I couldn't tell if it was okay for Clare to ask you to join us, or if you have rules against fraternizing."

Kent crossed her arms over her chest and looked toward Denny. "It's not always clear, especially when there's mobility in the department and people get promoted reasonably often. I went to the academy with some people in this department, and one is my superior, two are below me in rank, and the other works in HR and is sort of outside the hierarchy. We don't have to pretend we don't know each other well, and at various times I've had drinks or dinner with all of them. Tonight was fine with Sawyer, but becoming besties would be an issue. A romantic relationship would definitely be out. I've been on promotions panels before where one member will excuse themselves because they're close to the person being considered, and that's fine, but she's in my direct chain of command, so anything that goes beyond casual wouldn't be appropriate."

"Wow, that's confusing. It'd be tempting just to keep to yourself and avoid all the possible pitfalls," Tig said with a laugh. Kent gave her a look, and Tig switched to a frown. "Oh, that's what you do, isn't it?"

Kent shrugged as if it was inconsequential, but Tig sensed how lonely that must be. "Most of the time, yes. But like I said, I have casual friends scattered through the department. If I want to go out on a Friday night, I know the places where they hang out and I can always find someone to share a conversation or a drink."

"And dating?" Tig asked, hoping she sounded simply curious, but not sure if she pulled it off.

"Within the department? Not at all. I sometimes meet women from other departments during trainings or conferences, and when I was on patrol I dated a couple of people I met on campus, but those connections haven't ever felt important enough to be worth juggling time and distance to maintain a relationship when my work life is so busy."

Kent paused, then turned toward her. "This one does."

Tig turned to face her, too, leaning against the car mere inches away. "I might have to leave. I won't have a choice."

"I remember," Kent said. "From two minutes ago when we last talked about it."

Tig smiled. "Deflecting with sarcasm?"

Kent shrugged and grinned back at her. Tig raised her hand and brushed the pad of her thumb across Kent's lower lip. "What exactly are you proposing? Just a fling?"

"No," Kent said firmly. "That implies that this doesn't mean much, and that we can rush in and rush out without getting too close. It's the opposite. I think you're something special, and that under other circumstances you could prove to be very important in my life. Even though we might not have forever to explore that, I don't want to pretend I'm not feeling this."

Tig moved her hand until she was cupping Kent's cheek. "Do you mean dating? Letting this progress like normal, like we don't know how it might end?"

Kent nodded, her skin brushing softly against Tig's palm.

Tig frowned, wanting to say yes to anything Kent might be offering, but also needing to protect her heart—and Kent's, too. "Do you realize how much it's going to hurt when it ends?" she asked.

"Yes, I do. I already feel it. And I don't care." Kent closed the distance between them and kissed her.

Tig felt herself melting into the pressure of Kent's lips against her own. The physical sensations were powerful enough—she smelled good, she tasted *so* good—but there was something more, something Tig had never felt before because it had everything to do with Kent herself. She had held beautiful women in her arms in the past, and had enjoyed kissing them, but there was always something missing. Tig had thought the lack of real passion had been her shortcoming, that she wasn't responding the right way or feeling enough attraction, but now she knew the truth. Other women weren't Kent, and therefore they'd never be enough for her.

Damn it.

Tig fought to keep some part of her mind rational and detached because she'd never make it through this if she didn't, but the moment she felt Kent's tongue brush against her lips, she gave up the attempt. She turned until she had Kent pressed against the car, the full length of their bodies in contact, and met Kent's tongue with her own.

Somehow, with some superpower she hadn't realized she possessed, she managed to pull back an inch or two. Kent wasn't in uniform, but Tig knew she wouldn't want to be caught by any of her officers in public like this. She braced her hands on the car on either side of Kent's shoulders and rested their foreheads together as they both fought to catch their breath.

She brushed her nose against Kent's. "So," she said, "Does this mean I get to call you Adi?"

Kent laughed, and Tig felt the warmth of it against the chafed, sensitive skin of her lips. "Go right ahead," she said. "As long as you don't mind being arrested."

Kent gave her a quick kiss and playfully pushed her away. "You'd better get in your car before this gets any more out of hand and we both get arrested. If my officers see me having my rights read at the station, it will seriously undermine my authority."

Tig gave her hands a squeeze, then let go and fished her keys out of her pocket. "I'm going. But I'll see you tomorrow?"

Kent nodded. "See you tomorrow."

Tig got in her car and buckled her seat belt. She waved at Kent as she pulled out of her parking place and drove calmly toward the campus exit, trying to ignore the fact that she had just willingly signed on for a broken heart.

Chapter Eleven

Kent sat at her desk and did nothing. It was becoming a habit. Last night after Tig drove away, she had spent about two hours walking around campus, and then had gone home instead of doing the work she had intended to do before Sawyer intervened and got her to join her friends. Against her better judgment. She congratulated herself on that—she had known it wasn't a good idea to sit down next to Tig and lose herself in laughter and companionship. Yes, how very wise of her to have recognized it as a mistake.

And how very foolish to have done it anyway.

Now she was sort of in a relationship with a woman she barely knew, who would leave as soon as the university decided that having a Classics Department wasn't worth the high body count. She had blurred the lines between her and Clare. Libby probably thought that having a meal together with Kent meant she was officially part of the police force. She'd likely show up in uniform today.

Kent smiled. She wasn't sorry. Not about any of it. Sawyer was a savvy enough officer to keep their relationship professional. A one-time dinner was fine, and they wouldn't make a habit of it. And Libby? Hell, Kent might as well send her out on patrol and let her get it out of her system. Once she realized that police work was usually highly repetitive and boring, punctuated by brief moments of screeching excitement, she'd probably lose interest. She had been brought in to help solve a murder, and the experience had made her think that kind of complex case was the norm, when in truth the norm was drunk college kids who needed a ride back to the dormitories.

Which brought her to Tig. Kent kept waiting for regret to kick in. Why start something they wouldn't be able to finish? Why sign up for the pain of good-bye?

But regret didn't come, and neither did answers to those questions. All she knew was that she was going to say yes to Tig as long as the option was there. Yes to kissing her, to laughing with her, to spending time with her.

Someone knocked on her door, and she made an effort to force the smile off her face and return to her usual scowl. Or at least a neutral expression. She figured she was about as successful as Tig had been when she was trying not to look shifty during their interview.

Damn, she was smiling again. This really needed to stop.

"Come in," she said. Not bad. She sounded reasonably annoyed, which was her usual tone.

The desk officer opened her door and came in, with Sawyer on his heels. He handed her an envelope with her name on it in elegant script and left. Kent waved Clare toward the chair opposite her and slit the envelope with her letter opener.

She skimmed the note from Professor Matthiou, reading the key parts aloud to Clare.

"Circa 560 BCE, but some of the repair work is more modern. So far, no indication that it was stolen or that it's gone through an auction house, but they're still running it through a variety of databases to find out for sure." She looked at Clare. "I'm not sure what that means. How the hell did he get it, then?"

Clare shrugged, taking the letter when Kent offered it to her and reading through it. Kent figured the ornate handwriting would be challenging for someone with dyslexia, so she kept silent and gave Clare time to work through the letter. "Tig will probably know what this is about," Clare said, when she had finished reading. "She'll be here any minute, as soon as she finishes her class, so we can go to Davies's house."

"That's…good," Kent said, running through several other

word choices before settling on that one, deciding it was relatively neutral.

"Yes, very good," Clare agreed with a smirk.

"Watch your step, Sawyer, or I'll tell your doctor I saw you clutching your stomach and moaning like you were in pain. That ought to earn you another two weeks off to make sure that wound is fully healed."

She was losing her touch. Clare just laughed instead of quailing in fear.

Luckily, Tig arrived just then, before Kent had to come up with an even more threatening form of punishment for Clare to completely ignore. She came into the office wearing sunglasses and perched on the edge of Kent's desk. The action felt somehow intimate, although her expression—at least what Kent could see of it—didn't look romantic at all.

"Cool shades, Tig," Clare said. "You do realize it's raining outside, don't you?"

"Yes, I do. I was just wearing these so I could walk through Denny's halls without drawing too much attention to myself." Tig sighed and pulled off the glasses, revealing bruises that had gone a sickly shade of yellow-green around the edges.

"Oh…well…the bruises seem to be healing quickly," Kent said, trying to be diplomatic. "They must not have been too deep and should be completely faded…soon."

"You look like a raccoon with jaundice," Clare said, apparently not trying to be diplomatic at all.

Tig pointed at her eyes. "By rights, these should be on Kam's face, not mine. That's the last time I try to break up a fight."

"Maybe this will help you forget about your bruises," Kent said, gesturing for Clare to hand her the letter from Matthiou.

"You were right about the vase thing," Clare added.

Tig read the letter, tapping her lips absently with the sunglasses. Kent knew she wasn't intentionally doing it, but it made it difficult for her to keep from staring at Tig's mouth, which made her think of their kiss, which made her want to kiss her again.

She searched through some paperwork on her desk, pretending

she was looking for a Very Important Folder, while she mentally lectured herself about self-control and the dangers of wandering thoughts.

Tig put the letter on Kent's desk with a sigh. "Well, so much for me ever getting that amphora," she said.

"That was never a possibility," Kent reminded her. "But can you explain what it means that they can't find records of it?"

"It was probably part of a find from an illegal or unregistered dig and smuggled into the US. Unless Chase has official paperwork hidden somewhere that gives its provenance and proves he bought it legally, it'll most likely be returned to its country of origin, probably Greece. I'm not sure of the steps they'll need to take with it, but I doubt it will be part of his estate anymore."

"They can't just send it back if it's connected to a murder, can they?" Clare asked.

Tig shrugged. "That'll complicate matters, I suppose."

"Is there any way you would be able to buy something like this and not be aware that it was stolen?" Kent asked.

"Papers can be forged. Even though most auction houses dealing in this type of antiquity do their best to make sure items are legally able to be sold, some slip through. I wouldn't trust myself to be knowledgeable enough about verifying provenance to be sure I wasn't making a mistake. And then, some people don't care enough to look very thoroughly into an item's past, if they want to possess it badly enough."

Kent rubbed her temples. "We'll need to get the department's legal advisors to start working on this. Then we can get out to Davies's house. Maybe we'll find another artifact there, or some sort of bill of sale for this one."

Clare stood up. "I'll take the letter to the admin office and let them know what's going on. I need to go up there, anyway, to hand in my medical paperwork. Meet you in the parking garage?"

Kent nodded and handed her the letter, shutting the door after she left and turning to face Tig. She was a little nervous to be alone with her after last night, in case Tig had suddenly changed her mind about the two of them, but mostly she felt relief that they were finally together.

Tig gestured at her eyes. "Are you sorry you suggested that we get together now that I look like this?"

Kent laughed and walked over to where Tig was still sitting on her desk, stepping between her thighs and rubbing her thumbs gently over Tig's bruises, from her nose to the corners of her eyes, then sliding her hands farther until they were cupped behind Tig's neck.

"Yes. That's my deal breaker. I was perfectly okay with the thought of you moving out of the state and leaving me with a broken heart, but if your bruises are slightly more alarming than yesterday? That's it, then. I'm through."

Tig smiled, putting her hands on Kent's hips and pulling her close. Kent closed her eyes, shifting slightly against the warmth of Tig and wrapping her arms around Tig's neck. They stayed that way for a moment, just leaning into each other, before Kent pulled out of the embrace. She didn't want to, but Clare would be waiting. They had work to do.

She was about to open her office door, but Tig put a hand over hers.

"Dinner tonight?" she asked, standing close beside Kent. "Just the two of us?"

"I'd like that," she said. Such mild words, which didn't nearly describe how much the idea appealed to her. Tig smiled and stepped away again, pocketing the sunglasses and following Kent out of the station and into the small garage behind it where a few patrol cars were parked.

Clare met them at the entrance and handed a thick manila envelope to Tig. "These are from Larson," she said. "Printouts from Davies's thumb drive. Do you mind going over them again, see if anything stands out to you?"

Tig took the packet and got into the back seat of the patrol car. Clare looked like she might try for the driver's seat, but Kent beat her to it. "Get in, Sawyer," she said, pointing at the passenger side.

"Fine, but I get to drive on the way back."

"No way," said Kent, turning the key in the ignition. She pulled out onto the road and turned the wipers on. "Last time I saw your car at the station, you were parked up on the curb."

"You mean last month? When I was rushing to Gould Hall to save Libby from a murderer? I think one little tire up on the curb was justified in that situation."

"Maybe. Or it might be a sign that your skills are slipping. I think I'll need you to do another EVOC course before I let you drive me anywhere." She looked in the rearview mirror and saw Tig reading one of the pages and frowning. "Anything interesting, Tig?" she asked.

"Yeah, Professor Weston," Clare echoed, "anything interesting?"

"You can call me Tig, Clare. And I'm really not sure what I'm looking at here. I know Chase was doing research for a paper on the *Odyssey*, and several of these documents seem to be his notes from that. There are also a few similar files from papers he's already published. But there are also lower-level essays in here, which look like they're written by grad students for other professors' courses. I'm pretty sure this one was for Luke's seminar on Cato from a couple of years ago."

Kent met Tig's eyes briefly in the mirror, noticing some sadness reflected in them, then turned her attention back to the road. "Luke? Which one is he?"

"Lukas Rivers. He's on sabbatical because his husband hasn't been well. Laura Hughes was going to cover his classes, which was why she was on campus last month."

"I'm sorry," Kent said. She knew how much Tig cared about her friends, and how hard she tried to protect her faculty. Losing someone who straddled both roles couldn't have been easy on her.

They were silent for a moment, then Clare spoke again. "Are you sure those aren't his old grad school papers?" she asked.

"The others might be, but I can't tell for sure. There's nothing on them besides the essay—no names, dates, course numbers. But just going by the topics, they all match classes we've offered over the past few years at least."

Kent turned down a narrow street in the residential neighborhood of Pinehurst, watching the house numbers as she drove, and finally parked in front of a bright blue Cape Cod bungalow. It was boxy, with a natural wood door and a brick chimney on one side. White trim and white blinds made the windows seem large for the size of the house. It was small, but the lot was a decent size for this neighborhood. Davies's lawn was patchy and mostly brown, and a few evergreen shrubs were planted on either side of the front door. The house didn't seem to fit what she had been picturing, and she wasn't sure why. Something just seemed wrong.

She let that vague uneasiness simmer in the back of her mind and turned in her seat to face Tig.

"Could he have been selling essays? Another side hustle to add to his blackmail money?"

"Maybe," Tig said, and the upward inflection of her voice let Kent know that she didn't really think this was a plausible answer. "I don't know if he'd make enough for it to be worthwhile, and if he was going to do it anyway, he probably wouldn't have sold them to our students. It would be too risky. He'd sell them online, anonymously. I can check with Lukas about the Cato essay, and when I get back to my office I can look through our past course offerings and give you the names of the other professors whose classes match the papers."

She gathered the papers and tucked them back into the folder, then the three of them got out of the car and approached the house.

"Have you been here before, Tig?" Kent asked. Apparently, she had completely given up on the pretense of calling her Professor Weston. Clare didn't tease her this time. She was pulling a stack of envelopes out of the mailbox and didn't even seem to have noticed.

"No," said Tig. "That's not uncommon, though. A few of our faculty members like to host parties or have meetings at their houses, but others tend to be more private. It's about fifty-fifty."

"Is this what you expected? Or were you picturing a different kind of house?" Kent asked, still turning over the question in her own mind as she handed gloves to everyone. "What about you, Sawyer?"

"I don't know that I was picturing anything in particular," Clare said.

"Me neither," agreed Tig. "I thought it might be fancier, more suited to his style, but given the prices around here, this seems to be a stretch for his salary as it is."

Kent opened the door, and they walked in, turning on lights as they went. They split up and wandered around on their own, each collecting first impressions and looking at the house with their unique perspectives. Kent figured Clare would be the type to come in with as few preconceived ideas as possible, preferring to let her intuition guide her as she walked through the two bedroom, two bath house. She knew Tig was focused on finding more artifacts, probably hoping to find the Elgin Marbles clustered in the bathtub.

Kent's approach was based on the gut feeling that something felt out of place, even though nothing she saw supported that. One bedroom was being used as a study, with books everywhere, and a stack of essays in the process of being graded on the desk. The other bedroom was decorated in blues and browns, simple in style, but comfortable looking. Both shallow closets were filled with clothes, neutrals for the university, and brightly colored patterns for golf. She found tees and golf balls scattered on surfaces, and shoes with cleats in the closet.

She walked into the kitchen, which looked to have been renovated more recently than any other room. Grayish hardwood floors and marble countertops. White subway tiles on the backsplash. It looked like the design concept had been pulled directly from a display at a home furnishings store. She looked out the window into the back yard, where there was more dead grass, some sad-looking rose bushes, and more of the low maintenance evergreens like the ones out front.

No houseplants, no garden shed, no elaborate yard.

Kent opened a few drawers until she found his junk drawer. As she'd expected, there were take-out menus, various pens and batteries and rubber bands, and a stack of business cards. One of the top ones was for a lawn service company.

"Hey, Sawyer," she started, then paused when she saw Clare on her knees by the back door, peering at the locking mechanism. "What are you doing?"

"Come look at this, Sergeant," she said. "I think someone's broken in."

Tig joined them, and they used the beam of Kent's flashlight to see the small scrape marks next to the lock.

"It's a flimsy lock anyway and probably didn't take much manipulating to get it open. These grooves look recent, though. With all the rain we get around here, we'd be seeing some rust on them if they had been here for long."

"Not your average burglar," Kent said. "The television and gaming systems are still here, and nothing looks ransacked. This was someone careful, who might have been searching for something in particular. What made you think to look for this?"

Clare shrugged. "Something felt off. Some piles of papers were too tidy, that sort of thing. Just a feeling."

Tig straightened up from where she had been looking at the doorjamb. "I didn't find any other artifacts, but if there were some here, then maybe the person who broke in took them."

Kent shook her head. "Maybe they were already hidden. Let's go out back. We'll use the front entrance and leave this back door as is for now. I'll need to alert Seattle PD about this."

She led them through the front door again and around to the backyard. It only took a quick glance before she found what she was looking for.

"Remember his hands, Sawyer? The nails were dirty and uneven. When I saw them, I was thinking he might be someone who likes to garden, but that obviously doesn't fit with this house. He's done the bare minimum with landscaping, and I'll bet most of these shrubs were here when he bought the place."

She knelt next to one of the bushier shrubs, ignoring the light rain and the cold dampness from the ground that soaked into the knees of her uniform pants. She scraped her hand over the spot where the soil looked as if it had been turned over recently, and didn't have to dig far before she felt the edges of a brown plastic tarp. She moved enough dirt until she was able to lift the bundle out of its shallow grave, and she handed it to Tig. Clare got on the ground next to her, and together they unearthed two more packages.

She looked up as Tig was unwrapping the first one, carefully keeping it under the plastic to protect it from the rain.

She could tell it was something special before Tig even spoke, just from the look of awe on her face.

"A red-figure bell krater," she said. "They were used for mixing wine and water. My God, it's incredible."

Tig only had eyes for the large vase, but Clare and Kent looked at each other and frowned, neither of them knowing yet how all these pieces fit together.

Kent ran a hand over one of the bundles still on the ground next to her, feeling the curve of the vessel inside it.

"What were you up to, Professor Davies?" she muttered. The vase gave no answer, and the only sound was the light spatter of rain against its plastic covering.

Chapter Twelve

Later that afternoon, the three of them gathered in Tig's office. Kent and Clare rehashed the details of the case so far, and Tig half listened to them while she searched old course catalogs and matched classes to the papers Chase had on file.

She could see the appeal of detective work and wasn't surprised that Libby had been drawn to it when she helped Clare solve the previous murders. Looking for clues, piecing them together once found, and using deductive reasoning to fill in the gaps…it was like putting together a jigsaw puzzle when you had lost the box it came in and didn't know what the final picture would be. But, at the same time, there were moments that dragged for her.

When the Seattle PD officers had arrived at the house, Kent and Clare had to go over the entire story several times until everyone was on the same page with the events surrounding Chase's murder and the buried artifacts. She noticed Kent had left out key details, like Kam's involvement, the fistfight in Denny, and the documents Chase had been storing. She had to let them take over what was in their jurisdiction, but she wasn't going to let them touch what was in hers. Tig had watched this for a while, impressed by Kent's masterful ability to keep details sorted in her mind and to cagily only reveal what she wanted the other officers to know.

After the third explanation to yet another officer, however, Tig lost some interest in the dry recitation of facts and she wandered over to sit next to the three red figure vases, just appreciating being close to them without museum glass in the way. Kent glanced over at her occasionally—Tig wanted to think Kent just couldn't take her eyes off her, but she figured she was actually watching to make sure Tig didn't grab one of the vessels and run. Really, Kent needed to work on those trust issues. Tig wouldn't even consider trying to do such a thing.

Unless, of course, someone had let her hold the patrol car keys, which both Kent and Clare had refused to do. She doubted she'd make it far on foot given the number of cops lounging about the place.

Sad as she was to leave the vases behind, she was relieved to be back in her office and doing some work that required her expertise, rather than just observing the others.

Kent paged through the essays while Tig worked. "Do you think these were written by actual students? Maybe he kept them as mementos of his favorites."

"Or trophies," Clare added, and Kent nodded in response, as if this was a perfectly normal idea for someone to have.

"Trophies?" Tig repeated, looking up from the list she was making. "Do you mean from affairs? I hope that isn't the case, but I guess it might be possible. Maybe, if the people involved gave him the essays, but I can't see him going to other professors and asking for them. That would have seemed suspicious if he'd come to me."

She didn't want to even think about the repercussions if this turned into some sort of sex scandal. She might as well start packing up her desk right now if that was the case. She hated the thought that it might be true, but she didn't have any real reason to say it was an impossibility. She knew Chase had gotten divorced at least three years ago, but she didn't have any details about his personal life beyond that.

"Do you keep papers your students have written?" Clare asked.

"I do. I have them scanned and digitally filed, in case a student ever contests a grade or something like that. I don't have any papers they would have written for other classes except my own, though. Oh, and I have one that Laura's fiancé sent me just the other day, from one of her first classes with me. When I graded it, I wrote that she would do well in this field. She kept it through all these years, and he wanted me to have it."

"I'm sorry about your friend, Tig," Kent said. "We're going to do our best to solve this quickly, so that no one else gets hurt this time."

Tig smiled her thanks and changed the subject off Laura and back onto the current victim. Kent was right about them needing to focus on the current situation. She'd had time to mourn Laura's death, and now she needed to concentrate on helping Clare and Kent as much as she could. That was the only way she might make a difference and protect her people, and possibly rescue her department.

"You're assuming they were written by students," she said, "but I think they were Chase's."

Clare frowned. "You think he wrote all these essays himself? Is that normal? Would you want to…Oh, judging by your expression, I'll assume the answer is no."

Tig figured she must have looked horrified at the thought of going through that again. She loved school and had enjoyed her graduate courses, but she had no desire to revisit the assignments she had done. She wanted to move forward, not backward. "I can only give my opinion, so I'm not sure whether or not it counts as normal, but I would not sit around and write lower-level essays for fun."

"I think in this lone, isolated case, we can consider you to be fairly normal. So, what makes you think he wrote them himself?" Kent asked.

Tig was about to protest that she was normal more often than this once, but she decided to take Kent's comment as complimentary. Tig doubted she was the type of woman who'd be attracted to ordinary, so she focused instead on answering the question. "There are similarities in sentence patterns, and he repeats a few words and phrases in different essays. He has a couple of grammatical quirks that show up in almost all the papers."

"Are they good?" Clare asked. "How would you grade them?"

Tig had a ready answer since after so many years teaching, she didn't think she was capable of reading an essay without assigning it a grade out of habit. "Mostly As, and maybe a couple of A-minuses. They're well-written and carefully researched. The topics are interesting, and I'd consider them to be relatively advanced graduate level work, but at the same time they're not as insightful and innovative as the papers he's had published."

"He's dumbed down his writing?" Kent asked.

Tig shrugged. "More like he's simplified it. And he's limited the themes and sources to what a grad student would know how to access." She struggled to explain the nuanced effort she saw him making through these papers. "A professor with ten years of experience would cast a wider net than someone who's had a year or two of graduate work. But they'd also delve deeper into the topic."

Kent gave a low whistle. "Judging by what you're saying, he put a significant amount of effort into these papers."

"Do you think they were done as an exercise, then?" Clare asked. "He might have been challenging himself, for writing practice."

Tig sent the document she had been working on to her printer. "Colossal waste of time, if that's the case. Why go through this much trouble, fussing around with graduate level exercises, when he could have been researching and writing publishable material? He hadn't been publishing as many articles as usual over the past few years, but he kept talking about the research he was doing, so I assumed he'd release several in a short period of time as soon as he had them finished. I thought he was in a slump, not spending his time writing student-level papers."

"The other option is that he was writing them *for* students," Kent observed, echoing the thoughts Tig had been having.

"I agree, but like we said earlier, why do that at his own school, for colleagues to read and grade? He couldn't have made enough money for that to be a worthwhile risk." Tig took the page off the printer and walked over to Kent.

"We'll know more once we find out whether these papers were turned in as assignments, and by which student or students," Kent said. She took the sheet of paper from Tig, letting their hands brush against each other as she did, and then scanned the page.

"Huh," she said quietly, then gave the list to Clare. Tig's mind was focused on the touch of her hand, and the question of whether they'd still be able to have dinner together tonight, and when she looked up again, Kent and Clare were watching her with unreadable expressions.

"Tig, did you happen to notice anything unusual about this list?" Clare asked.

She looked at her computer screen and read the chronological list of courses and professors again. "Well, these date back to the time when I started to notice a drop in Chase's rate of publishing. Not surprising, I suppose, since they would have taken a considerable amount of work."

Clare looked at Kent and shook her head. "You try."

"Does anyone seem to be missing, Tig?" Kent asked softly.

"Well, Chase, of course. But why bother writing a paper for himself to grade when he could just give an imaginary paper an A-plus?" Tig asked rhetorically as she scrolled through the list again. "Then he'd…Hey, I'm not on there, either."

"Brilliant observation, Tig," Clare said.

Tig stared at the screen, unsure whether she was supposed to feel flattered or insulted that her colleague hadn't written a fake paper for one of her courses, which was a bizarre question to be considering.

"Maybe he thought you'd catch on," Kent said, and Tig heard a whisper of pride in her voice. Okay, she was going with flattered, then. "You seem confident that all these papers were written by him, and he might have known you wouldn't be fooled like the others."

Tig sighed and gave Kent a rueful smile. "As much as I want to say you're right, and that I have some sort of gift for ferreting out the author of a piece of writing, I had an unfair advantage over the other professors. I read a dozen of these papers one right after the other, along with some research notes that I knew were written by him, so the clues were all there, right in front of me. If I'd been given one of these essays in isolation? I might not have suspected anything, unless it was a drastic departure from the other work of whichever student turned it in."

"You're always unflinchingly honest, aren't you?" Kent asked with a smile. "I get what you're saying, but I also believe you're more perceptive than you give yourself credit for. He might not have wanted to risk it."

Tig returned her smile. "Are you saying I have a knack for detective work? Do you think I should consider a career change?"

Kent laughed. "Don't try to fool me into thinking you're becoming another Libby. You'd hate this line of work, and you know it. You love when there are puzzles to solve and the fact that there are ancient artifacts involved in this particular case, but the rest of it bores the crap out of you."

Tig didn't bother denying it. Even five minutes of standing around waiting for other officers to arrive or to examine every little clue, like the scrapes on the door lock, drove her crazy. Luckily, there had always been books within reach for her to read, whether they were in Chase's office or his home. "Maybe. But even though I don't want your job, I love watching you do it. You get very stern when you're talking to other cops, and it's impressive how even the higher-ranking Seattle officers defer to you. And a little adorable."

"I'm still in the room, you two," Clare said, rudely interrupting the moment Tig and Kent had been sharing. "And my sergeant is *not* adorable. She's irritating and abrasive and really needs to go back to calling you Professor Weston."

"All right, Professor Weston," Kent said, saying Tig's name in a slow, sultry way that made Clare throw a pen at her. She laughed and caught it with one hand. "I don't want to contact all the professors on this list just yet," she resumed in a normal voice. "If you trust your friend Lukas, let's start with him and see what he can tell us about this paper. Then we can decide from there which of the others we'll ask, if any. If it doesn't seem that any of the papers were actually submitted, then we can drop this line of investigation. Even if he was up to something inappropriate with them, it might not have anything to do with his murder."

Tig nodded. "I'll call Lukas, and I'll also do some searching online and see if I can find the papers on any of the sites that sell college essays. Not that it would make much difference now, with Chase…gone."

Tig hesitated over the last word. She sometimes found herself wrapped up in the live mystery and forgot that the reason behind it was her dead colleague.

When they got up to leave her office, Kent held back and let Clare go out first. She put her hand on Tig's arm and gave her a light squeeze. "Don't worry if you feel that you're treating Davies's death with a more clinical attitude than you think is acceptable. That's what we need you to do right now—to keep your head clear and to focus on the clues and what they mean to you. After this is over, you'll grieve for him the way you would any other close acquaintance. You're not doing anything wrong."

Tig smiled her thanks, covering Kent's hand with her own. "You're right," she said. "I want to find out who did this to him. Sitting around crying won't get that done."

"Exactly. Are we still on for dinner tonight? I should be out of the station by seven."

Tig nodded. "Do you want to try the new Vietnamese restaurant on Fiftieth? I can meet you there to avoid running into everyone."

"Yes, I've noticed that your friends have begun to use my station as some sort of staging area before every lunch and dinner."

She sounded annoyed, but Tig was starting to see through that. She had a feeling Kent liked having Libby around because she didn't treat her with deference like most of her officers did, but as a friend, with Clare starting to follow suit. And Ari and Jazz didn't care about her rank or the boundaries Kent needed to hide behind within her department. She thought Kent could use more easy friendship in her life, and this group was the epitome of that.

Still, she'd be glad to have Kent to herself for the evening.

Once Clare and Kent were gone, Tig called Lukas and left a voicemail for him to call her back. She wasn't surprised when he didn't answer, because he and his husband had been in and out of hospitals and medical appointments during Trevor's recovery, and Luke's priority wasn't jumping to answer his phone. She didn't want to give details about the paper until they were in person, although she still didn't think the stack of essays would prove to be a reason for someone to have killed Chase. Writing them was a weird hobby, maybe. Or a really poor choice in a side hustle. But not a cause for murder.

Chapter Thirteen

Tig got to the restaurant a few minutes early and sat at a table near the back, fidgeting with her cup of jasmine tea as she waited. She and her friends hadn't been here yet, but the place looked similar to many of the U District eateries. It was fairly small, which was typical since the main section of the business district only consisted of a few blocks along the western edge of campus, and space was at a premium. The décor was simple, which was also common in this high-rent area. The bottom half of the walls was covered with dark faux-wood wainscoting, and the top half was painted a rust color with the occasional picture or map making up the sparse decorations. Laminate covered tables and wooden ladder-back chairs were crammed together to seat as many people as possible. A few of the tables were empty, but most were filled with groups of students and locals.

Tig felt a hint of nervousness that was both exhilarating and worrisome at the same time. She was looking forward to spending time with Kent outside of the investigation, but she wasn't quite sure what to expect since their conversations so far had mostly been connected to it. Sometimes indirectly, like when they had discussed Tig's career prospects, but always within that context. She hoped they'd have enough to talk about that didn't involve Chase Davies's murder.

Those concerns fled from her mind the moment Kent walked into the restaurant. She had changed into black pants and a wine-colored sweater, and she looked surprisingly slim without her wool uniform and bulletproof vest. She draped a damp black jacket over the back of her chair and sat down.

"So, Libby was behind the front desk with Larson when I was leaving," she said. "*Behind the desk.* I think my officers are planning to adopt her. You look beautiful, by the way, multi-colored bruises and all."

Tig laughed, no longer worried about the potential issues with conversation now that Kent was here with her. They were going to be just fine. "I was thinking the same about you, but I don't look any different than I did this afternoon."

Kent shrugged. "I know, but I couldn't say anything before, with Clare hanging about. It was very rude of her to tag along with us today, just because she's my partner and we're supposed to be handling this investigation together."

"Third wheel," Tig said with a shake of her head. "She has no shame."

They paused to order their food, and then talk turned to the basic getting-to-know-you questions they had bypassed given the way they had met.

"Do you live near campus?"

Tig gestured vaguely in the direction behind her. "Just across the freeway. Wallingford."

"I'm in Fremont," Kent said, naming the adjacent neighborhood. "We're close."

For now. Tig hated that she heard those words ghosting after Kent's comment. She wondered if Kent sensed them, too.

"I'd describe my house to you," she continued, wanting to get her mind off the sad prospect of leaving Seattle. "All I need to say, though, is that it looks like my office, but slightly larger, and you can form a good picture of it. Books, replicas of busts and statues, papers everywhere." She paused and laughed. "And now you've gotten the description of every room and every house I've ever lived in. Most people go through stages, I suppose, with rooms decorated with ponies when they're little, then maybe all black when they're a Goth teenager, and so on. Not me. It's like I live in this bubble filled with pictures of the Acropolis and stacks of Greek and Latin grammars, and it's followed me my whole life. It's just the world outside it that changes now and again."

She sighed. She needed to stop making references to moving. She wasn't doing it intentionally, but it was weighing on her mind and affected everything else.

"Your parents must have been proud that you followed in their footsteps," Kent said, diverting the conversation slightly. She seemed to either sense Tig's worry about the future or she was feeling it herself. "Did they encourage that, or was it mostly your choice?"

Tig remembered when she had first started looking at colleges, judging each by the merits of their Classical Studies programs. Her parents had treated this as something unexpected, which seemed odd to Tig since she felt she had always known the direction her future would take. "They were proud," she said, slightly glossing over how excited her parents had been. "But they were really surprised that both of us became classics professors, too. Ismene teaches at Reed, in Portland. They said they figured we'd be likely to choose something in academia, but they never pushed us in that direction, or any other. Apparently, neither of us went through one of those rebellious stages where we wanted to do anything as long as it was completely different from what our parents did."

She paused and took a drink of her now-cool tea. Even her memories seemed wrapped in a haze of Mediterranean blues and whites. "Our childhood was very immersive in ancient cultures, especially Greek, so it shouldn't have been a shock that we absorbed it like we did. Myths were our bedtime stories, and our vacations were spent in Greece or touring museums or visiting universities where my parents could do research while the two of us wandered around."

She shrugged, unable to remember a time when her world hadn't been enmeshed in ancient cultures. "What about you?" she asked. "Do you come from a long line of cops? I thought it was common for it to be a generational sort of career. Is this what you always wanted to do?"

Kent waited as their food was set on the table, then she answered. "I'm the only cop in my family. Two of my brothers were military. Both Navy, one career and the other is now a civilian contractor in the Middle East. My oldest brother is a football coach and PE teacher in a high school. My parents own a construction company." She paused and took a bite of caramelized shrimp before continuing.

"My brothers are six, nine, and ten years older than I am, and they pretty much raised me since Mom and Dad were busy with the company. My dad was a carpenter, and my mom was a housewife until Jimmy, my youngest brother, started school. Then they bought the company my dad worked for and had to figure out how to manage it. It was a lot of work, so they didn't have much spare time, but my brothers took care of me."

She hesitated again, adjusting the jacket behind her and adding some sauce to her rice. Tig watched her quietly, learning as much about her from her behavior in between sentences as by the words themselves. Where Tig was more than happy to spend as much time as her listeners would allow chatting about family trips to Delphi, or the time they got to go into the staff-only areas at the Getty Villa Museum in Malibu, Kent seemed far more reticent about her past. Tig guessed that her hesitating delivery was due more to her being out of the habit of sharing personal details than that she was harboring some childhood pain, but Tig wasn't sure. All she knew for certain was that it meant a lot to be hearing these details from Kent. She had no doubt that they weren't offered to everyone Kent met.

"Were you lonely?" she prompted when Kent fell silent again.

"No," Kent said slowly. "It's just not easy to talk about…with you. You and I had such different experiences growing up. It was a long time before I realized that my life was unusual, and that most kids had parents who were more involved in their lives. And siblings who didn't want them around, not ones that did. My brothers took me everywhere with them. I got very good at playing video games, at having serious discussions about the plays called during football games, and at entertaining myself with cards and books when my brothers had friends over. I even went on the occasional date with one of them if the others were busy and couldn't watch me." She laughed. "Talk about an awkward third wheel. But to me, it was normal life."

She shrugged and took a sip of water. "I was kind of small for my age, and some of the kids at school tried to take advantage of that. I was getting bullied, and my teacher called the house and told Justin, my middle brother. She probably thought my mom and dad would come and have a nice chat with the principal and the other parents, but instead my brothers showed up on the playground the next day." She grinned at Tig. "Don't look so worried. They didn't beat up a bunch of first graders. They just let it be known very clearly that I had back-up, and that anyone who messed with me was going to have to take them on, too. Word must have spread, because I never had a single problem with bullies from then on. If I'd been a different sort of kid and had taken advantage of the situation, I could have made a fortune collecting lunch money. I probably would have retired by now on my savings alone."

"But instead of doing that, you chose a life path that would give you a chance to protect other people like they did for you." Tig had let her food sit, unnoticed, while Kent was talking, marveling at the thought of little Kent, small and weak, being protected by her brothers. She was right that her childhood had been about as different from Tig's homeschooled early years as it could get, but that childhood had produced this strong, fierce woman who defended others. That made it seem as magical as Tig's had been. She took advantage of another of Kent's long pauses and picked up a spring roll, taking a bite and enjoying the crunch of spicy, fried tofu combined with mango and cool cucumber. "Trade?" she suggested.

Kent nodded and spooned some of her rice and shrimp onto Tig's plate before taking a segment of spring roll. "Oh, that's very good," she said after trying the roll. "Mine's better, though."

Tig sampled the crispy shrimp and sighed. "You're right. Not by much, though."

"It started with me simply wanting to be physically strong

like they were," Kent said, continuing her story and responding to Tig's comment. "When my family noticed my interest in developing myself that way, my parents signed me up for Tae Kwon Do and karate, and my brothers started coaching me at the gym instead of having me sit and read while they were working out. I couldn't do much with weights because I was still so young, but they taught me technique and form. At some point in there, my goal became less about wanting to protect myself and more about taking care of other people. I saw cops who were regulars at the gym and added them to the list with my brothers as people to admire and model myself after. Eventually police work started to feel like a natural fit, career-wise."

Tig was starting to get a picture of Kent as a child and teenager. Intense, reserved, determined. All traits she would continue to develop as a woman and a sergeant. She also recognized the values Kent had internalized from a young age. To be self-sufficient and self-contained when necessary, and to protect others with no hesitation. She personally thought Kent carried it a little too far now that she was a sergeant, falling into the habit of holding herself back and remaining aloof partly because it was necessary when her co-workers were often off-limits as friends or potential dates, but also because it was the easy path to take. Tig would do her best to bring as much friendship and companionship as she could into Kent's life—not trying to pull her out from behind the barriers she'd been building for years, but going behind them herself. And even if she wasn't able to stay long-term, she knew Libby and the others would continue in her place.

"What do your parents think of your job?" Tig asked carefully, assuming they would have been as indifferent about it as they seemed to have been for the rest of Kent's life.

"Strangely enough, it brought us closer," Kent said. She looked up from her plate at Tig and smiled. "I can see you weren't expecting that, and neither was I. I felt like sort of an afterthought to them most of the time when I was a child, but when they saw how dedicated I was to my martial arts training and my desire to become a police officer, they seemed to develop more respect for me, I guess. Those were their values—to work hard and drive themselves toward a goal. We've grown closer over the years, but it's a slow process, and I'll always think of my brothers as my real parents."

Tig handed her empty plate to her server, and they ordered sweetened iced coffees for dessert even though it was long past summer. When they arrived, she stirred hers and watched Kent thoughtfully, finally voicing a question that had been on her mind.

"Your brothers sound great, and I'd love to meet them sometime, but I can't even imagine what it must have been like to come out to them," she said. Now that their plates were out of the way, she gave in to the temptation to touch Kent and reached across the table, resting her hand over Kent's. "How uncomfortable was that conversation?"

Kent gave a snort of laughter as she turned her hand in Tig's and laced their fingers together. "Are you kidding? I was raised by three teen and young adult aged males. They were so relieved when I told them I wasn't interested in dating men that they immediately started planning what to wear at the next Pride Parade." She shook her head. "You're laughing like you think that's a joke, but it isn't. We had to wear these horrible matching rainbow sweaters Kyle picked out. I felt very loved and very humiliated at the same time." She winked at Tig. "I met my first girlfriend there, though. She thought the outfits were cute, so I got over the humiliation real quick. So, what about you? Was this another surprise for your parents?"

Tig shook her head. "Hardly. My sister and I were reading texts like Ovid's *Art of Love* and Sappho's poetry before we hit puberty. The rule was, we could borrow anything from our parents' bookshelves as long as we discussed what we were reading. I must have made my preferences very clear in this case, and I'm sure there were other signs along the way, too. As you may have noticed, I'm not exactly a closed book when it comes to my feelings." Kent grinned and squeezed her hand gently in acknowledgment. "A few years later I approached my mom and told her I was attracted to girls, thinking I was unleashing some majorly dramatic news. She just said *Yes, dear, we know. Can you hand me that translation of The Iliad?*"

Kent laughed along with her. "What did you do then?"

"I handed her the book and walked out of the room. I was sort of in a daze after anticipating this confrontation for weeks just to have it be so casual, but then life went on exactly the same as it had been. In time, I've come to realize just how fortunate I was to have been so wholly accepted by my family. I'm glad to know that you had that kind of experience, too."

"It should be the norm, and not the exception," Kent said with a nod. "What about your sister?"

"Married to a man and has three kids. Mary, John, and Bob, if you can believe it. She never fully appreciated having such a unique name."

"I imagine that being called Meany by you didn't help much."

Tig sighed. "I know, I was awful. I still call her that, of course, but I try to be a really amazing aunt to make it up to the kids since it's mostly my fault that they have such ordinary names."

Her phone vibrated in her coat pocket, and she reluctantly disengaged her hand from Kent's to reach for it. "I'm sorry about that," she said as she pulled it out. "I would have turned it off while we were together, but I'm waiting for Lukas to call back. I thought you'd want to hear what he has to say right away." She looked at the screen and frowned. "Oh, it's Kam."

She looked up at Kent, uncertain what to do. She didn't recall him ever calling her before. If he wanted to talk, he'd catch her during office hours.

"Is this normal?" Kent asked quickly.

She shook her head, and Kent told her to answer.

"Hello? Kam?"

His first, whispered words were unintelligible, and she pressed the cell tightly to her ear, straining to hear him.

"…being followed. I was running…fell, and I needed to stop the bleeding…shouldn't have come here alone. Help me, Tig, please."

"Where are you, Kam?" she asked, then realized how much her voice had risen above its normal tone. Kent was already on her feet, tossing some cash on the table and reaching to take Tig's hand. She let Kent guide her out of the restaurant, ignoring the curious stares of the other diners and concentrating on her conversation.

"Can you get away from there?" she asked. "Get somewhere safe. Scream. Do something. I'll stay on the line."

She heard a grunt and what sounded like his phone hitting the ground and then the connection went dead.

Well, that couldn't be good.

CHAPTER FOURTEEN

Kent could feel Tig's hand trembling in hers as she pulled her out of the restaurant and into a small alcove in the building next door that served as the entrance to some upper-level businesses. Luckily, they were closed at this time of night, giving them some privacy.

She had a fleeting thought that it would have been nice to have had a normal date, when she would have led Tig into this darkened space for a very different reason...

She shoved that notion roughly to one side. Tig was still holding the phone to her ear, but she was no longer saying anything.

"Is he still on the line?" she asked softly. Tig shook her head, and Kent pried the cell from her stiff hand. She double-checked to make sure the call had ended.

"What happened, Tig?" she asked. "What did he say?"

"He sounded scared," Tig said, looking over her shoulder. "I need to find him. Do you think he's okay?"

The answer was obviously no, but Kent didn't say that. She put her hand under Tig's chin and turned her head to get Tig to look at her.

"We'll help him, but first I need to know what happened. You looked at your screen. You thought it would be Lukas, but you saw Kam's name. What did he say?"

Tig nodded and took a deep, shaky breath, as if Kent's words had settled her somehow. She recounted the short conversation, then Kent asked her to repeat it while she took quick notes.

"Think, Tig," she said, deliberately keeping her voice calm. She wanted to immediately start searching, too, but start *where*? He could be anywhere on campus or in Seattle. Hell, he could be anywhere within driving distance from the time Tig had last seen him, if he'd been scared enough to start running then. She was frustrated by her inability to help, and she didn't want that to seep into her tone while talking to Tig. "Where could he be? He said he was bleeding, so maybe he's near the medical center?"

"No, he said he was alone. It would still be busy there, even in the dark," she said. "Besides, he hates doctors. He said..." She paused, and then her expression brightened. "Oh, the Medicinal Herb Garden! He's into naturopathy, and he likes to brag about how he can get what he needs from the garden at night without needing to go to a pharmacy. What was it that stops bleeding? Maybe yarrow?"

"You're brilliant, sweetheart," Kent said, handing Tig back her phone and giving her a quick kiss on the cheek. She got her own cell and speed-dialed Clare. When she answered, Kent heard a murmur of sound in the background, most likely from whichever restaurant she and her friends were at this evening.

Kent told her where they were and about the phone call, including Tig's theory about where Kam was. Somewhere toward the beginning of the tale, she heard Clare whisper *Gotta go*, probably to Libby, and then the sounds of her running while Kent continued to talk.

"I'm just about a block away, so I'll come get you," Clare said. The slam of a car door punctuated her sentence.

"Good. I'll call dispatch, see if anyone's on patrol in the area."

They ended the call abruptly, and then Kent called in the location. When she finished, she and Tig stood facing each other. The sudden silence after the frantic calls and rushed words of the past few minutes fell heavy around them, sucking them into a small, private sphere that only they shared, but she knew the explosion was coming that would thrust them back into the world.

"Maybe he fell again," Tig said quietly, as if unwilling to break the spell around them. "He tripped and fell and broke his phone, and now he can't call me back. We'll find him sitting there on the path, wrapping yarrow leaves around his calf."

"Maybe," Kent agreed. It wasn't the most implausible prediction she'd ever heard, but neither of them seemed wholly convinced. She reached for Tig and pulled her into a tight hug, not ever wanting to let her go. Tig remained stiff for a moment—Kent knew she was trying very hard to keep herself pulled together— before tucking her head into Kent's shoulder and wrapping her arms around Kent's waist. How had it only been three days that they'd known each other? Kent never wanted to let her go.

She understood that relationships tended to intensify quickly when they were grown in stressful situations like this one, but nothing about her feelings for Tig felt contrived by circumstances. They were living with a clock ticking relentlessly beside them— with a murder that needed solving and Tig's potential departure— but even though they might have fallen more deeply and more quickly than they would have otherwise, Kent had no doubt they were falling into something real.

And the clock was about to get louder if her fears about this phone call came true. If Kam, alleged plagiarist and plant thief, wasn't as okay as they wanted him to be.

Clare screeched to a halt beside them in her God-awful green car. At least she parked on the street this time and not up on the curb. In another situation, Kent would have joked with her about getting to be the driver, but not now. She climbed into the back seat, letting Tig sit next to Clare and give her directions.

What would have been a long run across campus turned out to be a quick drive in Clare's car. She turned east on Pacific, bounded on one side by health services and the medical center and on the other by the science buildings, and pulled her car as far off the road as she could, parking on a narrow grassy verge. The three of them got out and crossed the Burke-Gilman Trail, skirting the Life Sciences Building and arriving at the entrance to the herb garden. She wanted to send Tig away, or at least have her wait in the car until they were certain Kam was even here, let alone alive and well, but she didn't want Tig out of her sight right now. She and Clare automatically flanked her, protecting her from both sides without needing to say a word.

The sign identifying the garden sat at the head of a path lined with delicate shrubs. Delicate, yes, but still obstructive. This was another of those hidden areas on campus, where you stepped beyond the border and felt cut off from the bustle outside it. That was fine during the day, when other people were a mere shout away, but on a dark and rainy fall evening like this one, the garden was full of shadows and blind spots, and even the well-traveled footpaths around it were practically deserted.

The crunch of boots on gravel was startling to all three of them. Kent and Clare already had their guns in hand, and they turned to face whoever was coming toward them.

"It's Pickett and Larson," Katie Pickett called quietly. The two officers approached them, and Kent lowered her weapon. "Didn't mean to sneak up on you, Sergeant. We didn't see you with all these bushes."

"The damned things will be gone tomorrow, if I have to pull them myself," Kent said. This fucking garden was probably identified on campus maps as *a very convenient place to stage a murder*. "Larson, I need you to stay back here with Professor Weston. Tig, please," she said when she started to protest, not caring who heard her use Tig's given name. "Let us do our job. If Professor Morris is hurt, we'll be there to help him."

Tig didn't look happy with the decision, but she finally nodded and stayed next to Miles as Kent and the others walked farther along the path. Kent still hated leaving her behind, even though she trusted Larson to protect her, but she needed her focus to be on her job, not on her...well, whatever Tig was to her. She barely managed to stop herself before letting the entire word *girlfriend* form in her mind.

The walking path meandered for a few yards before opening up to a more ordered garden area. Neat rows of rectangular herb beds were lined by white gravel paths that glowed faintly under scattered and largely ineffective lights.

Dim as they were, they still managed to reveal the dark form of a body lying between two of the beds, standing out in sharp relief against the white stones.

Kent sighed. "Call it in, Pickett. Come on, Sawyer."

They approached slowly, their flashlights skimming over the scene and into the surrounding shrubs and trees. Kent figured whoever had done this was long gone, but they didn't want to be surprised by either a lingering attacker or a wandering innocent student. They stopped several feet away and surveyed the scene.

This was becoming far too big a part of her job. She had seen only one murder since coming to this department until this year. She was up to four for this quarter alone, and it wasn't even the end of October yet. Three were from the Classics Department, making it the most dangerous job on campus at the moment. Kent pushed away the sudden image of Tig lying on the ground in some secluded part of campus. Focus. The only way to keep her safe was to figure out who was doing this and stop them.

"It's Kam Morris," Clare said, which wasn't a surprise. She was reciting the details more out of habit than a need to explain what Kent was perfectly capable of seeing, too. Still, Kent let her talk without interrupting. "Bullet to the forehead, but he also has a nasty-looking wound on his right cheekbone. There's his phone, too. Looks smashed."

"Tig said she heard a sort of grunting noise, then a crash, like his phone fell," Kent added when Clare was finished. "He said he was being followed, so maybe whoever it was approached while he was talking and pistol-whipped him across the face to knock the phone out of his hand. Then shot him and crushed the phone."

"Quick and quiet, if you're strong and ruthless enough," Clare said. "And then you just stroll away down the garden path."

"You're becoming our best customers."

Kent whirled to find the forensics officer from Davies's scene standing behind her. His team swarmed into the area, setting Kent's teeth on edge.

"You probably can holster that now," he said, nodding to her gun. She sighed, lifting her sweater slightly and tucking the weapon back into place. Clare did the same, with a look of resigned annoyance on her face. She was getting to be as territorial as Kent. "Stay here, and I'll be back soon with a preliminary report." "Is that a class forensics people take for their degree?" Pickett asked, stepping up beside them. "*How to make other officers hate you in five easy steps.*"

Clare grinned at her. "I was thinking it'd be *How to be a condescending ass.*"

Pickett nodded slowly, as if considering Clare's choice. "Yes. Less wordy. It'll look catchier in the course catalog." She laughed, then cleared her throat and turned toward Kent, her face serious again, as if she'd momentarily forgotten that her sergeant was standing next to her.

"We've got three more officers on the way, to control the perimeter. Should I have Larson escort Professor Weston back to the station?"

"She can go home for the night, and we can get her statement tomorrow," Kent said. She didn't bother to add that Tig wasn't a suspect since she'd been holding hands with Kent on the other side of the U District seconds before the murder occurred. Airtight alibi. "I'll go talk to her, so don't let Officer Arrogant give his report until I'm back."

She hurried back down the path, both because she wanted to see Tig and reassure herself that she was safe and sound, and also because she hated leaving her crime scene for too long. The first was a more pressing need, but she was bothered by how quickly Tig had become the center of her focus. She used to be far more single-minded, and keeping watch over her scene would have been more important than anything...

She paused on the path, still hidden from the entrance by bushes. Her words weren't quite true. During the last investigation, she had been concerned about Clare when she was hit on the head by the killer, and even more so when she was shot by her and attached to numerous drips and machines in the hospital. And about Libby when she was missing because she'd gone traipsing off into the woods with the same killer. The whole group of them were starting to matter too much. One would think she saw them as her friends, too. Not just as a random group of women who happened to have a knack for being around when horrible crimes were happening.

Good thing they weren't really her friends. They were a risky group.

She got back to the herb garden sign and found Tig sitting on a bench while Larson circled around her like an animal protecting its young. She glared at him until he got her message and moved out of earshot.

She sat next to Tig and took her hand. "Kam's dead, Tig," she said, figuring Tig could read it on her face and in her demeanor. No sense in dragging out the news. "He was shot."

Tig gave a weak laugh. "Yeah, I assumed the forensics team wouldn't be here just to help locate the correct plant for a scraped knee," she said.

"Always with the sarcasm," Kent said. She raised her hand and held it against Tig's face, trying not to see an overlay of Kam's wounds where she touched her. "I'm sorry this happened. I wish I'd…"

She let the sentence trail off, not sure how to end it. She wished she'd caught the killer already—if it was the same person, of course. But she still felt far from figuring out this case.

"You need to get home and get some sleep since I have a feeling tomorrow will be a long day. Miles will take you to your car. I would do it myself, but I—"

Tig covered Kent's hand with hers where it rested against her cheek, then kept hold of it and lowered both of them to her lap. "But you need to be here. I understand."

"I'll call you tomorrow. We'll need you to come down to the station and give a formal statement about the phone call, but can you stay with someone tonight? With Libby or one of the others?"

Tig held up her phone. "I've already had texts from the three of them, one fishing for information and all three offering to let me come over if I need to. Somehow they put it together that we're connected to Clare's abrupt departure from dinner." She laughed. "And don't worry, I'm not texting Libby a play-by-play account of my evening. I'll probably stay with Ari since she lives close, and she'll be less inclined to badger me."

"Ari," Kent said with a nod. "The one you have no chemistry with. She's my favorite."

Kent gave Tig's hand a squeeze, then let go and stood up. "I'm sorry about tonight. This isn't the way I wanted our date to end."

"Well, that's good," Tig said. "If it was, then I'd have to insist that I plan all our dates from now on, from beginning to end."

"Just as long as there's going to be another one, I'm happy."

Kent stepped forward and brushed a quick kiss over Tig's lips, not even bothering to care if Larson saw her. "Sleep well, Tig. I'll see you tomorrow."

CHAPTER FIFTEEN

Even though they were back at the station by eleven, Kent felt as drained as if it was three in the morning. She heated up two mugs of over-roasted coffee that had probably been sitting in the break room pot since early afternoon and joined Clare in the meeting room where she had first interviewed Tig. She handed Clare one of the mugs, then sat in Tig's chair and draped her legs over the arm. She was too tired to make the effort to sit up straight and look imposing. Besides, the pretense would have been wasted on Clare.

Clare sniffed at the coffee, made a face, then drank it anyway.

Kent waved the piece of paper she was holding, then tossed it onto the table next to her. "Ballistics report," she said. "Inconclusive whether it's the same weapon from Davies's murder. No match to other crimes."

"Eh," Clare said dismissively.

Kent sighed, agreeing with Clare's muttered opinion. The report wasn't surprising, nor was it helpful. It was far too easy to get an unregistered .22, and the killer could either have used a different gun for the second murder or scrubbed the barrel to change the resulting stria enough to keep the bullets from seeming to be a perfect match. Since the victims were professors from the same department who had recently been in a fight with each other, the likelihood of these being two separate murderers was ridiculously low. Especially considering the similarities between the killings.

"The autopsy will probably show a similar angle of entry, so that'll connect them," Clare said with a shrug. "What the hell is going on in that Classics Department?"

Kent didn't answer because she had no idea. Whatever it was, she was going to make sure Tig stayed with friends—if not with her, which was preferable—until the killer was caught. After that... well, classics had seemed doomed before, and now she was rapidly losing any of the hope she had still harbored that Tig might still have a place at UW when this was finished.

"It probably won't be a department anymore, given the rapidly growing ratio of murdered professors to live ones."

"Right," Clare agreed. "But if the new program does survive, I don't see them letting Tig lead it anymore."

"You think they'd blame Tig for this? Replace her as director?" Kent asked, startled by Clare's comment. She had been assuming either Tig would get to stay, with her current title, or she'd have to go. As much as she wanted Tig to remain at the U, the thought of her being demoted over something that was clearly not her fault... well, if that happened, she'd maybe become the most unlikely of supporters for Tig's move to a new university. Tig would probably be able to live with the public embarrassment of the situation, but the unfairness of it would be hard for her to bear. Tig took her role as department leader as seriously as Kent did as sergeant. She remembered Tig's unconvincing expression when they last spoke in this room, and she said she'd be happy to give up the position of director to—

"Professor Ayari," she said, finishing her thought out loud. "She thought she'd possibly be named director before Tig was, and she might be pleased to see her lose her title. I have a hunch she still wants the position."

Clare snorted at that. "Do you think anyone would volunteer for the job with all this going on?" she asked, but then her expression sobered. "Still, I read Tig's statement from the night Davies was killed. You seemed to think she was making some sort of threat toward Tig when she talked about wanting to head the department."

Kent nodded. "Tig didn't see it that way, but when she was

relating their conversation, it sounded like a vague threat to me. Or maybe a warning."

"She was close enough to the scene to have killed him, pulled him into the bushes, and then strolled away until…"

"She met Tig, alone on a dark path," Kent finished, feeling nauseated at the thought. She wanted Tig with her right now, where she could protect her. And if Tig decided she preferred living with Ari until this was over? Well, Kent might just decide to move in, too.

Clare paused, clearly considering this possibility. "Do you believe she's strong enough? Kam was hit fucking hard."

"I don't know…maybe? She was wearing loose clothing the only time I saw her, so she might be hiding some serious muscle under there. Plus, anger and ambition can augment physical strength significantly, if they're powerful enough."

Clare still looked unconvinced. "I understand wanting to be the one in charge. I'm ambitious, too, but I'm not planning on hurting you, or knocking off Landry and Pickett just to make it look like you're a bad leader and should be replaced. That seems extreme."

"Well, I'm relieved to hear that," Kent said drily. "Although admittedly a little alarmed that you already had two victims picked out."

Clare waved Kent's comment aside. "I don't, really. If I was willing to kill to get your job, you'd be my victim, not a handful of the people I'm hoping to lead."

"My relief was short-lived," Kent said. "And remind me to pick up a restraining order next time I'm at the courthouse. Seriously, though, I believe you're right. She'd be risking having the entire program shut down, let alone quite possibly being caught and spending her life in prison."

"That would be stupid," Clare said. "And she definitely doesn't strike me as stupid."

"No, but these people aren't acting predictably anymore," Kent said. She felt like an outsider peering into Tig's world through a smudgy window. "This curriculum shift has everyone so far on edge that they're toppling off one by one. To me it seems like a gross overreaction to a few course changes, but Tig and her faculty seem to be reacting like there's more meaning under the surface than I can see. There's subtext that I don't understand, and it's difficult to decide who's capable of which actions under these circumstances."

"We should talk to Tig about this."

Kent shook her head. Tonight had scared her. Davies was obviously mixed up in something outside of class, with his vases and grad school papers, but now they had another victim on their hands. It looked less like a murder specifically aimed at Davies and more like a killing spree focused on the classics faculty. "She's already too involved in this case. It's Libby all over again, and I don't want to put Tig in the same kind of dangerous situation."

"I understand," Clare said, her voice softening. "I still have nightmares about walking into that clearing and seeing her...seeing her tied up, with Angela aiming a gun at her. Believe me, I don't want to let anything like that happen to Tig. But without Libby's help, I wouldn't have figured out what was going on. I wouldn't have known how to find her, or even have known that Angela was a threat and Libby was in danger, if she hadn't been working on the case with me."

Clare paused, looking away and obviously collecting herself after dredging up that memory again. Kent stared into her coffee cup, letting her have some mental space.

Clare sighed. "I thought it would be simple to come here and do the same work I'd been doing with Seattle PD, just on a different scale. And most of it is similar. Drunk kids are drunk kids, whether they're university students or not. People need directions, stuff gets shoplifted or vandalized, arguing lovers have domestics. Most of the time we're just police officers doing the same job cops are doing everywhere else. But when it comes to the inner workings of these departments, the heart of the university, we're outsiders. Like you said, there's subtext here. And history and tradition. We might struggle to understand motive, but Tig won't. It's part of who she is."

Kent knew this was true, especially in Tig's case. She had been dismissive when Tig first told her how much the conflict over her department's new image meant to the people involved, and how serious the issue was to them, but it seemed she might have seriously underestimated the level of emotions the transition had triggered. Tig hadn't. She understood her faculty more than Kent and Clare could because she had lived inside this academic life since childhood—she lived and breathed it, while Kent and Clare looked in from the outside.

She looked up and realized that Clare was contemplating her coffee cup, giving her space to process what they were talking about, just as she had done for Clare.

"You're right," she admitted. "I don't understand enough about the situation to explain the murders or to guess where—if anywhere—the killer might strike next. Ayari might be a potential victim more than a suspect since she represents change, and a lot of people seem angry about the new department."

"People like Chase, you mean," Clare reminded her. "He was the opposition. They're pulling from both sides of the debate."

Kent sighed, giving in to the inevitable decision she needed to make. "Okay. We'll talk to Tig about all this and get her input, plus I think we should have her come with us to search Morris's office."

Clare gave a derisive laugh, breaking the serious mood that had settled over them. "Well, yeah. I wouldn't be the one to try to stop her if we *didn't* ask her to come. You know she thinks everyone's hiding ancient artifacts in their offices now. She wouldn't trust us not to use a priceless Greek column as a footrest while we're searching, or something."

"She goes with us," Kent agreed. "But when she's not at work or with us, Libby and your friends will watch out for her, won't they?"

Clare watched her in silence for a moment. "Yes, of course they will," she said. "Can I…um, permission to speak freely, Sergeant?"

"Can I say no?"

"Sure."

"And if I do, will you stop talking?"

"Probably not."

Kent rolled her eyes. This ought to be good. She'd been expecting this talk to come sooner or later, though, so she might as well hear Clare out. She waved a hand at her, giving her permission to continue.

"So, Libby's kind of being playful about wanting to be a detective," Clare said, starting the expected lecture in an unexpected place. She frowned. "Mostly, I think. But at the same time, it wouldn't surprise me if she quit the university and dived into police work. Or if she decided to become a sheep farmer because she wanted to make her own wool and knit architectural elements into sweaters. Or any number of other choices."

Okay, they were apparently going the roundabout way to their destination. Kent sighed, waiting for Clare to make her point.

"She sees patterns everywhere," Clare continued. "She loves teaching a variety of classes because she connects elements from all of them, and she does the same thing in life. But that's not how Tig works. She has one focus, one passion. Yes, she likes learning new things, and she's leading the diversification of the classics curriculum to embrace a diverse community of scholars and scholarship, but that's all peripheral." She hesitated again, watching Kent as if she might start yelling at her, when none of this was a surprise to her.

"Look, Sergeant, we both know there's a good chance the Classics Department could close. Or that it will survive this mess, but Tig's job won't. If that happens, well, I worry that—"

Kent held up her hand to stop Clare from finishing her sentence. "I know, Sawyer. She and I have talked about this. I understand that she might have to leave the U, leave the state. You and your friends are understandably worried about what will happen if she and I get close before then, and I don't want her to be hurt either, but I believe she'll be okay. She'll have a new department and a new university to focus on."

Clare frowned at her. "Yes, she will. That's what I've been trying to say. Sergeant, she's not the one I'm concerned about."

"You're worried about *me*," Kent stated. She had been prepared for the *What are your intentions toward my friend* speech, and it hadn't occurred to her that she could possibly be the one Clare felt the need to protect.

"Yes, a little. And please don't fire me for it," Clare said with a smile. "I absolutely believe that Tig is capable of loving someone deeply, but I also know she already has that depth of commitment to her field. Maybe if the two of you had met a long time ago, things would be different, but…Well, I think that intellectually knowing someone might walk out of your life because of their career is far from understanding just how painful it will be when it happens. We just want you to know that we'll be here for you, if you ever need to talk, or anything."

"We," Kent repeated, still feeling off-kilter from Clare's talk. "I suppose you and Libby have discussed this?"

Clare shrugged. "Yes. I've been worried, but she's the one who pushed me to actually say something to you. I told her I was too scared of you to bring it up, but she insisted."

Kent laughed humorlessly. "You're not scared of me, Sawyer. Not anymore. It's one of your most aggravating traits. Well, tell Libby I appreciate her concern, but I'll be fine."

"She'll be glad to hear that. She likes you, you know. It's one of the reasons she hangs around the station." Clare grinned. "You do realize she's been trying to set you up, don't you? She wants to integrate you into our group, and she figured getting you to fall in love with one of her friends was the best way to do it. She just picked the wrong one."

Kent frowned and had to think about the comment before she figured out what Clare meant. That afternoon already felt so far in the past that she had nearly forgotten the brief meeting. "Oh, do you mean when she brought Jazz Harald to the station? What did she expect? That we'd say nice to meet you, and then suddenly be in love? Ridiculous. I don't work that way."

"Oh, really?" Clare asked with raised eyebrows. "What if she'd had Tig meet her here instead? You've known her for, what, three whole days now? And if I'm not mistaken, when I came to get the two of you tonight, you had obviously been on a date and were just as obviously making out on the street."

Kent laughed in spite of her attempt to look outraged at Clare's insubordination. "There was no *making out*. There was possibly a hug, but I had no choice in the matter because she was worried about her colleague at the time. It was a very professional hug, like we offer any of our citizens when they are in distress. Just part of the job."

"If you say so," Clare said, with skepticism dripping from her words. "Although I didn't see you offering Professor Itori a hug when he came by because he was worried that his neighbors wanted to steal his dog. I just remember you telling him we're a police station, not a doggy day care."

"Yes, well, next time he comes to the station, I'll give him a big hug, and you can take the damned dog on patrol with you."

Clare held her hands up in mock surrender. "I'm just saying, if we're going to be doling out professional hugs as part of our job, maybe we should be in uniform while we do it. And not in the nicest outfit I've seen you in since I started working here."

"That's quite a compliment coming from the woman who showed up to work in her pajamas last month."

"Hey, it was the middle of the night, and I thought Libby was being attacked. I didn't have time to get all dressed up for a date."

"Right. That was your excuse for parking on the curb, too, wasn't it?"

They continued their banter while they waited for the forensics report to come in, and Kent let the playfulness distract her for just this moment. She still had two murders to solve, and a department to save. And Tig. She had to protect Tig no matter what—protect her from losing her job and possibly her life. She didn't have energy to spare for protecting herself, too. Besides, she was already too far gone to stop her growing feelings now. In fact, she wasn't sure she'd ever had a chance to do so. Like Clare had said, if Libby had replaced Jazz with Tig that afternoon, the outcome would have been very different. Maybe an offer of a private tour of the station, or an invitation to meet for coffee...

But not a polite hello, followed by an easy good-bye. It would never be that way for her where Tig was concerned, so she might as well accept that now and learn to live with the hurt later. Maybe when Tig left, she'd turn to Clare and her friends for commiseration, or for a drunken night of wallowing, but probably not. More likely, she'd tamp down her heartache and life would go on as it had before Tig stepped into it, just a little emptier.

A whole lot emptier.

She laughed at something Clare said and felt a pang of sadness when she did. This was another ending she'd have to face. As soon as Cappy was back, she and Clare would go back to being partners on cases like this—although God forbid they had any more murders on campus. They'd had their fair share, thank you very much. And while the two of them worked together to solve crimes, Kent would be relegated to her role of overseer again, facing her mounds of paperwork and occasionally checking in on their progress, snapping at them to get a move on.

She could turn her back now, on Tig and Clare and the whole lot of them. Get the good-byes over with sooner rather than later and get back to normal life. But she wouldn't. Maybe she was greedy, or maybe foolish, but she was going to accept these people in her life as long as she had the option. She'd deal with the fallout when it came.

CHAPTER SIXTEEN

Tig somehow made it through her eight o'clock class the next morning, but she had a feeling her students hadn't learned a thing and would have been better off sleeping in for an extra hour rather than showing up in her room. She kept losing her train of thought during her lecture, and she was sure she had inexplicably mixed up Plato with Pindar more than once. The students had been unusually subdued, though, and most of them probably didn't notice or care about her mistakes. These were graduate students, and they had all taken classes with both Chase and Kam, so they were naturally shocked by their murders. Several were their advisees, too, which reminded Tig that not only did she need to scramble to get professors to cover their classes, but she also needed to reassign students to new faculty advisors.

All of which was seriously cutting into her staring into space time. She really seemed to require a lot of that these days. Some of it was okay, like when she was thinking about Kent and how good it had felt to be held by her outside of the restaurant last night, but most of it was a fairly useless waste of time. Still, it beat dwelling on death by a long shot.

She hadn't yet gotten past the numbness following Chase's death, and now she had another murdered colleague to mourn. She hadn't been Kam's biggest fan, but they had always gotten along well enough. Same with Chase. She didn't know how to grieve for them—she had to acknowledge that they had likely been involved in something that had gotten them killed—and she was unprepared for how angry she was at them for dying. It wasn't her most rational moment, but not only did their deaths mean a lot of extra work for her, but it was all but guaranteed that the department would be shut down for good. They were going through professors at an alarmingly rapid rate. If this kept up, she'd be trying to run the department on her own, teaching every class and spending every waking moment grading papers...

Or she'd end up dead along with the others.

Somehow, she managed to conveniently forget that possibility for the most part, but then it would pop back into her mind at inconvenient moments. Kent and the police didn't know why her faculty members had been killed, so how could she be certain she wasn't next on the list? She was the public persona for the new Med Studies program, which might make her a target if someone was angry enough about the change, but then why kill Chase? He was just as public in his opposition.

She sighed and resumed staring into space, trying not to think at all.

A tap on her open door brought her attention back to the present in a heartbeat. These weren't her normal office hours, but she hadn't closed the door because she wanted to be available in case any of her students needed to talk. She would have preferred to see any one of them rather than the man who stood on the threshold of her office, wearing his usual expensive-looking black suit.

She stood and forced her lips into a smile. "Max, good to see you," she lied, shaking hands with Max Adel. She knew why he was here, and she wasn't glad at all about it.

"Hello, Tig," he said warmly, shaking her hand. He gave it a gentle squeeze before he let go. "I heard the news about Kamrick Morris. I'm so sorry. How are you holding up?"

That was the world's most inane question at a time like this. How was she holding up? She was losing it, that's how. Her career was flashing before her eyes, she might have to do the work of three professors for the foreseeable future, and she might be the next victim on the Classics Killer's hit list. She was pleased with the name she had thought of last night, in a morbid sort of way. Libby would appreciate it, although she would probably be jealous that she hadn't already thought up a name worthy of a true crime paperback for the murders she had solved.

"I'm fine," she said, gathering her rambling thoughts and giving the bland, expected answer. She gestured toward a chair. "Have a seat, Max. What can I do for you? Although, I have a feeling I already know why you're here."

He nodded, not trying to pretend she might be wrong. "You know how much this department means to me," he said, crossing his legs and resting his hands on his thigh, fingers laced together. He was not the type of man who gestured as he spoke—he always stood or sat with an odd sort of stillness when they were talking. "My classics degree opened doors for me because it's well-respected. It proved I honor tradition and value education, and that I'm a hard worker. I have been proud to support students who showed the same dedication to their studies that I did when I was a young man, giving them a chance to receive some of the same opportunities I did, no matter what career path they chose to follow, since this is the epitome of a liberal arts education."

Yes, yes, yes, she thought impatiently. *Just get on with it.* She wished he'd stop sounding like he was delivering a promo for the full scholarship he had offered and get to the part where he told her he wouldn't be funding it anymore.

"You have to understand, I'm sure, why I can't offer the scholarship any longer."

Yep. There we go.

"I have a reputation to uphold," he continued, "and to have my name connected with this department during such a disastrous, albeit tragic, time would be inadvisable. Fist fights in the hall? Childish name-calling by two professional adults? A director with a bruised face because she valiantly tried to break them apart? And now two murders in less than a week? I don't mean to sound selfish, but I've worked hard to build my business. It has to be my priority."

The phrase *you selfish bastard* was echoing through her mind, but then she remembered her conversations with Kent about moving for her career. Was she any better than him? She had practically said she didn't care how close she and Kent got—she was fully prepared to leave to find a new job.

Well, that was an uncomfortable revelation to have while she was trying to hate him for making a similar decision to put career above all else.

She sighed. She doubted there was anything she could do to change his mind. Everything he said was true, and as much as she hated to have him pull his support, she understood. Maybe someday, if the Med Studies program actually came to fruition and faculty members were once again safe to walk UW's paths, he might reconsider. She couldn't say anything now to jeopardize that hopeful future, even if she wasn't around to see it.

"I understand, Max. I won't lie and say I'm happy about your decision, but I respect it."

"Thank you, Tig. You've always been a straight shooter, and I admire that." He unlaced his fingers and picked at the fabric of his trousers before settling his hands again. "I'm excited about the new, more inclusive program you've been developing," he said. "How marvelous, to modernize the Classics Department and keep it relevant to today's world while still honoring its heritage. I've tried to follow the same vision with my company. You have my continued support for the work you're doing, although I might not be as vocal about it as I was before. I must maintain a certain…distance. But I believe in you and what you're doing."

And what the hell good did that do? Nothing. Having him support her only in his mind was completely useless, unless he was able to telekinetically build a beautiful new wing of offices and classrooms onto the back of Denny Hall—a project she had secretly been hoping he might consider funding. She had been going to suggest they call it the Adel Wing, in an appeal to his vanity. Now it was nothing more than the Figment of Her Imagination Wing.

"Thank you, Max. Your support means a lot to me."

Okay, she had promised she wouldn't lie about being unhappy that he was pulling the scholarship. She never said anything about not lying during the rest of their conversation. Diplomacy was all she had left right now, and she had to protect the future doors it might open.

He stood up and they said quick good-byes. He seemed as anxious as she was to end the meeting and go their separate ways now that the distasteful business had been settled. She paused in her doorway, debating whether she should shut herself in now or not, and saw Lukas Rivers peering around a corner at the end of the hall.

"Luke?" she asked. "What the hell are you doing down there?"

"Shh," he said, hurrying toward her and practically pushing her into her office. He shut the door behind them. "I saw Max leaving and wanted to avoid seeing him, so I was hiding around the corner. Thanks for shouting my name and drawing attention to my cowardice."

"God, I've missed you," she said with a laugh.

"Me, too," he said, pulling her into a squeezing hug. He leaned back a little and scanned her face. "Nice look. You've got quite the rainbow of colors on your face. Too bad it's not Pride Month."

They sat down across her desk from each other. "I happened to have earned these by stepping in front of Chase Davies's fist. Just another day as department chair. Max even called me valiant." She paused. "Hey, why are you hiding from him? I thought you liked Max."

"I like him," Luke said with a shrug. He leaned back and crossed his legs, managing to look as different as possible from Max. Where Adel was all neutrals, from his gray eyes to his black hair and clothes, Luke was color. Bright red hair, a riot of freckles across his pale skin, and green eyes that looked like they must be colored contacts but were really his natural color. He was wearing jeans and a sweater striped with multiple shades of blue and green. Luke talked with his hands, too, and there was nothing still about him.

"I ran into him in downtown Seattle about two weeks ago," he continued. "I was walking around, looking for a place to have lunch while Trevor had some tests run at Virginia Mason, and he was just coming back to his office after a meeting. We talked for a while.

He'd heard about Trevor, and he offered to help pay some of our hospital bills. I said no, thank you, and now I'm trying to avoid him so I don't risk changing my mind."

Tig waited for a moment, then realized she had the full story. "How rude of him. Don't worry. If he comes back here and offers to buy us lunch, I'll chase him away with one of my statues."

"Smart-ass. It was a nice gesture on his part, and more tempting than I care to admit, but Trevor would hate it if he thought we had to borrow money just because of him."

Tig frowned. "Is he okay? I thought he was doing better. Do you need money? Because I can…"

She faltered to a stop when he gave her a sardonic look.

"Oh, sorry. Now I'm doing it. We all care about you and want to help if we're needed, you know that."

"I do, and we both appreciate it, but we're doing all right." His expression brightened again. "And yes, he's doing much better. We're counting down to the final treatments, and his test results have been promising. I should be back here before you know it."

"No." She startled them both by saying the word vehemently and unexpectedly. But even when her brain caught up to her mouth, she was sticking to her response. "Luke, something bad is happening here, and for some unknown reason classics professors are being targeted. Or maybe it was just about these two, and they happened to be classics professors. Either way, I'll feel much better if you stay away from here until the police figure out what's going on. I'm sure Trevor will back me up on this, if you'd like me to call him and ask?"

He whistled. "Low blow. You're right, though. I need to stay safe for him right now. Still, I'd feel better if I was here keeping an eye on you, since you're one of those professors, too."

"Don't worry about me. I have all my friends looking out for me, as well as the police. They'll protect me."

He nodded, watching her silently for a moment. "What's her name?" he asked after a pause.

"I have no idea what you're talking about," she said, although she was pretty sure she did.

"You smiled in kind of a goofy way when you talked about the police protecting you. I doubt you're in love with the entire department, so what's her name?"

Tig sighed. She needed to take some acting lessons because apparently everyone could read her every thought. "Kent," she said. "Sergeant Kent. And I do not look goofy."

"You look happy," he said. "That's a good thing, Tig."

"It's a complicated thing," she corrected, then she changed the subject back to the reason she had asked him to come by the university when he had a chance.

"Do you recognize this paper?" she asked, getting the essay out of her desk's top drawer and handing it to him. "I thought it might be from your class on Cato."

His brow furrowed as he read quickly through the pages. "It seems familiar, but that was two years ago. No, wait. I remember this paragraph. Very insightful." He reached into his pocket, pulling out a small black thumb drive. "Here, I put my class files on this flash and brought it like you asked. Can I borrow your laptop?"

She spun her computer around to face him, and he plugged the drive into the USB port. After a few moments of searching through files, he nodded and looked up at her. "Spencer Cassidy. Good student," he continued, as if connecting the name to the paper jogged his memory. Tig had had the same thing happen to her before, when all the details about a student came back to her years later, triggered by a random memory.

"He got an A on this paper, and in the course," Luke continued. "I almost dropped him down a grade because he was so shy he didn't participate much in class, but he did outstanding work when he was able to write out his thoughts."

Tig sighed, jotting down what he said because she'd need to share it with Kent and Clare when she went by the station later. She turned her laptop back to face her and did a quick check on past graduate students. Then she got out two more papers.

"What about these? Do you recognize them?"

"They're not from my classes, but they seem similar in style to Spencer's. Both his, I expect?"

She shook her head, tapping her finger on the two papers. "This one was written for a class offered three years before the Cato. The other was just last spring, after Spencer had already graduated with his master's."

She handed him one more small stack of pages. "Now this."

"Research notes? Wait, isn't this the paper Chase Davies was working on? I remember him talking about doing...What the..." He fell silent as he picked up the Cato paper again and looked through it. Soon he was moving from one to the other among the four samples, probably connecting the similarities the same way she had done until...

"He wrote all of them?" he asked incredulously. "Chase wrote that paper for Spencer? He got a good grade, he got a fucking degree...Tig, what the hell is going on here?"

She felt the heat of his fury as if it was a physical flame, and his reaction terrified her. Not because she was afraid of him, but because he was as outraged as she needed to be by this situation. When she had been discussing it with Kent and Clare, they hadn't fully recognized the ramifications of Chase's actions if the papers turned out to have been actually used by students, and she had let herself ignore the full consequences, as well. Now she couldn't, not when she was sitting across from someone who understood. Fraudulent degrees, accusations of complicity. Add those to two murders, and her department was starting to collapse in front of her eyes.

For the very first time, she wondered if the university really *should* shut them down, if they were too far gone to ever come back to any semblance of credibility.

"What do we do now, Tig?" he asked, seeming to deflate right in front of her as the enormity of the situation sank in for both of them.

"You go home and take care of Trevor," she said firmly. He was looking to her to be a leader, but she didn't have much to offer him, except to remove him from the situation. She couldn't face another death like Laura's, of someone she truly cared about. "Don't say anything about this to anyone else, okay? And just...just stay away from campus for now, please. Let me worry about this mess, and the police will worry about catching the murderer. Then we'll see if there's anything salvageable left in the department. Oh, and you might want to update your CV while you're at it. Just in case."

He nodded, then piled the papers back into a neat stack and handed them to her. They stood up and hugged once more.

"Be careful, Tig," he said, and then he walked out of her office.

She sank back into her chair and rested her forehead on her desk. With all that was going on, her foremost thought was how much she missed Kent, even though they'd only been apart for less than a day. She had been concerned last night when Kent hugged her, and she had momentarily given in to the desire to rest near her, let her be the strong one. She couldn't just sit back, though, and let someone else take care of her. Not anymore.

Being the head of a Classics Department had long been a goal of hers. She had imagined herself solving disputes with the wisdom of Solomon and lovingly guiding her students and faculty to new heights of academic achievements. Her parents had both had long, happy careers as professors, and never once had they mentioned that the job might entail murder, fraud, and some sketchily acquired ancient vases.

The next position she got, she was going to be damned sure to read the job requirements more carefully than she apparently had for this one.

CHAPTER SEVENTEEN

Kent opened the glass front door of Denny Hall and held it for Clare, but she paused on the top step instead of following her.

"You go on," she said. "I just need to tie my boot lace—then I'll meet you in Tig's office."

Kent sighed. "Is this some juvenile attempt to give us time together? Because it's really not necessary."

Clare shrugged. "Fine with me. I just thought, because you haven't seen her since last night, and there's a lot going on, you might want a few minutes to be alone. But I guess I was wrong."

Kent held out her arm to block Clare's entrance. "Oh, tie your damned boots," she said. "But don't take too long, or I'll write you up for insubordination."

"Tig's a lucky woman to have found someone so charming," Clare said, turning away before Kent could say anything else.

She smiled and shook her head as she headed toward the stairs, the sound of her boots echoing as she walked across the marble floors. She was going to find it more challenging than she cared to admit to go back to being mere coworkers with Clare, leaving behind their teasing and relaxed relationship when they were no longer partners. She'd have to make more of an effort to make friends outside of the department. And possibly to find someone else to date, if Tig was gone.

Maybe just the friends. If she wasn't with Tig, dating didn't seem appealing at all.

She got to Tig's office and found the door open. Tig was inside, her head resting on her desk atop her folded forearms. She looked defeated.

Kent stepped inside and quietly closed the door, glad now that Clare had given them some time alone. She leaned against the desk, her hip resting against Tig's arm, and placed her hand on the back of Tig's neck, ruffling softly through her hair.

"Bad day, sweetheart?" she asked.

"Horrible," Tig said, her voice muffled since her face was still burrowed into her arms. "But no one on my faculty has been killed yet today, so I really can't complain."

Kent gave a short laugh. Then they sat in silence for a few moments. Tig moved one arm and placed it over Kent's thighs, pulling her closer.

Eventually, she sighed and sat up, keeping her hand curved around Kent's hip. "Sorry," she said. "It's just too much to handle at times."

Kent leaned over and kissed her softly, letting her lips linger against Tig's for far too short a time. She should have sent Clare back to the station to tie her boots. She pulled back again.

"Sawyer is just behind me. She'll be here any minute."

As if on cue, Kent heard a knock on the door. Tig waited for her to move to the other side of the desk and sit down before she called out for Clare to come in.

"Hey, Tig," Clare said as she came in the room, shutting the door again behind her. She walked over and gave Tig's shoulder a squeeze before joining Kent on the far side of the desk.

"So, what's been going on, Tig?" Kent asked. Tig seemed noticeably lower in spirits than she had been last night. Either the shock of Kam's death had worn off and she was suddenly feeling the full force of grief, or she'd gotten more bad news today.

She listened as Tig told them about Max's visit. She couldn't help but admit to herself that his reasons were valid, but she hated him for abandoning Tig and her department. He could have used his reputation to support her, but instead, his desertion only made the situation look even worse.

"Just how important was this scholarship, anyway?" Clare

asked, with an angry edge to her tone. She apparently shared Kent's opinions of this jerk.

"It was a nice opportunity for select students," Tig said, rubbing her hand wearily over her eyes. "But it was more about his endorsement than that single scholarship. A lot of people who either were connected to him in the community, or who wanted to be, gave to us because of him. Money, artwork, reference materials. The ripples from his one endowment—sizeable as it was—far outweighed it. I don't know what will happen, but I'm assuming most of the others will pull their funding after hearing that he did."

"Who got these scholarships?" Kent asked, taking notes as usual. She had pages and pages of them by now but felt no closer to finding the connecting lines that would lead to the killer—or killers—than before.

"It was a typical selection process," Tig said. "Need and merit were both considered. Chase Davies actually was his representative and handled most of the details, but there were a couple other professors on his committee. I've had a few of the recipients in my classes, and they were very bright, enthusiastic students. To be honest, though, most of our grad students are here on grants or fellowships or scholarships, so I can't always keep track of who belongs to which funding source. I can compile a list of the winners, if you'd like."

"Maybe. I'm not sure if it would help. Were Davies and Max close?" Kent asked.

"Not especially, I don't think," Tig said, frowning as if she was trying to recall. "When the scholarship was first proposed, he volunteered to be in charge. Chase volunteered for a lot of things. He liked to be involved."

Kent personally doubted whether his intentions were altruistic. What better way to find out about rumors and other things that might prove to be sources for blackmail than by insinuating himself into every aspect of the department that he could reach?

"After he left, Lukas Rivers came by." She looked at Kent, her expression weary. "Here's where you'll want to take lots of notes, by the way. He recognized the paper as one he got from a student named Spencer Cassidy."

"Huh," said Clare. "So he did give the essays to students after all. Do you think he was charging for them, or just doing special favors for ones he liked?"

"I'll bet your friend Lukas wasn't thrilled about being fooled by Davies," Kent added with a bitter laugh. She stopped at the look on Tig's face. "What is it? Is there something else?"

"No, but this is serious enough. Take Spencer. He graduated and received a degree from the university, but if he really did cheat, then that class grade is invalid. There will be hearings, investigations, possibly charges filed, degrees revoked. If they can prove anything, that is. I'm exhausted just thinking about all the actions that will have to take place if word gets out about this."

Kent watched Tig talk, only now realizing what a fiasco this would be for Tig and the struggling department. Clare was right—they really did need Tig to help them see the complete picture when they were dealing with university life. Tig related her full conversation with Lukas, then stopped and stared at her desk.

"I'm sorry, Tig. I hadn't fully grasped what this would mean to you or the university. I was thinking about the papers as potential clues, in a detached way, but they mean something more real and immediate to you."

"I'm sorry, too," Clare said. She looked at Kent. "Can you imagine if someone helped a bunch of people cheat on their police academy entrance exams, and then those people got jobs with different departments using those fraudulent scores? What a mess."

Kent sighed. She didn't even want to think of the time it would take to untangle and fix such a disaster, and she wished Tig wouldn't have to deal with all this. Of course, by lateraling to another university, she might be able to avoid it altogether...

Kent didn't want to think of that, either. She turned the conversation around to the subject she and Clare had discussed last night. "Which brings us to another topic we need your opinion on, Tig, because the nuances of university politics aren't always as clear to us as they would be to you. Remember the comments Professor Ayari made about wanting to be director? Well, we were thinking…I mean, it's a possibility that even if the department doesn't close completely, that you still might be…"

Kent faltered to a stop and looked at Clare, who didn't seem sure of what to say either because she just shrugged unhelpfully at Kent.

"Don't bother dancing around it," Tig said. "I know the likelihood of me remaining in my position is slim, even if we make it through this intact. Are you asking if Sami would kill me to get my job?"

"No," Kent said. She decided to take Tig's advice and stop prevaricating. "If she had wanted to kill you, she's already had plenty of opportunities, including the night of Davies's murder. But you might still be the indirect target. Someone could have killed Davies and Morris to make you look bad. Your people were causing a public spectacle, then they end up dead—it looks like you've completely lost control of your department."

"Not that *we* think you have, of course," Clare chimed in. "You're doing great."

Kent was so relieved to see Tig laugh at Clare's comment that she joined in, too. The laughter didn't last long, but Tig's smile seemed more natural after it ended.

"Thanks for the vote of confidence, Clare," she said. "So, would Sami kill them to get me demoted?" Tig paused for only a brief moment. "No. She wouldn't risk the department. I'd bet she'd rather be demoted to TA as long as our vision for Med Studies remained intact."

"Really?" Clare asked, sounding as surprised as Kent felt. "Do you feel the same way about this?"

Tig shrugged. "Probably not. If for some reason the new program was abolished, I'd be disappointed, but it would be on a much different level from what Sami would probably feel. Look, I love Classical Studies, especially Ancient Greek literature and languages. They speak to me, and something inside me responds. But even though I appreciate and study Greek things, I'm not Greek.

Sami is from Northern Africa, from Tunisia, so this is more than her field of expertise. It's her culture. A culture whose historical and literary significance has too often been subverted and erased by a Eurocentric focus on Greece and Rome."

Tig gestured at a map on her wall, showing a depiction of the Mediterranean region in ancient times. "Other Classical Studies programs across the country are changing to Mediterranean Studies, like we're planning to do. Too often, though, they only include the bare minimum of those less European focused courses. For someone like Sami, that kind of token change is nearly as problematic as being ignored in the first place. It's just a way for some universities to prove how modern and relevant they are, while nothing much changes in terms of course offerings and professorial positions. We talked about that quite often when we first started planning how our department would change, so I'm not putting words in her mouth here."

She turned in her chair and pulled a thick binder off the shelf that was next to her desk, tucked under her windowsill. She opened it and flipped through pages of lists and charts. "Ours was going to be different. We're adding more faculty positions, several underrepresented languages, and a variety of inclusive history and comparative literature classes. It's an important program—it's groundbreaking in a lot of ways. Just to be part of it is something special to her and to all of us. It would be a professional coup for her if she was named director of all this, but just helping create this program means more to her on a personal and cultural level than it could for me. It matters more to her that the program *exists* than that she's the leader of it."

Kent didn't speak right away. With every step of this investigation, she felt farther from figuring out the truth, yet closer to understanding Tig. She had assumed Tig was a well-respected and excellent professor to be named director of the new program, but Kent hadn't realized what a significant impact she was having not only at the UW, but on Classical Studies programs everywhere. She kept finding more to admire about Tig. More to love.

Like. More to like.

"Wow, Tig," Clare said. "Libby told me this transition was a big deal, but I thought she meant that in relation to you, that it was going to be a lot of work. This really is a big deal."

"It is," Tig agreed. "I'm worried about losing my job here, but it's even more important that the curricular changes happen, either with or without me."

With her, Kent vowed to herself. That was how it should be. She meant that in more ways than just with her changing department, too. How much more? She wasn't sure yet.

"Then let's get busy and solve these murders," she said. "First, we need to check out Morris's office. I get what you're saying about Ayari, but I'd still be interested in having a chat with her about what's going on. Not as a suspect, but as someone who might be able to shed more light on this case."

She reached out her hand and pulled Tig to her feet. She almost forgot where she was and kept Tig's hand in hers, but remembered to let go as they were going out the door. Morris's office was one floor down from Tig's, and she opened it with the key she had gotten from admin.

Her first thought on opening the door was that the place had been tossed, but Tig followed her in without comment and started poking around. Kent figured she'd seen his office before, so this must be his version of normal. Books were askew on the shelves, and several jackets and scarves were on the floor next to an ironically empty coatrack. And there were papers everywhere. Some of the ones on the top layer of the desk had coffee mug rings on them, and others were crammed into file folders that seemed sadly insufficient for the job he had expected them to do.

"This is…" Clare hesitated, apparently searching for the right word. "Appalling."

Kent agreed. Davies's office had been similar to Tig's. Lived in, with piles of books and ungraded papers lying around, but an ordered sort of chaos. This was simply chaos.

"There's a computer under here," Tig said, peering under some papers on the desk with her gloved hands. "Can I look at what's on it?"

"Yes," Kent said. "If you need help getting passwords, I'll bring Larson in."

Tig started up the computer and tapped a few keys. "No need. I'm good."

Kent walked over and stood by her shoulder. She had done the same with Larson in Davies's office, but with more distance between them. Now, she stood close enough to touch Tig, to place her hand on Tig's shoulder.

"No passcodes needed, or did you guess the correct one right away?" she asked, looking at the screen. It was crammed with icons, none of which were in a straight row.

Tig shook her head. "Looks like he disabled the lock screen or had someone do it for him. I'll see if I can find out how he stored papers and class lists."

Kent brushed against her gently as she walked away, giving Tig time to search his computer. She started straightening papers, trying to sort them into more comprehensible piles that they could go through in more depth later. Clare was pulling books off the shelves, skimming through their pages, then replacing them, probably hoping to find a note or other message tucked inside one of them.

"Look at this," Tig called, and both of them clustered behind her chair. "I found his class folders from two years ago. See this one on Herodotus? Look who took the class."

She pointed the cursor at Spencer Cassidy's name.

"Can you find a paper he wrote?" Clare asked. "Something to compare to the one Davies wrote?"

"No," Tig said, searching the folder again to show them that there were no results. "I can find papers from other students, but nothing for Spencer."

Kent frowned at the screen, not really seeing anything on it as she tried to piece together the clues. "Do you think someone else removed the essays? Maybe someone knew we were looking into the papers Davies wrote."

Tig gestured at the screen again. "There's nothing recent in the document history. Maybe someone who knew how to cover their tracks could have done it, but that's beyond my level of skill."

Plagiarized articles, ghostwritten essays, missing papers. Kent let the three simmer together in her mind. "Oh," she said, as a thread wove its way among them. "What if this was the price of blackmail?" Tig and Clare turned to her, not following her train of thought yet. "Davies wants this Spencer kid to succeed, so he writes his papers for him. But why bother with Morris's classwork if he has the goods on the professor?"

Tig nodded, her expression admiring as she looked at Kent. "He was blackmailing for grades, not for money. That actually makes a lot more sense since we're talking about Kam."

"There's a kind of elegant reckoning there, if that's really what happened," Clare said. "Using a plagiarized paper as a way to force Morris into giving falsified grades on nonexistent ones."

"That would have appealed to Chase, I think," Tig added. "It would maybe have given him a way to justify what he was doing, in his own mind."

"Okay, then," Kent said. "Let's look deeper into Spencer Cassidy, and maybe try to get names to go with a couple of the other examples, too, but only if some are connected to professors you trust, Tig. We'll talk to Ayari today, and then we'll see where these two leads take us."

Kent felt more positive than she had over the past few days. They were getting somewhere and finding some connections. Was it too little, too late for Tig's future here? She hoped not.

Chapter Eighteen

Tig had another class to teach, so Kent and Clare went back to the station to prepare for their interview with Ayari. They walked along paths dotted with sodden leaves and puddles, relieved to have a brief respite from the near-constant rain of the past few days. They were in civvies since Clare didn't have to work patrol today, and street clothes helped them get across campus more easily, without people stopping them to ask for directions or to handle other cop-related issues.

"It feels like we're trying to fit two different sets of puzzle pieces together," Clare said with a frown. "On the one hand, we have Morris and Davies who are rivals in the Med Studies debate, and on the other we have them mixed up in the same cheating scandal."

Kent agreed. The pieces didn't match up. "Don't forget your third hand," she said. "The vases. Are they connected, or were they just another scheme Davies had going?"

Clare shook her head, no more able to answer that question than Kent was right now. "And the person who killed them," she continued. "Why pick those two? Is it just coincidence that they murdered the two who were involved with the papers?"

"Don't forget, there were more papers. If they were the only two involved, then it would seem unlikely the murderer would randomly have chosen them as sacrifices. But if there were more professors connected to the falsified papers, then the odds would have been higher that any two chosen would have been part of that, too."

They walked in silence for a while, both stewing over the disparate elements of the case. Kent's mind was torn between turning the clues over in her mind and thinking about Tig. Tig was in the lead so far, in terms of the amount of time Kent's focus was on her. She had looked so exhausted and worried, overwhelmed by the amount of work required of her because of the two murders, and now the possibly far-reaching cheating scheme. Not to mention the ever-present concern that one university decision could mean that she no longer had to worry about either of those because she had lost her job. Kent felt the weight of that concern, too.

They came to the stoplight on Fifteenth and stood to one side, out of earshot of other pedestrians. "You know, if someone really wanted to discredit Tig or the department, what better way to do that than by bringing the scandal to the university's attention? Why bother killing two of the men involved if the same result can be achieved with just an accusation?"

"Good point," Clare conceded. "That would have eliminated the risk of being caught, and would have made the accuser seem like a hero for uncovering this mess."

They started walking again when the light changed. Kent kept her voice low with so many people around them. "Plus they would still have had the satisfaction of getting Davies and Morris fired or investigated, if their intention was to harm them. Tig said once that the effects of accusations such as plagiarism never really go away, even if charges are dropped, so they would have tainted their reputations, maybe even permanently, no matter whether they were convicted or not."

"You'd think that would have furthered the cause to take away some of the prestige of studying classics in the traditional way and to open the door for a more relevant approach. Much simpler than killing them and maybe turning them into martyrs." Clare held the door to the station open and they walked inside. "Which brings us back to it being a coincidence that someone murdered the two members of the faculty who were involved in the cheating thing. And I remember from our last murder case how little either of us likes coincidences."

"We hate them," Kent confirmed. "They're messy, and they usually are indications that we're heading in the wrong direction. Don't forget, though, that we only found the evidence from Davies and Morris because they were murdered. We might have found similar proof if two others had been chosen."

"Great, now it's a which came first, chicken or egg scenario. I hate those, too. Did we find the evidence because they were killed, or were they killed because of the evidence we found?" Clare clutched the hair at her temples in her fists. "I'm getting a headache."

Kent was, too. "Go get some water. Or caffeine. Take a break. Ayari will be here in an hour, and maybe we'll be able to learn something from her perspective when we talk to her in person." She sighed. "One of us needs to be on her game, so it'd better be you because I have to go do some admin work and make my headache even worse."

She and Clare parted ways, and Kent went into her office. She'd been neglecting her regular work, and even after a mere few days it was beginning to create alarmingly high piles. One stiff breeze when someone opened the door, and her office would look like Morris's did, minus the clothes on the floor. She did have some standards.

She checked her watch, and then pulled out her cell instead of getting to work. She had five minutes before Tig's class started.

"Hey," she said when Tig answered.

"Hey, yourself. So, are you calling to tell me you and Clare solved the case?"

Kent laughed, suddenly feeling very glad that she had made the call. "You mean, on the walk from Denny to the station? Yes, we did. Everything's neatly wrapped up, and this is all over."

Tig laughed, too. A welcome sound over the phone. "Well, that's a relief. Good job, you two. Now I'll be able to sleep more peacefully."

"Speaking of sleeping," Kent started. Or not sleeping. Either one. "I wanted to ask if you'd come stay at my house tonight. I'll feel better knowing you're safe."

"With you?" Tig asked, then another laugh. "Sorry, stupid

question. Of course you'll be there, too. Yes, I'd like that. Just for safety's sake, of course."

"Of course," Kent agreed. "There's no other reason I can think of to have you spend the night with me."

"I'm hanging up now. If we talk about this much longer, my cheeks will turn bright red. Pair that with these bruises, and my students will think our department is becoming a clown college, not Med Studies. I'll see you tonight."

"I'll pick you up at Denny after your last class," Kent said before ending the call.

She spun her phone slowly in her hand as she replayed the conversation in her mind a couple of times, then she resolutely put the cell to one side and pulled the first paper off the stack. A request for a shift change, how exciting. She signed the form and moved it to one side before reaching for the next task.

She happily locked the door on the rest of her work once the desk officer let her know Ayari was in the conference room. She joined up with Clare on the way, and they entered the room together.

While Clare handled the introductions and the forewarning that the interview would be recorded, Kent observed the professor. She was wearing a similar outfit to the one Kent had first seen her in, but this time instead of reds and purples, she was in a sunny yellow shirt and banded trousers with a bright spring-green head wrap. The hint of yellow undertones in her light brown skin and the etched laugh lines on her face gave a sense of warmth to her black eyes. She had a ready smile and seemed amused by the experience of being called to the station. Kent remembered reading the same tone into her expression when she saw her at the Davies v. Morris bout. Her demeanor was relaxed, and Kent wondered what she thought about the chaos occurring on campus. She seemed detached, but this was meant to be her new home. The demise of the Classics Department—and by extension, the Med Studies program—would mean a shift in her personal career, as well as a major roadblock to the exposure these university students would have to her culture.

She would have thought Ayari would at least seem mildly concerned.

"I understand that you were instrumental in designing the expanded Mediterranean Studies department at UW, weren't you, Professor Ayari?"

She inclined her head, as if graciously receiving Kent's accolades. "I proposed the concept, yes, but there were many at the university who had already been considering the change. I merely provided some guidance in terms of courses and ways to integrate the various cultures into the existing program. Professor Weston had been working on a similar project, and she and I have worked together to design the new curriculum."

"This would be an important move for you career-wise, wouldn't it?" Clare seamlessly stepped in. "Not to mention it being a positive step toward more recognition of your culture, your heritage."

Ayari shrugged. "I had a good position at Berkeley, so it is a step sideways for my career. For my culture, though, yes, I agree with what you are saying. Our early literature and history have been hidden behind those of the Greeks and Romans for far too long, and it is good to give them a chance to stand side-by-side."

"Would they really be balanced?" Kent asked, making a weighing motion with her hands, and tipping the scales to the right. "Or would the current Classics Department still be considered to be the main focus, with its faculty holding more leadership roles?"

"One would hope that discrepancy will even out over time. Many of the professors for the specializations other than classics will be new to the university. It will take time for them to be seen as equals with the more entrenched members of the current faculty."

Kent had a feeling that not all of those more entrenched faculty members would be open to their new colleagues. "You're no stranger to such unfairness, are you? Even here, where some people like Professor Weston are open-minded and welcoming, I'm sure there are others who disagree with this change."

Her words finally sparked a change in Ayari, albeit a small one. Just a flicker of the eyes and a brief tightening around the mouth to show that Kent's words had hit home. Ayari nodded. "You are correct, Sergeant Kent. I was an external member of the committee that designed the program, and I have been to the community and faculty meetings. Some claim that the transformation would make the classics degree seem less revered than in the past. They say we are teaching revisionist history, not facts. That we are something new and unproven as a culture, when we have been in existence—writing and creating and living—for many centuries."

Clare pretended to look through some notes, although Kent knew they were following an agreed upon direction with this interview, and she didn't really need to consult them.

"Professor Chase Davies was opposed to the new program, wasn't he? Did he ever confront you with his concerns?"

Ayari laughed softly. "Ah, are you suggesting I murdered this man because he did not agree with my dream?"

"You are not currently a suspect, Professor. We merely wanted to discuss the current situation and see if you might have a different take on it since you are new to the university."

Ayari inclined her head, acknowledging Kent's point. "As you mentioned, Sergeant, I am no stranger to such attitudes as he possessed. He had lost, though, and the transformation was already in motion. Killing him would have made no difference."

She maintained her dismissive tone throughout her last few sentences, but Kent finally understood what Tig had been trying to say about her. If she were in Ayari's position, pushed to the edge by constant confrontation with demeaning attitudes toward her culture and her history, Kent might relish the chance to commit murder, and she admired Ayari's equanimity in the face of such opposition.

"Do you collect any artifacts from your country's past, Professor?" Clare asked, changing the subject. "I've noticed that many of our faculty members who study ancient cultures choose to do so."

Kent mentally commended Clare for asking a good question. She had let the thread of the vases slip from her mind, and she was impressed that Clare had remembered to allude to it obliquely enough not to give any information about the find. Otherwise, Tig might have competition in her attempts to steal them.

"I have many replicas of statuary and models of temples and other ancient sites," she said, with the same sort of expression Kent had seen on Tig's face when discussing this topic. Her enthusiasm seemed real and not forced. "I will be bringing them with me when I move to Washington. I am afraid that I do not have any true artifacts. I believe such things should remain in my country. Too much has already been plundered, and we must do what we can to protect what is left."

Kent asked a few more questions about the Med Studies curriculum, glad to have a chance to learn more about Tig's project. Ayari was obviously impressed with Tig, and her tone was warm whenever she praised her. Kent had originally been dismissive about the impact of this new program when she first met Tig, but she was rapidly learning how important and influential this had the chance to be. Eventually, the desk officer came to escort Ayari out of the station. Kent leaned back in her chair, stretching her lower back, and skimmed through the notes she had taken during the interview.

"First impressions?" Kent asked.

"I like her," Clare said, tapping her pen on the table and making little metallic pings as she did. "I think Davies annoyed her more than she's letting on, but do I think she got an unregistered gun and silencer, and then stalked and killed him? Not so much."

"Same here," Kent agreed. "She has a mean handshake, but I have trouble believing she could have inflicted those wounds on Morris."

She glanced back through the autopsy report that revealed that Morris had suffered several fractures to his right cheekbone before being shot. "Caused by a pistol-shaped object, possibly the same weapon used to fatally shoot him." She shook her head. "They can't just come out and say the obvious. Do they really think it's a possibility that the killer had two guns, one to hit with and the other for shooting?"

"Maybe someone offers etiquette lessons for serial killers," Clare said with a laugh. "You wouldn't want to embarrass yourself at a murder by using the wrong gun for the first course." She paused. "Joking aside, she's a force, and I wouldn't want to be her enemy, but I feel the same way about Tig. I believe they'd both do their fighting on an intellectual level."

Kent nodded. "Good question about the vases," she added. "She could possibly have smuggled them into the country on one of her international trips, but I believed what she said. I know these specific ones are Greek and not from her country, but I think she'd make the same ethical choice with any cultural artifact. I can't see her giving Davies anything like that."

Clare nodded. "Especially not to him. She seemed very Tig-like when she answered me. I got the feeling she desires objects like these, and enjoys having the replicas surrounding her, but I believed her, too, when she said she would want them to stay in her country. I imagine she'd extend the same respect to Greek or Roman items, too."

Kent stacked their notes together again. "Well, we still have no suspect. This was productive."

"It'll all come together, somehow," Clare said, with an optimism Kent didn't share.

"And if it doesn't?"

Clare met her gaze. "Then we figure out a way to get Tig out of here, even if we have to fill out job applications ourselves. Or whatever one fills out to apply at a university."

Kent doubted they'd be able to land Tig a job on their own, but she couldn't disagree with Clare. If the killer wasn't caught soon, she'd rather have Tig safely teaching in Boston or wherever than here, in danger.

❖

Kent managed to get a significant chunk of work done in between her interview and picking up Tig. For once, she was happy to have the piles of paper on her desk because the work helped the time pass and kept her mind from obsessing over the night ahead.

She paused once, to debrief the chaplain and liaison officer who had gone to Morris's house to speak to his sons. He might have been a slob at work and a probable plagiarist, but from the sound of it, he had been a loving and beloved father to his three boys. He didn't deserve to have died the way he did, alone and terrified in the dark. She needed to solve this case to protect Tig, but now she also wanted to give those boys some closure and to bring his murderer to justice.

She stopped work once more to call Jimmy, the youngest of her brothers, who was currently stationed north of Seattle, at the Naval Station in Everett. Just to say hello. They spent about half an hour catching up, and she was tempted to mention Tig but decided against it. If she managed to solve this case, and if Tig's department survived and she stayed local, and if their relationship continued, *then* she would tell her brothers about her.

For now, there were too many *if*s for her to believe they had a chance.

But they had tonight.

CHAPTER NINETEEN

Tig waited by the front door of Denny until Kent came to pick her up after her last class. She'd had a tiring day, from her first class to the series of midmorning visitors, to her two-hour block on Callimachus. Luckily, the latter was a translation class, so she didn't need to be able to coherently lecture for that length of time. She had started the class by answering some questions the students had about the murder—although there wasn't much she could say that they wouldn't have already heard through the campus grapevine. She had to concentrate to make sure she didn't let anything inadvertently slip, like the existence of some gorgeous ancient artifacts, and by the time the students had settled enough to begin their translations, she was too exhausted to really focus anymore. They muddled through together, though, and she was grateful for the patience the students had shown, as well as their obvious sadness over losing two professors.

She wanted to make this right for them. To keep the department going because the students who loved these ancient words and works deserved a place where they could pursue their passions. And those words and works deserved, in turn, to be studied and dissected and not cast into oblivion, as did the products of the other ancient Mediterranean cultures. This hopeful place that had been her home for so many years couldn't be lost, relegating Denny to the ranks of existing merely as overflow space for other departments or to being yet another admin building.

Jazz had apparently already been hatching plans to annex

Denny to Suzzallo Library, turning it into a specialized reference library. Tig told her to keep her grasping Viking paws off her building, although Jazz's proposal beat out the other options by a landslide, and Tig could imagine how beautiful it would be with the interior opened up more and filled with books.

She was happy when Kent came up the stairs, dispelling her gloomy thoughts about the fate of Denny. Well, she was just plain happy to see her.

"Hi," she said when Kent reached her. She was still in uniform, so Tig resisted the urge to reach for her, but it was a close call for a moment there. Kent looked as if she felt the same, and they stood facing each other in silence for a few heartbeats.

"Good thing we didn't kiss each other hello," Tig finally said. "People might have gotten the impression that we're in a relationship or something."

"Dodged that bullet," Kent said. She winced at her own comment, likely said out of habit, and hurried to get past it. Tig understood, since she had made similar remarks over the past few days, when she spoke without thinking. "No one would ever guess if they just saw us standing here like this," Kent continued. "About half an inch apart and staring at each other."

"We're very subtle. And I'm assuming nothing in my expression gives away the fact that I really want to touch you right now."

Kent cleared her throat and took a step back. "I can't see anything of the sort. Come on, let's get out of here. I can carry that for you."

She took the messenger bag off Tig's shoulder, and laughed as she hefted it onto her own. "I'm assuming the dead weight in here is books, and not an ancient vase that you picked up in the Museology Department. How many of them are you planning on reading tonight?"

"None," Tig admitted. She had all night with Kent, and she wasn't going to spend it reading. "It's just a habit to bring them."

Kent had moved her car to the lot behind Denny, and she led them to a nondescript brown Camry.

"I could easily have met you out here, you know," Tig said as

Kent unlocked the doors and put Tig's bag on the back seat. "It's still daylight."

Kent shrugged. "We don't know for sure that our killer is solely nocturnal, so until we find out their habits, you should be careful about walking places alone. Did you need to stop by your house for anything?"

"No. I went right before my last class and picked up what I needed. Don't glare. I went with Jazz."

"Jazz," Kent repeated. "The librarian with the axe on the wall in her office? Do you realize that's ill…Oh, never mind. If I'm not around, stick close to her."

Tig smiled and settled back in her seat as they drove, looking around the car for clues about Kent and who she was outside of the police station. Unsurprisingly, there was little to go on, since there was no trash or anything else within sight.

"Did you deliberately tell the dealership you wanted them to remove any amenities that might make your ride more comfortable or enjoyable?" she asked, waving toward the unadorned dash and the simple radio.

Kent laughed. "Actually, I did. I wanted to pay cash, so I had them strip off any extras. My real vehicle is a patrol car," she explained. "This is just a way to transport myself from home to work."

Tig reached over and let her fingers trail down the side of Kent's neck. "You're a mysterious woman, Adi Kent."

Kent groaned, but it turned back into a laugh. "Not Adi," she said. "And I'm not mysterious, I'm just very simple. It sometimes gives the false impression of depth and mystery."

Tig let her hand settle at the base of Kent's throat, curling over the lapel of her uniform and dipping under the material to the soft skin underneath. Kent turned her head and kissed the top of Tig's hand, sending a shiver up her arm. "I can think of a whole lot of words to describe you, and *simple* is nowhere on that list."

Complex and intelligent. Brusque, but kind. Sexy as hell. Tig could go on for hours.

The drive to her house was a short one, and Tig was pleased

to see that they lived within only a couple miles of each other since they were both near the boundary between Wallingford and Fremont. Kent pulled into the tiny slip of a parking space next to her two-story contemporary style home. It was narrow and modern, with huge plate glass windows and an interesting two-toned siding consisting of horizontal honey-colored wood planks on the bottom floor and vertical, rich brown ones on the top. It was a small lot, and the neighbors were close, but the house was clean-lined and stylish.

Tig stood in front of Kent's home, looking up at the unique siding patterns.

"Well?" prompted Kent.

Tig shook her head slowly. "You asked me before if Chase's house was what I expected, and I think if I had been given pictures of both, I would have flip-flopped you and assumed you lived in the older home with the large lot. But now that I'm here, this feels right. It suits you."

It did, too, unassuming and elegant as it was. They walked inside, and the interior was as clean and modern as the outside. Everything was in shades of black, tan, and white with hints of gray in the geometrically patterned rugs and softening the harshness of the black kitchen cabinets.

Kent set Tig's backpack on the couch, and they stood in silence for a moment. Tig had the awkward realization that they really hadn't spent much time alone with only each other as company— except for last night's dinner, of course—and now she was here for an entire night with Kent. She wasn't sorry she had come, far from it, but she felt an unaccustomed sense of shyness settle over her.

Kent might have been feeling the same because she gestured upstairs. "I'm going to change and take a quick shower. Help yourself to anything from the fridge. I thought we could have pizza delivered for dinner?"

"Sounds good," Tig said. "Do you mind if I snoop around?"

Kent laughed. "Go anywhere you like." She pointed beyond the open concept living room and kitchen. "The room back there is a sort of den, and the main bedroom and bath are upstairs. I won't be long."

She headed upstairs, unbuttoning her uniform shirt as she went, and Tig was tempted to follow her. She didn't, though. She needed a moment to reconcile this beautiful space with the woman she was just getting to know. She wandered into the kitchen and chose a local amber ale from the fridge, finding a bottle opener in the second drawer she tried. She leaned on the counter and looked around. Framed photos of misty fir-covered mountains and a ferry boat moving through the fog had obviously been taken in the area. She walked over to one and deciphered the name Kyle Kent scrawled across the bottom corner. One of Kent's brothers, she assumed.

She hadn't been lying when she told Kent that her own office was basically a microcosm of her home. Her passion for classics was front and center everywhere she was, out in the open in the same way that her thoughts and emotions apparently were in her expressions. Kent's personality was hidden behind lovely details and tidily arranged, minimalist drawers. Tig really had expected Kent's house to look like her office, just as hers did. Bare walls and floors. A simple desk, and maybe a cot in one corner for sleeping. She wasn't sure how she'd come to the assumption that Kent lived in a monastic cell, but the realization made her laugh, which finally made her relax into this unexpected space.

She went into the den and found Kent's more comfortable side. A plaid pull-out sofa bed faced a large screen TV, and a shelf next to it was filled with video games and multiple controllers. Tig scanned the titles. They were foreign to her, but they seemed to mostly involve planes and sports. She had a feeling this was where Kent spent most of her time when her brothers came to visit. She peeked through a door on the far side of the room and found a combined bathroom and laundry room. Indications of her brothers' continued presence in her life were there, too, in the form of a couple bottles of shampoo, some shaving cream, and a razor.

She shut the bathroom door again and focused now on the pictures she had been hoping to see. They were in this room in abundance, scattered in randomly sized frames—not nearly as put-together and cohesive as the art in the living room. They weren't in chronological order, either, and a photo of an impossibly tiny

Kent standing near a merry-go-round with her three large brothers surrounding her sat next to an older Kent—taller now, and just coming into her present-day beauty—in graduation robes, clustered together with her brothers, their faces creased in obviously proud smiles.

She went from photo to photo, fleshing out Kent's childhood with the random jumps of a time traveler. In some of the photos, an older couple stood with the quartet of siblings, but they were always a little bit separate. Not quite part of the group.

She was looking at a picture of Kent and one of her brothers on what appeared to be an aircraft carrier when she sensed someone near. She turned around and saw Kent in the doorway, leaning against the jamb and quietly observing her. She had changed into a thick flannel shirt in a black watch plaid and black sweatpants. Her short, dark brown hair was still wet and slightly curled from her shower.

"That's Jimmy," she said, nodding at the picture. "My youngest brother. He's with a carrier strike group in Everett." She walked into the room and pointed at a different photo. "Justin is the middle one. He's in the UAE right now but is supposed to be back here for Christmas. And that's Mom and Dad," she said, almost as an afterthought. She picked up another with a boy in a football uniform holding Kent—tiny again—like a ball he was about to pass.

"My oldest brother Kyle, the football coach."

"And photographer," Tig added, nodding toward the living room.

Kent smiled, looking as proud as her brothers had at her high school graduation. "Yes. He's very talented." She shrugged and put the photo back on the dresser, and Tig stepped behind her as she did, wrapping her arms around Kent's waist and resting her chin on Kent's shoulder. "It was an unconventional childhood," Kent said, leaning into her, "but a good one."

She turned in Tig's arms and slid her hands around the back of Tig's neck, one hand nestling into Tig's hair and the other settling between her shoulder blades. "I'm glad you're here," she said.

"Me, too," Tig managed to say before the urge to kiss Kent

became too insistent to ignore. The kiss was soft, but deep, as their tongues played against each other, and Kent's hand on her neck pulled them ever closer. Tig moved her own hands lower until they were cupped around Kent's ass, holding them tightly against each other until every shift of their hips elicited a soft moan from both of them.

They slowly ended the kiss and just held each other close, breathing together as their foreheads rested against each other. Tig decided kissing Kent was her new favorite activity, but she also loved the moments they'd shared over the past days when they just melted into the stillness that settled so easily between them.

She pulled them together at the hips once more before loosening her hold and moving back. "Do you mind if I shower, too?" she asked, wanting to wash away as much of the day's troublesome moments as she could, leaving her with just Kent for the night, with just these few hours they had together.

Kent nodded. "I'll order pizza. Come look at the menu first."

They settled easily on an Italian meatball pizza with olives, then Tig reluctantly walked away from her and up the open staircase. The bedroom upstairs was as elegant as the living room, but in a warm, lived-in kind of way. The colors were muted sage and ivory, and Kent's preference for geometric patterns was apparent here, as well. There were stripes on the bedspread and interlocking diamonds on the throw rug beside it. The curtains were ivory, with a glossy, tonal Greek key design across the bottom.

Tig stared at the bed for a moment, hoping—and feeling it was highly likely—that she'd be sleeping there tonight, and not on the game room sleeper sofa. As long as Kent was with her, though, she didn't mind where she slept. Sofa, floor, kitchen counter. Wherever.

She took off her clothes and stepped into the large shower. She stood under the wide, rainfall showerhead and let achingly hot water blast the day away.

CHAPTER TWENTY

Kent tucked some wadded-up newspaper between two logs in her fireplace, then added a pile of shaved wood as kindling. She carefully stacked two more split logs on top before striking a long match and holding the flame against the paper. The fire caught quickly, then slowly spread from the kindling to the larger logs. She sat back on her heels and pulled the screen closed, savoring the rush of heat as the flames grew.

She turned at the sound of Tig coming down the stairs. The sight of her, in an oversized T-shirt and leggings, with her skin flushed from the shower, took Kent's breath away. The intimacy of having Tig here, of them wearing comfortable clothes and shutting themselves inside together, away from the night, was overpowering. She felt *right* here. Kent had been expecting attraction, and she hadn't been surprised by the sense of awkwardness they both seemed to experience in their first few minutes together in Kent's home, but this feeling of belonging caught her off guard. Tig belonged here, with her. And she belonged to Tig.

"Feel better?" she asked, relieved when her voice sounded fairly normal and didn't reflect the shock she felt at how easy it would be to have Tig simply live here now. She was here. She should stay.

But she wouldn't, and they both knew it. Kent dreaded the time when she'd have to admit to Clare that she had been right to be worried about her—because Kent was going to come out of this with a wound that would likely never fully heal.

She took a deep breath and exhaled slowly. She couldn't let her racing thoughts ruin the evening. She got up and sat on the couch facing the fire. Tig sat next to her with her legs tucked under her hip, her knees resting against Kent.

"Much better," she answered. "That's an amazing shower. I could have stayed in there for hours."

Kent smiled. "It was top on my list of must-haves when I was looking for this place. Those people I work with drive me crazy, and I need something to help me unwind at the end of the day."

Tig grinned at her, and Kent knew they were both thinking about a much better way to unwind. She put her hand on Tig's thigh, playing with the hem of her shirt. The pizza would be delivered soon, and so she decided to fill the time until then by telling Tig about the news she had gotten that day. If she didn't, she was worried they might start something and that neither one of them would be in a suitable state to open the door when their dinner arrived.

"So, it seems Matthiou might have found the route your vases took to get to the States. The authorities at the Port of Tyre in the Middle East confiscated some other artifacts being smuggled through the port on a fishing boat, and it seems the dates and descriptions of those might be a good match for the ones Davies had. Matthiou thinks they were originally found at an illegal dig in Izmir in Turkey, which she said would have been part of ancient Greece?"

"Yes, it used to be called Smyrna." Tig sighed. "I suppose they'll be sending them back, then? I won't even have a chance to say goodbye?"

Kent gave Tig's knee a nudge. "Sorry, but they'd probably ask me to vouch for you before you did, and I'd be lying if I said you wouldn't try to snatch them. I doubt I'll be kept up to date on the situation with them, but if I hear anything, I promise to tell you."

Kent came to the end of her story. "The frustrating thing is that the closest we've come to finding a guilty-looking person is Chase himself. The only one who can't be a suspect. The killer is likely someone close to the department, Tig. I know it's not in your nature, but please don't trust anyone completely, even Ayari. She's not a suspect, but still…if she comes to you some night and says she wants to show you an interesting shrub on an out-of-the-way campus path, please tell her no."

Tig laughed. "I promise. She has a fascinating approach to studying her culture, and I have a feeling she's going to be at the top of her field in a few years. If we can save our department and retain enough donors to be able to offer her opportunities to travel and continue her research, she has the potential to bring a lot of prestige to the university."

"More prestige than you bring?"

Tig scoffed at that. "Far more. Honestly—and this isn't meant to be an insult to myself, it's just a fact—I'm a workhorse sort of professor. I publish articles regularly, and they've been well-received, but I'm a better teacher than I am a writer. Managing the department and giving lectures are my strengths. Writing innovative papers is something I can do, but not as well as the other parts of my job." She shrugged, curving closer to Kent. "I'm fine with that, too. I enjoy sitting in a classroom discussing a poem or play with a group of students much more than sitting at my desk picking apart an ancient text. That's probably why the thought of going back and writing grad school level papers like Chase was doing is so unappealing to me. Even when I was working on my degree, I loved being a TA more than working on my thesis or on essays."

Kent had a feeling Tig was downplaying the accolades her writing likely received, but she admired anyone who had enough self-awareness to identify their true gifts. "So, Ayari is more of a writer than a teacher?"

"That's part of it," Tig said. "The other part is that my focus is on pieces of literature that have been studied by thousands of scholars over the years. It gets progressively more difficult to come up with earth-shaking new interpretations when we have a limited number of extant works. Sami's focus lies in directions that have often been overlooked, so she's in the vanguard."

"That makes sense," Kent said as the doorbell chimed. "Hold on, I'll get this."

She paid for the pizza, then set the box on the coffee table along with plates and napkins.

"So, what exactly is she studying?"

"Well, a brief recap of Tunisian history is that of conquest by different cultures, so they have a unique and multi-ethnic blend of cultures that make the Tunisian people who they are today," Tig said, putting a piece of pizza on her plate but leaving it untouched while she spoke. "The Romans were a major conquering force, when they destroyed Carthage and settled on its ruins. Sami's field is two-pronged. She studies pre-Roman art and inscriptions, really any surviving artifacts, which sadly isn't a lot since so much was destroyed. Many scholars are dismissive about these pre-Roman relics, claiming that Tunisia didn't offer anything significant to the world before the Roman conquest. But she also studies more modern art and literature, examining how aspects from the various conquering cultures were incorporated to become something uniquely Tunisian, rather than just being derivative. The combination of the two is providing some remarkable insights into the cultural identity of her people, and interest in what she's accomplishing is only going to grow."

Kent ate some pizza while she listened to Tig talk. Their legs were entwined together, and they had seemed to have quickly developed the habit of reaching out to casually touch each other every few seconds. As much as she enjoyed being physically close to Tig, she was loving the chance to learn more about her just by watching her talk. There was no sign of jealousy as she spoke about Ayari's bright future. Instead, she simply sounded fascinated by the prospects of the other professor's research, and happy to have a chance to help her fulfill that potential in their new department.

"I'm lecturing, aren't I?" Tig asked, with a sheepish grin. She picked up her piece of pizza and took a bite. "Thank you for being kind about it. My friends usually throw things at me to make me stop." She shrugged. "Of course, the main reason they want to shut me up is because they want the chance to lecture about their own subjects, and if I'm talking, they can't."

"I like it," Kent said. "I want to know all about you, and the university and what you do there are huge parts of who you are."

Tig balanced her plate on her knees, holding it in place with her right hand and draping her left across the back of the couch so her fingers barely brushed against Kent's neck. "I feel the same about you. So, you know my career goals, which are to study and teach classics and which haven't changed since I was ten. What about you? Do you like where you're at in your department? Or do you want to promote? Make it to chief?"

Kent groaned. "Not chief. Way too much paperwork." She sighed, leaning into Tig's touch. She loved hearing Tig talk about her job and her life, but she was less comfortable sharing parts of her own. She had let the habit of keeping herself closed off become too deeply ingrained, and even now, when she was sitting next to someone she was starting to truly care about, she was tempted to shut down. Give a shallow answer, or offer an expected, trite response. Not because she was afraid about Tig's response—that she'd mock her or think she was foolish—far from it, in fact. Clare was correct that Tig was single-minded in her personal and professional focus on classics, but at the same time she was one of the most generous people Kent knew when it came to supporting others and recognizing their talents in their own fields.

Rather, she was afraid for herself. If she offered too much of who she was to Tig, she'd be left with a hollow shell of herself when their relationship ended.

But that's what she had signed on for. If Tig stayed, they'd have built the foundation of something that overwhelmed Kent with the thought of how permanent and real it could be. If she left, then they'd have passed the point at which they could have ended without heartbreak. Kent had already passed it. Why stop now?

"I've stayed at this rank too long," she said, starting by admitting something she had barely acknowledged in her own mind. "I'm bored with it." She shrugged, and with the movement, she felt the gentle graze of Tig's fingernails along the side of her neck. She fought to recapture her train of thought. "It's been my choice, though. I've skipped opportunities for promotions because moving up would mean I'd move farther away from patrol and my officers. At least as sergeant, I'm still connected to the daily life of the campus police, and that's important to me. I've also stayed where I am because I haven't had any compelling reason to go higher in the department."

"But something's changed, hasn't it?" Tig asked. "That night at the station, after Chase's death, you were saying you were sometimes tempted to go back to patrol, but that's not what you're talking about now, is it? Have you found a reason to move up?"

"Exactly, yes," Kent said. She laughed. "I always tease you about being easy to read, but I never thought I was. You seem to be figuring me out."

"I want to learn all about you," Tig said. "And I always devote myself fully to my studies." She slid her hand to the back of Kent's neck, then leaned forward and kissed the place it had vacated, just under her ear. Kent gave a sharp intake of breath at the feel of Tig's warm lips, and the almost undetectable touch of her tongue.

Tig sat up again. "Keep talking," she said. "I didn't mean to distract you. Yet."

"If this is you *not* distracting me, I don't stand a chance in hell of resisting when you are."

"No, you don't," Tig agreed. "Now, go on. Talk."

Kent nodded, willing to do whatever Tig asked. "It's these two cases," she said. "The murders. I don't mean to sound callous, or like I'm enjoying this investigation, but there's been something… important about working to solve them. Working with Clare…I mean, Sawyer. Shit," Kent said, poking Tig in the arm. "Don't you dare tell her I called her by her first name. She'll think I like her."

Tig laughed. "I promise not to tell her, but she already knows. Hate to break it to you, but she likes you back. You need to get used to the idea that you have friends now."

"Anyway," Kent said, trying to hide her smile. "At first I thought I was just tired of the constant paperwork that comes with being a sergeant, and that I never should have left patrol in the first place. But something's been changing. Sawyer was part of it, because she came here with experience as a detective. Not as much experience as she wanted me to believe, but her instincts for the job more than make up for that, and she's been instrumental in keeping these investigations within our department instead of having them farmed out to Seattle PD.

"I have an idea for forming a squad, or task force, within our department," Kent continued, turning the half-formed ideas she'd been hoarding inside her head into a coherent plan as she spoke them out loud to Tig. "It would be made up of officers who get sent for specialized training in solving different types of crimes. Then, when something happens on campus, we'll have skilled people who can step into the role of detective as needed. We don't have enough call for this sort of thing to have dedicated detectives on staff, but we can have specialists who would assume those roles for the duration of an investigation, while still helping with patrol, like Sawyer has been doing. Not just with murders, but with other crimes, as well."

"You'd be a more self-sufficient department," Tig said. Her hand had been stroking Kent's neck, but it stilled as she considered Kent's suggestion. "I could see how hard it was for you and Clare when the Seattle officers came to Chase's house and took charge."

"We hated it," Kent said happily—not at the memory, but because if she could turn this dream into reality, she'd be doing something to change that type of experience rather than just having to accept it. "Plus it would help the officers who receive the training. They'd get experience in detective work, which would be helpful if they ever want to pursue that more fully in another department, and they'd probably be more likely to promote if they stayed with ours."

"So, if you promote, you'll be able to create something like this?"

"I'd have a better chance of making it happen," Kent said, not wanting to get too far ahead of herself. "But first I have to sit the next available test, which should be happening in December or January."

Tig stacked Kent's plate on top of hers and leaned forward to put both on the coffee table. "Sounds like you're going to be busy studying, then," she said as she moved one leg over Kent's thighs and straddled her lap. "If I'm going to distract you, maybe I should get to it now."

Kent moved her hands under Tig's T-shirt, holding her waist

and pulling the weight of Tig more solidly against her. "You can try," she said. "But I might not be ready to surrender."

"Oh, please," Tig said with a laugh. She resumed kissing Kent's neck, and this time Kent definitely felt Tig's tongue, and her teeth, against her sensitive skin. Tig pulled away ever so slightly, until Kent felt Tig's breath against her ear as she spoke. "You gave up resisting about ten minutes ago."

"Longer than that," Kent corrected, turning her head and capturing Tig's mouth with her own. She kissed her deeply, and what had been gentle play turned rapidly into something more urgent. Tig's tongue moved against hers, and the movement of her hips against Kent's became more insistent. Kent slid her hands up to cup Tig's breasts, teasing her until she was hard and moaning against Kent's lips.

Kent couldn't say exactly when she had stopped resisting what she and Tig had. She had been interested in her when they first met. Attracted to her, wanting her, needing her—those feelings had been growing more powerful as the past few days had gone by. But she knew the exact moment when attraction and need and interest were obliterated by the realization that she loved Tig. When the thrust of her hips and the heat of her drove them both to release, and she felt at once closer to Tig than she had ever been with anyone, and closer to having this love slip through her fingers and disappear.

She wrapped her arms around Tig's back, holding her close as they caught their breath. Tig burrowed her face between Kent's neck and shoulder, and one or both of them was trembling—Kent no longer could tell them apart.

"How can it be so wonderful and so sad at the same time?" Tig asked, her voice muffled against Kent's skin.

Kent didn't trust herself to answer, she knew her voice would give her away. Tig needed her to be close, but also to be strong. Not to make this time, when Tig's life was so uncertain, more difficult by having Kent profess her love and pitifully beg Tig to stay—which Kent would have been surprisingly willing to do if she thought it would change anything.

Instead of making a fool of herself by groveling, she vowed to herself to be what Tig needed her to be. She put her hands on Tig's hips and neatly flipped them to one side, shifting their bodies until Tig was lying lengthwise on the couch with Kent on top of her. Kent got the response she wanted when Tig laughed at the sudden move, then gasped when Kent slid her hand under the waistband of Tig's pants.

"Nice police move," Tig said, her voice catching when Kent's hand reached its wet and beautifully hot goal.

"Thank you," Kent said, pushing Tig's shirt up with her other hand, until her chest was bare and flickering golden in the light of the fire. "I've been preparing for this a long time. I knew all those bruises I got during training exercises would be worth it in the end.

"And if you think my strength is awe-inspiring," she continued with a laugh, inserting words in between kisses, starting at Tig's collarbone and working her way down. "You're going to be even more impressed by my stamina."

CHAPTER TWENTY-ONE

Tig woke in stages the next morning. The momentary confusion of waking up in a strange bed—with sheets that felt different against her bare skin, and a pillow that smelled woodsier than her own—was quickly eased when Kent shifted against her side. Then, memories of the night before pushed all other thoughts from her mind...

...until the unsolved murders and her uncertain fate at the university came barging unbidden into her head. She couldn't make them go away completely, but she could ignore them somewhat by not looking directly at where they lurked in the corner of her mind and focusing on Kent instead.

Kent was facing away from her, and Tig turned, reaching an arm around Kent and pulling her closer. She slid her thigh between Kent's and kissed her on the shoulder.

"Good morning," Kent said softly, lifting Tig's hand from where it rested on her stomach and kissing her palm. "Sleep well?"

"Very well. For about ten minutes." Tig laughed against Kent's shoulder. "You weren't kidding about the stamina."

Kent shifted to face her. "I'd never kid about something as important as that," she said with a grin. "Although you were more than my match in that category."

"I know," Tig said smugly. "Rather amazing considering that my main form of exercise is carrying books around. Of course, I have a lot of really heavy books."

Kent laughed, but it faded quickly into a sigh. "Why don't you cut class, and I'll call in sick to work, and we can stay here all day."

Despite her suggestion, she gave Tig a kiss on the mouth, and then sat up, stretching her back in a way that made Tig want to call Kent's bluff and cancel all her classes for the day.

"I have a good amount in savings," she said, abruptly bringing up a topic that had occurred to her during the night. She hadn't mentioned it then, partly because her mouth had been too busy to talk, but also in an attempt to keep the future as far from their night together as possible. How odd that the one time she was in a relationship that seemed loaded with potential to turn into something long-term, she desperately wanted to avoid discussing anything beyond the present moment.

But now, in the light of day, she had to bring it up.

Kent gave her a quizzical look. "Well, that's good, sweetheart. It's important to have savings."

Tig smiled. "Thank you, but I wasn't trying to impress you with my financial prowess. I meant that…well, if I do lose my job, I can take some time to find another one. I don't have to rush into anything, and maybe something closer to Washington, closer to you, would open up."

"No," Kent said quickly. She closed her eyes and took a deep breath before looking at Tig again. "I don't want you to go anywhere. You have to believe that. But I can't let you give up that much just to be with me."

She reached out and traced her fingertip along Tig's cheekbone. "You're the head of your department here, and I know it took a lot of effort to get to that position. If you have to start over at a new university, work your way back to the top again, then you won't want to waste a year or more sitting around here. You'd want to get started, to move forward, not to hang out where you'll have constant reminders of UW and your old life." Kent ran a hand through her hair. "Hell, *I'd* be a constant reminder of the U."

Tig hadn't thought of that. How comfortable would she be meeting Kent near campus for lunch? Or having dinner with her friends, when all of them were trying to skirt the topic of the university? It made up such a huge part of all their lives, and now she would be the outsider.

Her face must have given her away again, because Kent sighed and rested her forehead against Tig's. "Besides, when you say a closer position might open up, what do you mean by that? Seattle? Washington? The Northwest?"

"Maybe. Or California. But at least then it would be easier to see each other. Sometimes."

Kent pulled back a little, watching Tig's expression. "Is that something you'd want? A long-distance relationship?"

Tig wanted to say yes—anything to give them a chance, but she shook her head. "No. I want last night, every night." She smiled, and it only felt a little shaky. "Well, maybe with more sleep occasionally, but not often."

"That's what I want, too," Kent said. "If it were just for a year or two, then we could maybe make it work. But if you go to a new school and I promote, then we'd both be starting on new career paths. In two years' time, we'd be more entrenched in them, not less."

Tig knew Kent was right. She'd never get anywhere near her current position if she kept switching schools. And Kent had dreams of her own to fulfill with the campus police.

"Stay with me again tonight?" Kent asked.

Tig nodded. For now, that was as far ahead as they were able to plan. It wasn't enough, but it was all they had.

Tig was walking into her office after her last class of the day when her phone buzzed, and she pulled it out of her blazer pocket. Just the sight of Kent's name on the screen brought memories of their night together stampeding into her mind, and she was relieved to be able to shut the door and keep her suddenly flushed cheeks away from the public eye.

"Hey," she said when she answered.

"Good afternoon," Kent said, with decidedly less warmth in her voice.

Tig laughed. "Uh-oh, is your bestie Clare in the room with you?"

"I'm fine, thank you. The reason I'm calling—"

"Is it to chat about last night?" Tig interrupted. "Maybe the part where we were on your stairs, trying to make our way to the bedroom?"

"Hold on, Professor. Hey, Sawyer, get out," Kent said in her strident sergeant's voice. Tig heard a muffled reply in the background. "Stop that," Kent said to Tig when she came back on the line with Tig. "I'm calling on official police business."

She was still trying to sound stern, but now Tig could hear the laughter in her voice. "Okay, I'll behave," Tig said. "But not for long."

"I'll hold you to that. Right now, though, Sawyer and I are going to talk to Spencer Cassidy, and we thought you might want to come along."

"Yes, I'll come. Are you going to accuse him of cheating?" She definitely wanted to be part of that. Maybe they'd let her be the one to handcuff him, if it came to that.

"No. No accusations. We'll ask about his relationship with Davies, and see if we can learn anything more about why he was writing those papers. Just a casual conversation."

"I can be casual," Tig said. No problem. It was just a friendly chat with one of the people who might have sealed her doom at the university by being part of a cheating scandal. Nothing to be uptight about there at all.

Kent laughed. "Just don't *try* to be casual. We know how well that will work." She paused. "Look, I know this is a sore subject for you, and I understand if you're feeling angry toward him. If you'd rather not come…"

"I'll be fine. I'm just observing, right?"

"Right. So, we'll pick you up in the Denny parking lot in fifteen. And, hey. I've missed you today."

"Me, too. I'll see you soon," Tig said before ending the call.

She got out the paper Chase had written for Spencer—had allegedly, probably, maybe written, she reminded herself—and reread it. There was a chance she was wrong, that Spencer had written this himself, and Chase had kept a copy of this essay for perfectly legitimate reasons. But Luke had noticed the same similarities when he read the papers and research notes one after the other. Had she led him to that conclusion, though? Looking back, she wasn't sure.

She put the paper back in her desk drawer and hurried down the stairs and out to the parking lot, where Kent and Clare were already waiting for her. Clare had apparently lost the bid to drive yet again, and she got in the back seat so Tig could sit up front with Kent.

The urge to reach out for her, to give her a hello kiss, was stronger than she had expected. She managed what she hoped was a nonchalant greeting—although given Kent's apparent urge to laugh as she answered, Tig guessed that her attempt wasn't a success.

"Where does Spencer work?" she asked, turning the focus back to the job at hand to try to keep her mind off Kent.

"Vaughn and Keppery," Clare said from the back seat. "It's a law firm. He's a paralegal there, and he's in law school."

"That's a coincidence," Tig said. "Howie Keppery is one of our major donors, and he got his master's in Classical Studies, too."

"Maybe that's how they met," Kent suggested.

"Probably," Tig said. "Max always said that about his degree—that it opened doors for him. The local alums are an active group, so I suppose Spencer could have joined them as soon as he graduated."

She continued. "I looked up his records, by the way. He was an Adel Scholar. I should have remembered that, but if I didn't have those students in my classes, it was easy to forget which ones they were." She had files full of lists for each year—lists for everything from which students would be studying abroad to which ones were assigned to the various faculty advisors. Unless she had a chance to link those names to faces and personalities in her courses, they rarely stood out in her mind or were remembered for long. "He got decent grades," she said. "Nothing spectacular, but respectable."

Kent merged onto I-5, heading south toward Seattle's downtown. "The question is, how much those grades reflect his own work versus that of Davies. And why was Davies helping him and the others in the first place? We only have a small sampling of papers that he wrote, but there could be more on another flash drive, or others that he deleted."

Clare leaned forward from the back seat. "Maybe this will be one of those interviews where the person tells us everything we need to know and ties up all the loose ends, then we can have this case solved by lunchtime."

"Really?" Tig asked. "Does it ever happen like that?"

"Never," said Kent and Clare at the same time.

Kent parked the patrol car in a police-only zone in Belltown, and they walked the short distance from there to the building where the firm's offices were located. Eclectic stores and restaurants were packed tightly in the trendy, upscale neighborhood, and many of the second stories of those places were used as office space. Spencer's firm sat on top of a pet clothing store and a vegan bakery, taking up the entire second floor of the building.

Kent had obviously made an appointment to come here, because they didn't even have time to sit down and wait before the receptionist greeted them and asked them to follow him to Spencer's office. Tig wondered if they were trying to be extra accommodating for the police, or if they just didn't want people in uniform hanging out in their public reception area. The receptionist left them at the door and hurried to bring an extra chair to the office before disappearing again. Tig figured she was the unexpected guest, and wondered if Kent had purposefully not told them she'd be coming along, just to catch them off guard if possible.

Spencer came around his desk to greet them. He was a decent-looking man in his twenties with neat brown hair and a well-tailored navy suit. Tig had a feeling that if she ran into him with a group of similarly dressed men next week, she'd be hard pressed to identify which one he was. He blended. He seemed to be doing well with his life, though. His office was small, but having a private space that was bigger than a coat closet at one of Seattle's prestigious firms was quite an accomplishment for someone his age. She wondered if the firm was paying for law school, too, since he would likely remain with them once he graduated.

He shook hands with everyone, holding Tig's for a fraction longer than the others.

"Professor Weston, isn't it? It's a pleasure to finally meet you," he said before letting go of her hand. "Your reputation as a classics scholar is impressive, and I'm disappointed that I never had an opportunity to take one of your classes."

She smiled and thanked him but wasn't fooled. Her reputation was that she was fair, but students—especially at the graduate level—wouldn't make it through her courses unless they were willing to put in a lot of hard work. She was proud of that. If he had been trying to skate through his time at the U, he had been smart to avoid taking her courses.

"I assume you're here about the murders of Professors Davies and Morris," he said, getting directly to business as the four of them sat down. "Such a terrible tragedy. I took several classes from both of them, since my interests were in epic poetry and ancient history, and they will be sorely missed by everyone who knew them. I haven't seen either of them since graduating, though, so I'm not sure how I can help you today."

"How well did you know Professor Davies when you were at the university?" Kent asked. "Were you friends outside the classroom? Did he give you any advice or help as you progressed through the program?"

Spencer shook his head, his expression friendly, but not overly warm. "He interviewed me for the Adel Scholarship, but beyond that we were nothing more than teacher and student. Professor Morris was my advisor, and he helped me plan my schedule."

"Ah," Kent said. "I thought Professor Davies might have introduced you to Howard Keppery."

"No. We met at an alumni dinner. All the new graduates were invited, to give us a chance to meet the local group. Mr. Keppery and I share a love for history, and I was fortunate enough to be invited to interview with him and Ms. Vaughn."

Tig occupied herself with looking around the office while Clare and Kent asked questions that Spencer answered in unsurprising ways. For someone who loved classics and history as much as he professed, she didn't see any signs of either interest in this space, aside from the framed master's degree diploma hanging on the wall behind his desk. She was planning to take it when she left, if she could manage to distract the others somehow.

She knew that not everyone who appreciated classics had replicas from the Parthenon or photos of ruins in their offices, but she'd have expected some sign, especially with a recent graduate whose degree had opened a shiny golden door leading to a promising career. He had plenty of other pictures on the walls, of him skiing and hanging out with friends and family.

Clare must have been examining the photos, too, because when Kent paused in her interview, she pointed to one that Tig had noticed as well. It was of Max Adel and a clearly teenaged Spencer, posed smiling in front of a yellow and white private plane.

"You're friends with Adel?" she asked.

He only gave a hint of a frown as he looked over his shoulder at the picture before answering. "He and my father are business acquaintances, and I only met him that one time. He had flown down to Tacoma for the day to meet with my dad and some other local business owners. I was an undergrad at PLU at the time, a history major, and he encouraged me to apply for the scholarship when I graduated. Of course, I've seen him socially since I finished my degree, at the alumni get-togethers."

Pacific Lutheran University was a pricey private college in Tacoma. Tig wondered how much of Spencer's qualifications for the scholarship had been need-based and how much were based on his family connections to Adel.

Kent opened the folder she had been carrying and put the Cato essay on the desk in front of Spencer. "This is a paper you wrote for one of your classes. Do you recognize it?"

He frowned more deeply this time as he glanced at the first page. "Oh, yes. I believe this is mine, but it's been two years since I was in class. I don't remember the details, but I believe this was for Professor Rivers."

Kent nodded and took the paper back before he could read through it. "Interesting topic," she said. "Can you tell me how you came up with this idea?"

He laughed, although it sounded forced to Tig, and spread his hands in a helpless gesture. "To be honest, Sergeant, I don't think I can. Graduate school was such a busy time, with all my classes and homework. I was exhausted most of the time, and existing on cold pizza and very little sleep. If I could read through the paper, and maybe go through my notes I still have at home, it might jog my memory, but I can't recall off the top of my head."

"Oh, and I thought it might have to do with skiing," Tig interrupted with a laugh. She gestured at a photo of Spencer and his friends bundled in ski wear in front of a snowy backdrop. "Since it's obviously a hobby of yours."

She turned away from him to address Kent and Clare, who were staring at her like two people who had their interview dance carefully planned out, and who were surprised to suddenly have a third partner in the mix. Surprised, and not overly pleased.

"Spencer's paper is about Cato bringing the poet Ennius from Sardinia to Rome, and how difficult it is to separate actual history from the sometimes-altered versions given by historians and biographers," she said, then she shrugged. "It's just an interesting side note that Cato invented skiing on that trip."

She smiled at Spencer and gestured at Clare and Kent with her head. "Their expertise isn't in the field of classics, like ours. Not many people know about the origin of the sport."

He laughed, looking pleased at the answer she had given him. "Of course. That had slipped my mind, but now that you mention it, that's exactly why I picked this topic. Professor Rivers told us about it during one of his lectures, and the anecdote caught my attention. That's why I chose to write about that journey."

"Thank you, Mr. Cassidy," Kent said. "I appreciate you clearing that up. We don't want to take up more of your time, but I hope we can contact you in the future if we have further questions?"

"Absolutely. It's been a pleasure, officers, Professor Weston," he said as he stood up and opened the office door. As if transported by magic—or more likely because he had been standing outside waiting for them—the receptionist was there to escort them back to the lobby.

"What the hell was that?" Kent asked once they were in the stairwell. "Skiing? On the island of Sardinia?"

Clare was leaning against the wall laughing, having obviously held it in while they were in the office. "Maybe she meant water skiing?"

"Oh, that's right. Cato *didn't* invent skiing," Tig said, tapping her chin thoughtfully. "I was mistaken." She shrugged. "Oh, well, I was only off by about six thousand years and a few degrees of latitude."

"You're brilliant, Tig," Clare said. "I thought it was reasonable for him to say he couldn't remember how he got the idea for the paper, but then he pounced on the explanation you gave him."

Kent nodded, a smile tugging at her lips even though she kept her expression neutral. Tig was getting to know her well enough to recognize that she was pleased with Tig's contribution to the interview. "He should have stuck with his original *I can't recall* tactic instead of committing himself to the lie. He has a lot to learn in law school."

Tig smiled as they resumed their progress down the stairs. "Maybe Libby is on to something," she said. "This detective stuff is fun."

CHAPTER TWENTY-TWO

They got back in the patrol car, but Kent didn't put the key in the ignition right away. She turned so she was facing Tig, and Clare leaned forward from the back, resting her arm on the back of the passenger seat.

"Thoughts?" Kent asked.

"I think it's pretty clear that he didn't have any idea what was in that paper, or much of what was going on in class," Clare said. "But why bother with the degree, then?"

"Look where it got him," Kent said. "He's doing quite well for someone who recently graduated, plus he doesn't have any student loans. He probably wasn't lying about not remembering much of his two years at the U because he was most likely partying the entire time. It's not like he had to study. What I don't get, though, is how he made it through. Davies might have been writing his papers, but he couldn't sit in the classes and answer questions for him like a ventriloquist with his dummy."

"You'd be amazed at the ways you can either adapt or cheat the system," Clare said. "No one knew I was dyslexic until college, and it still might have gone unnoticed if I hadn't asked for help. I figured out tricks to help me through, and I carefully chose my classes based on which teachers didn't require lots of reading, that sort of thing."

Tig nodded. "When teachers cover the same topics year after year, they can get very predictable if they're not careful. Test questions might be repeated, and class structure can be routine. It's different, too, when we're talking about Classical Studies, which will cover art, history, and literature with everything in translation, as opposed to Greek or Latin language courses where there's usually more oral work done in class."

She laughed. "Although, there are ways to work around that, too. I had one class in grad school where the professor assigned massive amounts of Homer every night. Bear in mind, I had a heavy load of classes that term, as well as working on my thesis, so I was stressed and overworked. But every class, he'd ask for volunteers, then start calling on people to translate, so I'd make sure I knew just the first couple of paragraphs perfectly, then I'd volunteer to go first. Don't look at me like that," she said, shoving Kent playfully in the arm. "I'd spend the remainder of class finishing the assignment, and I learned a lot about how *not* to teach from him. I have an algorithm for calling on students to read which ensures that I get to everyone, but it seems random to the students." She smiled at Clare. "When I told Libby I did that, she insisted on sitting in on the class to try to figure out my pattern. Took her less than two days."

Kent shook her head. "I'm not sure why I keep fighting her on becoming a cop. This might be the career for her."

Tig laughed at the expression on Clare's face. "Don't worry, Clare. I doubt she'd truly want to give up her old buildings for a life of fighting crime.

"Anyway," she continued. "Spencer probably read enough to be able to keep up somewhat in class, or he was coached by Chase. Luke told me he was very shy, so he cut him some slack as far as class participation went. That might have happened in other classes, too. Plus, if he took every course Chase and Kam had to offer, he could have gotten good grades in them without even showing up or turning anything in."

"Shy?" Kent snorted. "He seems to have recovered from his reclusive ways. He didn't have any trouble communicating with us, and he hasn't exactly picked a great career for someone who's afraid of public speaking."

"What made Luke think he was shy, anyway?" Clare asked.

Tig shrugged, thinking back to their conversation. "He didn't say. He was rather furious at the time. It's not easy for a teacher to find out they've been played. It's a betrayal. I can call him now and ask if you want."

Kent nodded, and Tig got out her phone and dialed Luke's number.

"Hey, Lukas," she said. "You're on speaker with the police, so be careful what you say."

He laughed, his voice sounding tinny through her old phone's speaker. "Then I guess you wouldn't want me to tell the story about how you...um...*acquired* that bust of Homer you have on your desk, right?"

Tig shrieked, then laughed and waved vaguely at Kent. "He's just teasing. He has a weird sense of humor."

"Mm-hmm," Kent said, writing something in her ever-present notebook. "I'm kind of busy at the moment, but as soon as we wrap up the murder investigation, I'll look into this."

Tig grabbed the notebook and tossed it to Clare. "Burn that for me, will you?" she whispered before raising her voice again. Clare the Traitor handed the notebook back to Kent.

"Luke, you told me Spencer wasn't very outspoken in class. Did you notice just from his behavior, or did he talk to you about it?

"Neither," Luke said. "Chase told me at the beginning of the quarter. Apparently, he'd been through some tough shit when he was a child, and he had some residual PTSD. Chase said they found this out while going through his application for the scholarship, but they obviously weren't going to make it public since...Hey! That fucking liar."

"Sorry, Luke," Tig said with a sigh. "I didn't mean to dredge this up again, but we needed to know. I'll call you soon and explain, okay?"

She ended the call, and Kent started the car.

"Judging by those photos, poverty wasn't one of the childhood traumas he faced," she said, looking over her shoulder before changing lanes. "So, Davies picked Spencer for the scholarship, possibly because of his connections to Max Adel, and then helped him get his degree," Kent said as she pulled out onto the road.

"He was writing Spencer's papers, and Morris was handing out good grades," Clare continued. "They were also directing him toward classes where he'd have a better chance of getting through with minimum work, and spreading misinformation about him to professors like Lukas."

Tig nodded. In theory, every student should be graded equally, but she would have done the same thing Lukas had done. She made accommodations where she could, where there was truly a need, because the traditional school system didn't always take into account specific students and the challenges they faced. But being flexible and making occasional allowances required trust—trust in the student and in whoever shared the personal information. Trust that Chase had broken.

"Were these students more blackmail victims?" Kent mused. "If they owed their degrees—and therefore their jobs—to Chase, he might have demanded regular payments once they graduated and were bringing in paychecks."

"Invest a few hours in essay writing and reap the reward for years after," Clare added. "He kept all the evidence, so it would have been easy to threaten them with exposure. They'd lose their jobs, disgrace their families, and possibly face criminal charges for getting fraudulent degrees."

"Until maybe someone got tired of paying and living under Chase's thumb," Kent finished.

"Although exposing them would have gotten him in the same trouble," Tig reminded them, almost reluctant to break into the conversation while the two of them were bouncing ideas off each other. They made a good team, and she could tell that Kent was just as excited when Clare made a smart observation as when she herself did.

She continued. "Maybe he had some way of pinning this on Kam or the students themselves if one of them decided to tell the truth, by accusing them of stealing the papers or something, but I haven't seen any sign that he had been prepared for anyone but himself to look guilty if one of the students went public with this."

"People can be arrogant," Kent said. "He might have figured he could get away with it indefinitely, or maybe they had specific time frames and once they finished paying their dues, they were free."

"So, you think one of them decided to kill him instead of paying?" Tig asked, still finding it hard to believe that Chase had his own personal version of student loans operating in her department. Well, maybe not *hard* to believe. *Exceedingly aggravating* to believe, perhaps. "What about Kam, then? I guess he knew too much, if he was involved in the scheme."

"Or he could have tried to take over where Chase left off," Clare suggested. "But the killer wasn't going to pay him, either."

Tig thought back to Kam's shaky demeanor when he accosted her in the hall. "I don't know. He looked like he was about to have a breakdown just after Chase died. He didn't seem prepared to head a black-market scholarship program."

"Well, it's the best lead we've gotten so far, so let's run with it." Kent merged onto the freeway, heading back to campus, before glancing at Tig. "I'll check into young Spencer's alibis. Tig, you said before that you could get a list of the scholarship recipients. Let's see if the other papers from that drive belong to them, or if we're dealing with random students that Davies was *helping*. One of them might be our killer."

"I can do that," Tig said. "It's not much more than a dozen since Max started the endowment. Do you want me to ask other professors about the papers, then? See which students turned them in?"

Kent shook her head. "Not yet. But if we know the students and the classes they took, we should be able to compare that with the list of courses and years you gave us earlier."

"Ooh...smart," Tig said with a grin. Kent turned her head and gave Tig a quick smile.

"Stop it, you two," Clare said with a groan from the back seat. "Or you might have to pull over so I can be sick."

"All I did was smile at her," Kent said, giving Clare an unconvincing glare in the rearview mirror.

"I know," Clare said. "It's just wrong. It's destroying my image of you as a hard-ass sergeant who'd sooner fire me than give me the time of day."

"I don't know," Kent said with a shrug as she turned on her blinker for the exit to the U. "I'm perfectly capable of firing you and smiling at Tig at the same time. In fact, the firing part would make me smile even bigger. It might even coax a little giggle out of me."

Clare pretended to faint.

Tig watched their antics as they drove back to Denny. She had to admit that after this morning, when Kent had gently dissuaded her from using her savings to delay looking for a new job, she had been wondering if Kent might be convinced to leave *her* job and follow Tig. It seemed to be another option for them to explore. She was sure Kent could easily find another campus security job, or maybe switch to a different type of department where she might have more opportunities to advance as a detective. She had even thought about how she might phrase the suggestion when they were back at Kent's house tonight.

But watching her with Clare today had made her rethink the idea. Not that she wanted Kent with her any less, but because Kent was fitting in here in a new way. She and Clare seemed to have an intuitive sense of how to work together, like during the interview when Kent had peppered Spencer with questions he was easily able to bunt back at her, then she had paused and let Clare come in with one that took him off guard. They had switched roles and used the same tactic right before Kent brought out the essay.

They were both damned good at what they did, and they seemed to bring out the best in each other. Their bond would probably continue to grow, especially as Clare advanced in the department, putting them on more equal footing.

Kent had a good friend in Clare, even though they had to be respectful of their working relationship right now. Tig couldn't ask Kent to give up this partnership, or the friendships she was slowly forming with Libby and the others. All Tig would have to offer would be a new, strange city, and long hours apart as Tig struggled to get her own career back on track after such a major setback. This was Kent's home, and Tig would be selfish to ask her to give it up.

❖

The three of them headed back to Tig's office, where Kent and Clare pored over Kent's notebook and carried on a quiet conversation while Tig compiled her lists.

The first thing she did after printing the list of Adel Scholars was follow a hunch and send an email to a friend at the alumni association, asking for information on their current whereabouts. Then she accessed their degree requests, the formal applications for graduating that they made to the department when they were nearing completion of their degrees, which included the courses they had taken. After that, it was as easy as Kent had made it sound to match her new list to the one she had made after finding Chase's essays.

When she finished, she printed her final pages and laid them out on her desk so Clare and Kent could read them.

"So, here are the scholarship winners," she said, pointing at the first one. "Fourteen of them over the past six years that we've offered it. Four of them were in my classes, which didn't have papers written by Chase associated with them. The other ten took a disproportionate number of classes from Chase and Kam, plus they were in classes that overlap with the list I made before. None of the papers we found were for courses other than ones that had an Adel Scholar in them."

Clare shook her head. "So, he was choosing the recipients, then making sure they did well."

"Worse," Tig said. "He wasn't just padding their grades. He was doing the work for them. He was giving out degrees for nothing. I'm assuming the four who took my classes were legitimate recipients. He probably chose a few who actually deserved the award to make it look less obvious that he was cherry-picking the rest."

She felt justifiably proud of that, too. Chase must have known she would catch on to what he was doing if he let his favored ones take her classes.

"Oh, sweetheart," Kent said, looking at the list of her four.

Tig was surprised at the endearment—not because Kent hadn't

used it before, but because she didn't even seem embarrassed that she was saying it now, in front of Clare.

"Yes?" she asked suspiciously, drawing the word out because she really didn't want to hear what Kent was going to say next.

Kent set the list down and tapped one of the names. "Jessica Bower. She took your Ancient Theater course last spring."

"Yes, I remember her," Tig said. She had been a quiet girl but had seemed to adore Tig and enjoy the class. Her coursework had been mediocre during the term, but she had aced her final, proving to Tig that she had really absorbed the lessons during—

"Fuck," Tig said, as the memory of the Oedipus Rex file on Chase's thumb drive flashed back into her mind. Now she really wanted to smash something. "A kind of shy student who didn't contribute much, but managed to turn in a brilliant exam, thanks to the questions I willingly gave that bastard."

She rubbed her hands over her eyes, then pushed them angrily through her hair. "I've been so smug, feeling sorry for Luke because the poor guy had been fooled by Chase's essays and lies, and here I was doing the exact same thing."

"But he only let four take a class from you," Clare pointed out, kindly trying to make her feel better, even though it obviously wasn't going to work. "And we only know about one of yours getting help. The other three might have been exceptional scholars on their own. Like you said, legitimate recipients."

Tig shook her head with a rueful laugh. "It's humiliating."

"No," Kent interjected, using her sergeant's voice. "You will not feel sorry for yourself about this. You've been the one to figure out most of what we know in this investigation. You might have been tricked, but you have been instrumental in getting us where we are right now. You've understood clues that Sawyer and I wouldn't even have recognized as meaningful. The vases, the papers. Now, let's figure out what's going on. Why Davies was doing this in the first place."

Tig appreciated Kent's words, but she wanted to wallow some more, to protest that she had no clue how Chase could have managed to mastermind this scheme on his own. Or why he would have risked so much for a portion of a paycheck, even if it was a healthy one for a recent graduate—

"Oh," she said. *"The vases, the papers…* What if the vases were his payment?"

"How?" Kent asked, leaning toward her. "Did he get money from their parents to help the kids through, then use it to buy them? How was he managing to import stolen…Oh, shit. Adel?"

The man with money, connections at multiple ports around the world, and expansive pride in the way his degree had opened doors for him and launched his career. Tig nodded as she opened her email account and searched her inbox, running over past conversations in her mind. "Port of Tyre. That's where you said the vases were being funneled out of the country." She opened an email, then backed up and looked at the ones surrounding it. She was starting to get a headache as ideas popped into her mind with alarming rapidity.

She opened the email from Max again. "When I first wrote to him and told him we were seriously considering switching to the Mediterranean Studies program, he sent this. He said he'd talk to me when he got back into the country because he was on a business trip to Lebanon. That's where Tyre is. Then only two days later, I got an email from Chase saying he wanted to formally register his opposition to Med Studies. He hadn't seemed particularly concerned either way before that, but after, he became sort of the leader of the faction that wanted us to remain purely focused on Greek and Roman studies."

Clare exhaled with a huff. "So, Davies was organizing this scholarship in exchange for the expensive ancient artifacts, doing favors for Max's friends by helping their underachieving kids get this degree, and then…what, Max asks him to oppose the transition? I thought Adel supported you, Tig."

"In show, he did," Kent added. "But maybe not in his heart. This way, he could continue to look open minded and like he was on the side of inclusivity and change, while Davies did the dirty work of fighting against the inclusion of these overlooked and marginalized cultures."

Tig nodded. "That was part of Max's spiel every time he talked about his degree or the scholarship. What a proud place the Classics Department held at the university as a historically significant part of academia. How much the degree meant to him because of what it signified to other people about his traditional values and dedication to the pursuit of knowledge. Med Studies is meant to be relevant, to challenge preconceived ideas that certain cultures are more important or worthwhile than others just because history tells us that's how it should be."

She shook her head, wondering why it hadn't struck her as odd that the same man who always talked about the proud history of Classical Studies would also be supportive of significant changes to it. Maybe it was because she had been the same way—loving the way the department had always been, but reluctantly moving forward because it was the right and important thing to do. She had lived with that paradox and had been sympathetic when she saw others doing the same.

"He cared about the degree itself," she said sadly, "and not what he was actually learning along the way, which is the opposite of how it should be—and it's the opposite of the ideals he claims to value so dearly."

Kent nodded. "And when Davies failed, and the department transition was confirmed, the degree didn't mean as much to him, so why go through the expense and effort of offering it as a special favor anymore?"

"So, Davies becomes a liability," Clare added. "And without him holding Morris in line, what's to keep him from blabbing?"

Tig thought back to Kam's frantic conversations with her. She hadn't recognized the hints, then, but she could understand them now. "He wanted to tell me. I think he would have if he hadn't been killed, too."

She sighed and continued. "I asked a friend to send me a list of the current jobs the Adel Scholars hold. I'd be willing to bet we find that most of them are working with other alums, maybe even Max himself. And they probably have better job opportunities than most graduates can expect."

"So, how do we catch him?" Clare asked.

Tig shrugged. "We offer to give him back his degree, along with a professor who really needs his help and will likely do whatever she needs to in order to keep her job." She looked at Kent, who glared back and shook her head firmly.

"We offer him me," Tig finished.

Chapter Twenty-three

Kent somehow managed to compartmentalize her life for the evening. Tig's suggestion that she offer herself to Adel as a Davies substitute—and the subsequent, foolhardy plan she and Clare hatched—well, those belonged to her work life. Sergeant Kent would deal with them the next day, when she would be comfortably in uniform and prepared to ignore everyone's entreaties as she utterly rejected the idea of Tig going to a bar to meet with a potential cold-blooded killer. Tonight, she would just be Kent, deliriously happy to spend the evening with her girlfriend, and without a care in the world.

No cares, except for the fact that said girlfriend was likely moving across the country soon, and that she was currently planning on an ill-conceived rendezvous with a murderer, and that Kent wasn't sure she really had the power to stop Tig from doing anything she set her mind to.

Okay, maybe she wasn't compartmentalizing as well as she thought. Still, she was managing not to discuss the topic—aided by Tig, who seemed to have the same goal of not discussing murder cases or sting operations outside of regular working hours.

Kent was glad when Tig suggested they stay at her house for the night. A new environment with rooms to explore would help keep Kent's mind occupied and off the prospect of tomorrow's battles. And any opportunity to learn more about Tig was welcome. Kent didn't really need more evidence to prove to herself how devastated she was going to be if Tig walked out of her life, but she was prepared to find more when she saw Tig's home. Everything about her was special, and the more Kent learned about her, the more she found to admire and respect.

And love. But that emotion was going in its own special compartment because it had no place in their temporary relationship.

She followed Tig's directions and parked in front of a small Craftsman style home, painted cobalt blue in a neighborhood full of brightly colored houses. Willow branches draped over Tig's porch, and massive rhododendrons lined the borders between her and her neighbors. The yard would be a riot of color in the spring, and for a moment, Kent found herself longing to see it in that season. She certainly wasn't going to drive by if Tig was gone, just to see the flowers, and the hope that Tig might still be there, ready to give her a tour of her gardens, filled her with a sharp pang of hope. She shook it off and followed Tig into the house.

"Oh, it's beautiful," she said, pausing on the threshold and looking around. When Tig told her that her home was basically an extension of her office, Kent had pictured it in browns and dark cherry wood, with books piled everywhere and photos covering every wall. The reality was much brighter and tidier than she had been expecting, and much more colorful. She stepped farther into the room and examined one of the mosaics on the wall, this one of an owl with a Greek key design around it.

"This is gorgeous," she said, running her fingertips lightly over the tiny glass tiles. They were stuck directly onto the wall and not on a canvas or other surface, as she'd first thought. "Did you make this?"

"I did," Tig said, coming to stand next to Kent. "It's a hobby of mine, ever since I was a little girl. I recreate Greek and Roman mosaics. It's a good thing I own my home now, because I've never gotten a security deposit back in my life."

Kent smiled, sliding her arm around Tig and pulling her close until Tig's back was pressed against her chest. "So, you have to leave them behind every time you move?"

"I do, but I know it when I make them. It's sad, but I leave them for others to enjoy and I make more of my own."

"You're amazing," Kent said. "It's lovely work." Tig sighed in her arms, sinking closer against her. Kent loved the way Tig's body moved against hers, and she had no doubt the feeling was mutual, but she thought she knew why Tig had wanted her to come here tonight. Tig was immersed in the world of classics, from her job to her hobbies, to her home and family. Kent thought this might be Tig's way of reminding her about that—that she would follow her career because that's where her soul would lead her. She might have built something here with Kent, but she'd willingly say goodbye when it was time for her to go.

Kent understood. She had known from the beginning that Tig would follow her heart, and her heart was devoted to the world of classics more than to any one person. But that was just another thing for her future self to deal with. Right now, Tig was in her arms. She bent her head and kissed the top of Tig's shoulder before dragging her tongue lightly up the column of her neck. Each small bit along the way earned her a soft moan from Tig, and the sound of her obvious pleasure in Kent's touch was more arousing than anything Kent had ever heard before.

She gently pushed forward until Tig's body was pressed between her and the wall in front of them. Every breath Tig took echoed through Kent's breasts and hips, her entire body, until it took every effort to keep from gasping the words *I love you*. That wasn't what Tig wanted or needed, and Kent had to remember that even as her thoughts became less coherent and more wrapped up in the sensations she was experiencing. Tomorrow she'd have hell to pay, as she moved one step closer to watching Tig go, but tonight? Tonight, they could pretend nothing existed beyond this small pocket of time.

Tig bit her lip as Kent rocked against her. She felt Kent's nipples hard against her back, and her own breasts were pressed against the wall, so they were sensitive to every shift in their bodies. Kent's hand traveled from her hip across her stomach, and Tig moved her hips a little away from the wall, nestling her ass closer against Kent in order to give her room to unbutton Tig's slacks and delve between her legs. She gasped and arched her back as Kent's fingers slid deeper, gently exploring inside her and moving through slick wetness. Kent seemed to sense when she had had enough of *slow*, and her touch became more insistent, driving against Tig with an irresistible rhythm until she came, crying out as her body shuddered against Kent's.

Tig slowly caught her breath, grateful that Kent kept a firm hold on her while she did, or she might have slid down to the floor on legs too weak to hold her up. Eventually she turned around and put her arms around Kent's neck.

"So, this is the living room," she said, continuing on as if the tour of her house hadn't stalled on the edge of the foyer.

"I'm a fan," Kent said with a laugh. "The other rooms have a lot to live up to."

"Don't worry," Tig said, starting to button her pants again, and then changing her mind and letting them slip down her legs and onto the floor. "I'm sure the rest of the house won't disappoint. Especially the bedroom."

Kent stepped away but kept hold of Tig's hand as they wandered slowly through the rest of the house. Tig pointed out the occasional item or photograph, but her mind was distracted. She had meant the house to be a message to Kent—well, to both of them. A reminder that she was a classics professor at heart, and she had been since before she graduated from high school and went on to earn her degrees. Her job was as ingrained in her as her personality or her hair color. No matter how intricate the life she had built in Seattle— with her home and her friends and her position on campus—she was devoted to her calling above all else and would leave everything else behind if she needed to. She had expected Kent to come into her home and seem out of place. A wonderful visitor to have, but not a permanent fixture, and definitely not a tether to keep Tig here even if she lost her job.

Instead, Kent had walked in and looked immediately at home. She fit—and not just in the space, but in Tig's life. She wasn't displacing classics in Tig's heart, but she had definitely nudged the subject aside enough to make room there for herself.

Tig wasn't sure how she was going to handle this. She had been prepared to feel sad about leaving Kent if she had to move, but she hadn't expected to feel as if she was leaving a part of herself behind.

They finally made it to the bedroom and undressed in silence, climbing into Tig's bed and reaching for each other with the sort of desperation that let Tig know she wasn't the only one feeling the weight of their uncertain future. She felt something else, too, as an undercurrent to their passion, and again when they lay in each other's arms and talked quietly through the night about nothing in particular.

It was something unexpected. Something ill-timed and potentially heartbreaking. It was love—and Tig was powerless to stop it.

CHAPTER TWENTY-FOUR

I'm not letting you do this," Kent said, pacing back and forth in the small space behind her desk. Four goddamned steps each way. That wasn't nearly enough to work off her anger. She had managed to tamp down every feeling except for love and passion last night, but in the light of day—and while Clare was off preparing her fucking wires and recording devices—passion gave way to fear and worry and anger.

Tig sat calmly in the chair on the opposite side of her desk, watching her progress as she nearly bumped into the wall on one of her passes, wanting to break it down with her fists so she had more space to move.

She wasn't angry at Tig. Well, maybe she was, a little. Tig had no right to willingly put herself in danger, especially not since Kent was coming to care so much about her.

Mostly, though, she was worried. If Max Adel had coldly killed those two men because they were no longer of use to him, and because they knew the truth about who he was, then what would stop him from taking Tig out of the way? If he at all suspected she was being disingenuous, why would he hesitate before harming her? He wouldn't. Kent knew that with every instinct she had developed as a cop and as a person. Someone who had killed like she suspected Max had wouldn't think twice about sending Tig off the same way.

"We'll find another way," she said, turning to go the other direction again.

Tig stood up and came over to her, pushing her gently into her chair.

"You're making me dizzy," she said. "Look, Kent, this will work. Clare agrees, and you know she wouldn't let me do this if she didn't. Libby would kill her."

Kent refused to get sidetracked into her usual response that Libby had nothing to do with police business and shouldn't be used in an argument of this sort. She had a feeling Tig had thrown her name into the conversation like tossing a piece of distracting steak to a ferocious guard dog. Guard dogs were trained to ignore such tactics, and so was Kent.

"I'm not letting you do this," Kent repeated. She held up a hand to stop Tig, who looked ready to protest again. "And yes, in this case I *can* tell you what you can and can't do because it's a police matter and I outrank you and Clare and Libby. In all other aspects of your life, you are a free human being who is able to make her own choices. Not here."

Tig perched on the edge of her desk, facing Kent and with their legs touching. "I'll be in a busy, public bar, with you and Clare just outside, listening to us the whole time. I won't leave there without you, no matter what he says. But I'm the only one who can get him to admit what he's done. I'm the only one who would be able to keep Chase's scheme going, and who is desperate enough to make it believable."

Kent looked away as Tig spoke, but she couldn't keep from resting one hand on Tig's leg. Her plan was actually a good one, and if it had been any other person suggesting it besides Tig, she might have gone along with the idea. Have Ayari approach Adel and tell him—in strictest confidence, of course—that she had insider information that the Med Studies program was going to be shut down. There were too many issues facing the Classics Department, so having this transition piled on top was unwise. The university wanted to focus on getting one of its cornerstone degrees back on track.

"He'll never believe Ayari," she said, continuing to dissect the plan, but out loud now. "All those new professors, with their contracts and courses. He'll know the university won't just be able to ignore them."

"They'll still come to teach, but they'll be shunted into different departments. Languages, history, comparative lit. They'll be minor players in a bunch of departments instead of a significant part of the new one, but their contracts will still be honored."

Damn. Tig was making this shit up, but she sounded convincing even to Kent, who knew the whole thing was a lie.

"But I'm worried," Tig continued, her voice soft. "I might lose my job if they decide to make me the scapegoat in all this. And I'm desperate to keep it. I'd do anything to stay. Has he heard anything? Does he have any advice for what I can do?"

Kent raised her head and looked at Tig. She had spoken in a scared voice, perfectly matched to the words she was saying.

"How did you get so good at that? I've always been able to read you well, but your acting skills have improved overnight."

Tig cupped her cheek. "I'm not acting. I really am desperate to stay, because of you. I wouldn't compromise my career and my ethics to do so, like Chase did for the vases, and the parts about the department are false, but as long as I concentrate on what's true, on us, I'll be able to make him believe me."

"And you really think he'll make you the same offer he made Davies?"

"Yes. It's about control, and his identity. Bragging about the degree, dangling it in front of parents, magnanimously introducing new grads to powerful people. If we're correct about what's been going on? Then, yes, I believe he'll be more than willing to take advantage of my position and use me, as well."

"And if we're not correct?"

Tig shrugged. "Then he's not a killer, and I leave the bar. And then we keep looking for the truth."

Kent rested her forehead on Tig's legs, and she felt Tig's hand settle on the back of her head, gently playing with her hair.

"I don't want you to do this."

"I know," Tig said. "But you're going to let me, aren't you?"

Someone knocked on the door before Kent could answer, and then Clare popped her head in the room. Kent sat up—not even trying to hide the fact that she had been leaning her head in Tig's lap—and Tig pushed herself into an upright position.

"Ayari's here," Clare said, with no teasing or playfulness in her voice. She understood, probably more than anyone here, what Kent was going through.

"What should I tell her?" she asked.

Kent sighed and nodded her head, staring at the desk and not making eye contact with either of them.

❖

The next two hours were painful for Kent, made even more so because she was peripheral to the action. Clare stepped in as the leader of this little sting operation she and Tig had fleshed out after Tig gave them the initial idea. She went over the script with Ayari and led her through the call she eventually made to Adel. She coached Tig about what to say to Max and how to set up the meeting without sounding like she was up to something suspicious, and she monitored that call, too. She organized the cops who would be stationed in and around the bar. And then she fitted Tig with a wire and explained how to use it.

Kent knew Clare wasn't taking over because Kent wasn't capable of doing these things herself, but instead because she was worried Kent might change her mind and pull the plug on the operation at any moment—most likely when Adel was on the line and would be spooked.

She was tempted to do exactly that, but she had to admire the way the plan came together in such a short time. She listened in on the calls, and Ayari sounded genuinely pissed about the fucking university and its imbecilic new plan for her and the other new professors. In her own call, Tig sounded lost and a little helpless, and Kent hated knowing, based on their conversation in her office, that some of those feelings were genuine because of her—because Tig might really have to leave her.

As the time of the meeting neared, the other officers got in their positions, and Clare was about to sneak Tig out the back of the station, in case Max was anywhere near, so that she wouldn't be seen leaving the campus police headquarters and moseying to the bar like someone who was probably wired to the gills. Really, the worst that could happen was that Adel wouldn't bite, and they wouldn't get any information from him.

And the even-worse-than-that worst was that he'd get suspicious and casually shoot Tig in the middle of a crowded university bar.

Either one of those would fit with what she thought she knew of the man.

Tig's phone chimed, and she checked the screen. "Oh, it's Marie from the alumni association." She looked at Kent. "I asked her to get the current jobs for the Adel Scholars. She's on her way to my office with it now. She said it has something interesting I need to see. I'll bet it's that some of them are working for him now."

"Go," Clare said to Kent. "You have time to grab it, and then get to the bar."

"I'm not—"

Clare held up a hand to stop her. "You'll try to steal Tig away at the last minute. Or you'll run into the bar and karate chop Adel just because he says hello the wrong way. Please, work off some of that nervous energy by running to Denny and back. You're stressing Tig out with all the pacing you're doing."

"I haven't been pacing," Kent protested. She felt as if she'd been standing absolutely, helplessly still for the past hour.

"Yes, you have," said Tig and Clare in unison.

Kent gave Tig a kiss and as hard a hug as she dared with her wires.

"Don't you dare leave her alone," she said to Clare, in as threatening a voice as she could manage, which just sounded scared to her own ears.

"I won't. Not for one second," Clare promised.

Kent pulled herself away from them and jogged to Denny, relishing the physical activity even as she felt her stress increase with every step she took away from Tig. Most of Kent's department was there with her. She would be safe with them. She had to be.

She unlocked Tig's office and stepped inside, hoping she wouldn't have to wait long for this Marie person to arrive. She turned on the light and realized that she wasn't going to have to wait at all.

And that she probably should have worried a little more about herself, trotting across campus on her own, than Tig, who had all her back-up with her.

"Hello, Sergeant," Max said. He was sitting in Tig's chair with his legs crossed and his hands quietly clasped on his lap, wearing a long black coat over his suit, and black driving gloves. She was pretty sure he had a hearse parked out front.

Of all the things Kent should be concerned about right now, the fact that he had usurped Tig's chair should have been far down the list, bordering on insignificant. For some reason, though, it made her want to launch at him with a battle cry and take him down.

"You're armed, I'm not, Sergeant," he said, spreading his hands wide before clasping them together once more. "I'm not a threat to you right now." His laugh was shriller than it should be, considering the normal register of his voice, and it gave her the creeps. "Not a physical one, at least."

He indicated the chair across from him. "Please, sit. I'd like to talk about Antigone."

"The play?" she asked, refusing to move. "I'm afraid I don't have a degree like yours, so it'll have to be a one-sided conversation. Or wait...did you do your own work, or have someone do it for you?"

"Very amusing. Yes, I wrote all my own papers. No one cared about them once I graduated, but they loved the degree. It's a powerful one, when used correctly. But, no, much as I enjoy discussing Sophocles, I'm speaking of our mutual friend, Professor Weston."

Kent warily moved to the chair and sat, leaving the door open behind her. He smiled at that. "You're not a prisoner, Sergeant. You are free to leave at any time, although I'm sure you will want to hear what I have to say."

"I doubt it," she said, a cut of anger in her voice.

He reached forward and picked up a sheet of paper from the desk. "I believe you came rushing over for this." He handed it to her. "Go ahead, read it. I'm sure there's nothing there that will surprise you. Marie called to ask a question about one of the scholars, and let it slip that Tig had asked for this, so I offered to deliver it for her. I also got an interesting call from Spencer Cassidy today, telling me about your little visit with him. It wasn't difficult to put two and two together and realize that you had found out what Chase Davies has been up to."

"The email came from you, then, not from Marie," Kent said.

He nodded at Tig's laptop. "She really needs to make less predictable passwords."

"What were you planning to do to her when she got here?" she asked through gritted teeth. Kill her, most likely, although that wouldn't have undone what they had already learned about him.

"Ah, Sergeant, this is where I know more than you do. It's a delicious feeling, to best the cops. You see, while you have been investigating me because you want to charge me with murder, your girlfriend has another goal entirely. I know that she has other plans this evening, because they were with me, and I assumed she would send you here in her place."

"You wanted *me* to be here?" Kent asked, confused. He might try to shoot her, but she had a gun, too, and she wasn't half bad at using it.

"She was coming to meet me," Max continued. "She wants to take Chase Davies's place, in exchange for my help keeping her job."

That was the story Tig had given. Kent tried to get her mind to catch up to what was really going on. He had believed Ayari and Tig, just as they had hoped he would. He'd just deviated from the reaction they'd expected from him. "So you want to kill me?"

"How vulgar. No. I merely want to tell you what's going to

happen now. I'm going to give Tig exactly what she's asked for. My help. She is going to continue the good work I've been doing with my scholarships, helping young people succeed in life and keeping the beauty of this degree intact. We're going to save the department together."

"And me? Where do I fit in?"

"You're going to let her, if you want her to stay safe. Drop this investigation, or else take it in a new, dead-end direction. Don't interfere with what she and I are doing. And if you do as I say, you'll live a long and happy life together. That is what you want, isn't it?"

Yes, it was. But on their own terms, not his. She'd buy Tig a plane ticket to Boston before she'd let this man blackmail either one of them. "Actually, what I want is to arrest you. Tig has no intention of doing your dirty work and selling degrees. And I wouldn't compromise her by siding with you. This department, even her job—they aren't worth it."

She reached for her gun as she stood up, but before she could raise her weapon, the chair kicked out from under her, sending her backward onto the floor. Her head cracked painfully on the ground as the gun spun from her hand and slid across the floor, coming to rest out of reach against Tig's bookshelf.

He jumped on her, pinning her down with his hips and one hand on her throat as he stretched the other toward her gun, and she realized he actually hadn't come here ready to kill her. He honestly had believed Tig would agree to work for him, and that, after his little talk, Kent would look the other way to keep Tig alive. The belief hadn't kept him from rigging her chair, though, probably as a precaution against the very move she had just made.

She grabbed the hand on her neck and worked to get the other free, and he gave up on her gun and resorted to choking her instead. She was gearing up for one final fight to free herself when he collapsed on top of her with a grunt.

His hands loosened, and she gasped for air, pushing him to one side and off her. Tig was standing over him, holding her caryatid statue, one side of it now smeared with blood.

"I've been wanting to hit someone with this ever since Chase and Kam got in that fight," she said, reaching out her hand to pull Kent upright. "It felt fucking good, too."

She nudged an unmoving Max with her toe. "Do you think I should hit him again? Just in case?"

Kent laughed weakly, her voice sore. "I think the first one did the job."

"Sergeant," Clare said quietly from the doorway. "Are you all right?"

Kent nodded, then pulled Tig into a tight hug. She released her after too short a time, but she needed to ask. "How did you know to come back here?"

"I shouldn't have pushed you to go off on your own," Clare said. Her hand was trembling slightly where it rested on the door jamb. "I didn't feel right about it, and when I turned to say that to Tig, she was already saying pretty much the same thing to me. We ran out of the station without telling anyone where we were going, but you had a head start."

"We must have gotten here right after you did," Tig said. She held up the tiny mic from her wire. "I pushed this around the corner, and we waited while he talked." She shook her head, her eyes belatedly reddening as the adrenaline dumped out of her system. "I just stood out there. I should have come in sooner."

Kent shook her head, which didn't feel very comfortable. She was going to have bruises to rival Tig's. "You came in at the perfect time."

"Yeah, while I was around the corner, letting Pickett know what had happened," said Clare.

"The two of you look pretty gloomy for people who just saved my life," Kent said. She broke protocol and stepped over to Clare, hugging her quickly, then letting go. "Now, how about you get back to work, Officer, and zip-tie this man before he comes to and Tig has to hit him again."

Tig swung her statue like a baseball bat, swishing through the air. "I really don't mind," she said. "I'm happy to do it."

CHAPTER TWENTY-FIVE

Tig walked across campus with Sami, attempting to explain her plan as they passed Denny on the way to the U District, where her friends were waiting for them. She was wearing her best clothes—her lucky blazer and nicest pants and a pair of socks with images of Aphrodite's head scattered over them. After all, it wasn't every day one met with the president of the university, as well as an executive vice president, the provost, and a handful of deans. She had told Kent this morning that she felt quite honored that they had gathered such an illustrious group together just to fire her.

Kent hadn't seemed as amused as she was by the joke.

Tig fell silent as they crossed Fifteenth, focusing on every aspect of the campus that she loved, everything she would miss. Denny, of course, and the trees and squirrels, and the view of Mount Rainier from the east side of campus. Her nice parking spot, and the bench where she ate her lunch when the cherry trees were in bloom. She walked slowly down the Ave., noticing her favorite used bookstores, and each coffee shop, restaurant, and diner where she had eaten with her friends.

Come to think of it, they ate out a lot. They probably should learn to cook one of these days.

Of course, if she lived back east, without friends to meet for meals, she would probably want to cook more. Or she'd just microwave frozen pizzas.

Focus on Kent, she told herself. Not on food or what she'd like to eat for dinner. Focus on how awful it would be to leave her. In the three days between Max's ambush and today, they had been nearly inseparable, aside from the hours when they had to be at work. Tig had spent nights in Kent's arms, and days laughing with her as they talked about everything but the fate of Tig and the Classics Department. Even after such a short time, her sense of normal had shifted to include Kent. This was life now—the two of them together, and Tig felt as incapable of unraveling them in her mind as she would be imagining her arm or leg going to live a separate life in a different state. That simply wouldn't work.

Unless life had other plans.

They got to the café and stood outside for another moment, letting all the sad thoughts of leaving fill her until they reached her face. She felt close to crying, but that just made her congratulate herself on how good she was getting at controlling her expressions and what other people might read into them. She pushed aside her pride—she couldn't carry that into the restaurant if she wanted to have any hope of fooling her friends.

"Are you ready for this?" she asked Sami.

"I do not have to do anything? I just stand there?"

Tig nodded.

"Then I am ready."

Tig nodded, then went into the café, immediately spotting her friends. She walked over to the table and sat down without a word, not quite trusting herself to hold her act together and speak at the same time. She sighed, which seemed to go well. Kent put her arm over Tig's shoulders, and Tig leaned into her.

"Oh, sweetie," Libby said, leaning toward her. "I'm so sorry."

The others murmured their agreement. Sami raised her eyebrows but remained silent as she sat down in the chair Ari brought over to the table for her.

"So, Boston?" Jazz asked, obviously attempting to inject a note of optimism into her voice.

Ari shook her head. "Bryn Mawr. It's a great department, and a smaller school so she'll do more teaching."

Jazz looked at her as if she was insane. "Have you *seen* the libraries in Boston?"

"Stop it," Libby hissed at them before turning back to her. "We'll visit you all the time, Tig. And we can FaceTime you from restaurants, so you won't be eating alone."

Tig was about to tell them the truth when Kent spoke up. "She won't be alone. I'm going with her."

"What?" Tig asked, turning to face her. She didn't have to feign surprise.

"I decided yesterday and wrote my letter of resignation. I'm coming with you."

"You quit? Please tell me you didn't quit."

Kent frowned at her. "I want to be with you. I thought you'd want this, too."

"Well, of course I do," Tig said, exasperated. "I love you. But I'm not going anywhere. You didn't actually quit yet, did you?"

"You love me?" Kent asked softly. Tig just glared at her. "Oh, all right. No, I didn't send the letter yet. And I love you, too."

"Good," Tig said, giving her a kiss. "Let's love each other in Washington, okay?"

"So, you're just pretending?" Clare asked, interrupting their kiss. "You're not fired?"

"She told me this would be humorous, to pretend she had to leave," Sami said. She nodded at Tig. "You were correct. Their expressions were quite amusing."

Tig grinned at her before turning back to Clare. "No, I'm not fired," she said, reaching for Kent's menu. She hadn't been able to eat all day and she was starving. "They were planning to sacrifice me, just like I thought, but Sami did some heavy-duty threatening before I got there. They need her, and they need Med Studies to heal some of the scars these problems are causing, and she told them she'd pull out if I wasn't leading the program anymore. By the time I got in there, I had been turned into the hero who single-handedly uncovered a cheating scandal and solved two murders, while leading my department bravely into the future." She looked at

Kent, then Clare. "Sorry about that. I would have told them you two played a part in the investigation, too, but I didn't want to interrupt them while they were singing my praises. It was like having my own Greek chorus."

She laughed but sobered quickly. "It's going to be a lot of work to get us pulled together again, and to deal with the fallout from all this, although it's helpful that the cheating was confined to a specific group of students. I still don't know if I can heal this department, but at least I have a chance to try." Kent put her hand on Tig's thigh, squeezing gently.

"I'm happy for you," Ari said, although she actually sounded rather annoyed. "But why the pretend moping?"

Tig shrugged, reaching for Kent's hand and holding it tightly under the table. "Everyone kept saying how easy I am to read. I wanted to prove them wrong. It's exhausting, though. I had to spend the whole walk over here making myself really feel sad. I'm going to go back to being an open book."

Jazz fussed with her phone and reached across the table so Tig could see the picture on her screen. "Seriously, have you seen this library?"

"I'm not going to Boston, Jazz."

"I was right, wasn't I?" Ari asked, no longer sounding irritated. "You were going to pick Bryn Mawr, weren't you?"

Tig sighed and settled back in her chair as her friends chattered on around her, arguing over which of them knew her best and could predict where she would hypothetically move. They were a weird bunch, but they were hers. All of them, but especially Kent.

"It's really true?" Kent leaned toward her and asked quietly. "You're staying. We can plan more than a day in advance. We can be together?"

Tig smiled at Kent. "Yes, it's true. All of it, but especially the last one. That's really all that matters, isn't it?"

She hooked her finger in the turtleneck Kent had been wearing with her uniform to hide her bruises and pulled her close for a quick kiss. "That was the public part of my kiss," she said, letting go again and returning her hand to Kent's, where it rested in her lap. "You'll have to wait until we get home for the rest of it."

"Can you please stop kissing my sergeant in front of me," Clare said, groaning. "It's damaging to my psyche."

"I'd be fine with it if I worked for you, Sarge," Libby said. "You can kiss anyone you want, and you won't hear a peep from me."

"That's it, you're hired," Kent said. "We had a sudden opening, just a few minutes ago, so you're in. Sawyer, you're out."

Tig laughed, and then she and Kent leaned into the group and rejoined the conversation going on around them. They had the rest of their lives for this. Time to be with friends, time to spend with only each other.

Plenty of time for love, in all its forms.

About the Author

Karis Walsh is a horseback riding instructor who lives in the Pacific Northwest. When she isn't teaching or writing, she enjoys spending time outside with her animals, reading, playing the viola, and riding with friends.

Books Available From Bold Strokes Books

A Degree to Die For by Karis Walsh. A murder at the University of Washington's Classics Department brings Professor Antigone Weston and Sergeant Adriana Kent together—first as opposing forces and then as allies as they fight together to protect their campus from a killer. (978-1-63679-365-8)

Finders Keepers by Radclyffe. Roman Ashcroft's past, it seems, is not so easily forgotten when fate brings her and Tally Dewilde together—along with an attraction neither welcomes. (978-1-63679-428-0)

Homeland by Kristin Keppler and Allisa Bahney. Dani and Kate have finally found themselves on the same side of the war, but a new threat from the inside jeopardizes the future of the wasteland. (978-1-63679-405-1)

Just One Dance by Jenny Frame. Will Taylor Sparks and her new business to make dating special—the Regency Romance Club—bring sparkle back to Jaq Bailey's lonely world? (978-1-63679-457-0)

On My Way There by Jaycie Morrison. As Max traverses the open road, her journey of impossible love, loss, and courage mirrors her voyage of self-discovery leading to the ultimate question: If she can't have the woman of her dreams, will the woman of real life be enough? (978-1-63679-392-4)

A Talent Within by Suzanne Lenoir. Evelyne, born into nobility, and Annika, a peasant girl with a deadly secret, struggle to change their destinies in Valmora, a medieval world controlled by religion, magic, and men. (978-1-63679-423-5)

Transitioning Home by Heather K O'Malley. An injured soldier realizes they need to transition to really heal. (978-1-63679-424-2)

Truly Enough by J.J. Hale. Chasing the spark of creativity may ignite a burning romance or send a friendship up in flames. (978-1-63679-442-6)

Vintage and Vogue by Kelly and Tana Fireside. When tech whiz Sena Abrigo marches into small-town Owen Station, she turns librarian Hazel Butler's life upside down in the most wonderful of ways, setting off an explosive series of events, threatening their chance at love…and their very lives. (978-1-63679-448-8)

The Accidental Bride by Jane Walsh. Spinsters Miss Grace Linfield and Miss Thea Martin travel to Gretna Green to prevent a wedding, only to discover a scandalous passion—for each other. (978-1-63679-345-0)

Broken Fences by Jo Hemmingwood. Former army sergeant Seneca Twist has difficulty adjusting to civilian life until she meets psychologist Robyn Mason and has a place to call home. (978-1-63679-414-3)

Never Kiss a Cowgirl by Ali Vali. Asher Evans dreams of winning the National Finals Rodeo in Vegas, and Reagan Wilson wants no part of something that brings back the memory of what killed her father. (978-1-63679-106-7)

Pantheon Girls by Jean Copeland. Cassie Burke never anticipated the detour life is about to take when a meeting with a prospective client reunites her with a past love and reignites the star-crossed passion they shared twenty years earlier. (978-1-63679-337-5)

Roux for Two by Aurora Rey. For TV chef Chelsea Boudreaux and hometown boy Bryce Cormier, love proves as tricky as making a good pot of gumbo. (978-1-63679-376-4)

Starting Over by Nance Sparks. Jennifer has no idea if she can mend Sam's broken soul after the sudden loss of her wife, but it's never too late for starting over. (978-1-63679-409-9)

Three Wishes by Anne Shade. A magic lamp, a beautiful Jinni, and a cursed princess make for one unbelievable story. (978-1-63679-349-8)

Undiscovered Treasures by MJ Williamz. For Cyl and her friends Luna and Martinique, life's best treasures often appear when they're not looking. (978-1-63679-449-5)